“I, the great Kuu Taisei, show no mercy in the face of such insolence!”

“Yo… real… trying to force your way into Taru’s workshop!”

VII

HOW A REALIST HERO REBUILT THE KINGDOM

Dojyomaru
Illust. Fuyuyuki

Kuu Taisei

There were tens of small, fast boats decorated in gorgeous colors, and they shone brilliantly on the evening river.

Souma Kazuya
Roroa Amidonia

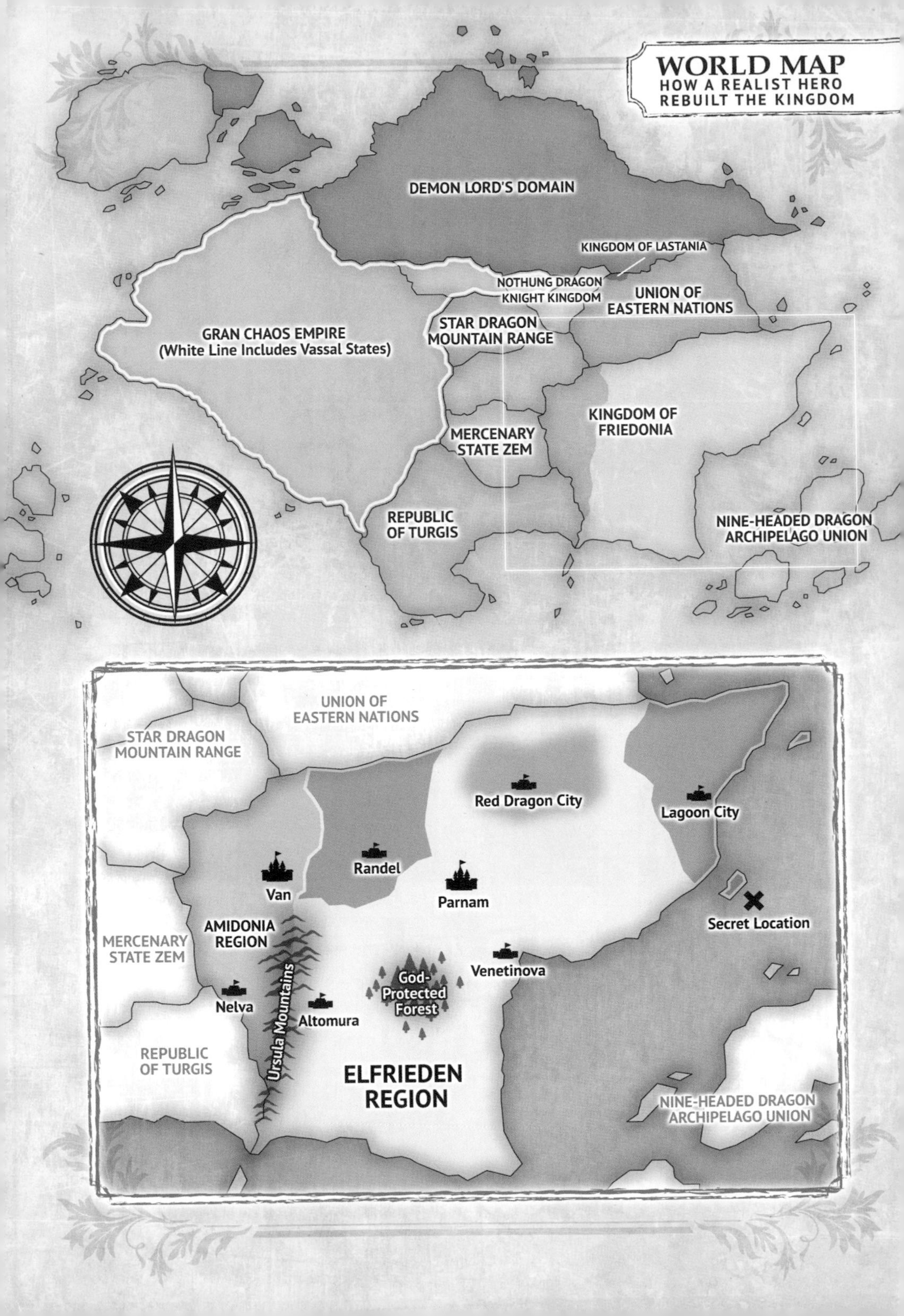
WORLD MAP
HOW A REALIST HERO
REBUILT THE KINGDOM
DEMON LORD'S DOMAIN
KINGDOM OF LASTANIA
NOTHUNG DRAGON
KNIGHT KINGDOM
UNION OF
EASTERN NATIONS
GRAN CHAOS EMPIRE
(White Line Includes Vassal States)
STAR DRAGON
MOUNTAIN RANGE
KINGDOM OF
FRIEDONIA
MERCENARY
STATE ZEM
REPUBLIC
OF TURGIS
NINE-HEADED DRAGON
ARCHIPELAGO UNION
UNION OF
EASTERN NATIONS
STAR DRAGON
MOUNTAIN RANGE
Red Dragon City
Lagoon City
Randel
Van
Parnam
Secret Location
AMIDONIA
REGION
MERCENARY
STATE ZEM
Venetinova
God-
Protected
Forest
Nelva
Altomura
Ursula Mountains
REPUBLIC
OF TURGIS
ELFRIEDEN
REGION
NINE-HEADED DRAGON
ARCHIPELAGO UNION

HOW A REALIST HERO REBUILT THE KINGDOM

11/3/20
I rg
$13.99

HOW A REALIST HERO REBUILT THE KINGDOM:
VOLUME 7

Illustrations by Fuyuyuki

First published in Japan in 2018 by
OVERLAP Inc., Ltd., Tokyo.
English translation rights arranged with
OVERLAP Inc., Ltd., Tokyo.

Follow Seven Seas Entertainment online at
sevenseasentertainment.com.
Experience J-Novel Club books online at j-novel.club.

TRANSLATION: Sean McCann
J-NOVEL EDITOR: Emily Sorensen
COVER DESIGN: Kris Aubin
INTERIOR DESIGN: Clay Gardner
INTERIOR LAYOUT: George Panella
COPY EDITOR: Dayna Abel
LIGHT NOVEL EDITOR: E.M. Candon
PREPRESS TECHNICIAN: Rhiannon Rasmussen-Silverstein
PRODUCTION MANAGER: Lissa Pattillo
MANAGING EDITOR: Julie Davis
ASSOCIATE PUBLISHER: Adam Arnold
PUBLISHER: Jason DeAngelis

ISBN: 978-1-64505-512-9
Printed in Canada
First Printing: August 2020
10 9 8 7 6 5 4 3 2 1

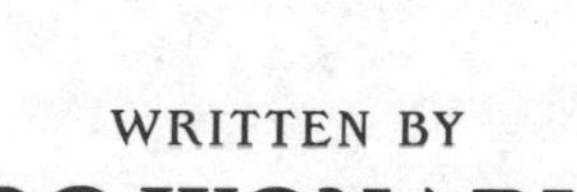

WRITTEN BY
DOJYOMARU

ILLUSTRATED BY
FUYUYUKI

Contents

PROLOGUE
Meeting Up
9

CHAPTER 1
From the New City, Venetinova
15

CHAPTER 2
Urgent News and a Meeting
39

CHAPTER 3
A Great Man Still in the Making
87

CHAPTER 4
To Know a Person
113

CHAPTER 5
Fighting Together
141

CHAPTER 6
A Trump Card in Negotiations
173

CHAPTER 7
The Tripartite Medical Alliance
189

EPILOGUE
An Unsettling Presence
215

SIDE STORIES
After Returning to the Country Arc
227

BONUS SHORT STORIES
325

PROLOGUE

Meeting Up

THE MIDDLE of the 5th month, 1,547th year, Continental Calendar:

Tomoe, who had been left in a town bordering the Lunarian Orthodox Papal State, came to the noon market with her bodyguard, Inugami. A messenger kui had delivered word that Souma and the rest were safe and would be taking Tomoe with them to their next stop, the Republic of Turgis. She was to wait in the town for them to meet up with her. However, it seemed like it would be a shame to just sit around and wait, so she and Inugami decided to look around the bustling market.

Thanks to being near the border, many merchants who traveled between the two countries gathered here, and goods from both nations were for sale.

"Hey, little girlie," said one of them. "Why don'tcha have your daddy buy you this hairpin?"

"I've got some me real fine dried foods here, y'know?" yelled another. "Have a look, would ya?"

While Tomoe and Inugami walked through the market, the merchants in their stalls called out to them in merchant slang. It seemed they were being mistaken for parent and child. Their faces were shaped very differently, but it was common among the beastmen races for men and women to have very different appearances, so that might be why they looked like father and daughter.

Tomoe looked up and giggled. "Mr. Inugami, they think you're my dad."

"Yes, ma'am," he said. "It's rude of me to say this, Little Sister, but it's convenient for us to have them misunderstand our relationship like that. If a man is seen walking with a girl who is young enough to be his daughter, but isn't, people start thinking things we don't want them to."

In other words, if the alternative was being mistaken for a kidnapper and victim, it was far better to be thought of as father and daughter.

Tomoe looked up at him. "Um... Then wouldn't it be better if you spoke to me less respectfully, and more like a father would?"

"No... I cannot do that..."

"You can't?"

"I-It's not that I...can't. You're probably right, Tomoe." Having relented, Inugami dropped his formal tone.

Tomoe giggled. "Okay then, 'Dad.'"

"What is it, 'daughter of mine'?"

"I want to see what kind of shops the merchants who come from other countries are running here today."

"Hm... In that case, that's probably one of them over there." Inugami pointed out a stall being managed by a fat man. It seemed he was selling dried fruits that would keep for a long time.

Tomoe tilted her head to the side. "How can you tell?"

"You see the accessory with the Lunarian Orthodox symbol he wears over his chest?"

Now that Inugami pointed it out, she could see the fat man wore an accessory with a symbol that looked like a combination of a full moon and crescent moon over his left breast.

Tomoe had no way of knowing this, but Mary, the person who had been sent as an envoy from the Lunarian Orthodox Papal State, had worn a necklace with the same symbol.

"The devout believers of Lunarian Orthodoxy carry those at all times," Inugami explained. "You can see the color on it is nice, too, right? That's also a mark of someone who's made significant contributions to the main church."

"Oh, I get it. That's how you knew he was from the Orthodox Papal State, huh?"

"That's right. Do you want to go take a look?"

"Yes!" she exclaimed.

The two of them walked over to the stall. There were dried fruits and nuts out front, and in the back were several barrels where the man kept fruits preserved in honey.

"Hey there, little girl, I've got some yummy honey-preserved fruits," the shopkeeper said with a grin. "Why don'tcha buy some?"

In response, Tomoe asked, "You're from outside the country, right, mister? Do you have any interesting stories about your country?"

"Huh?" The shopkeeper was confused by the sudden question.

"Hey, it's rude to suddenly ask him like that!" Inugami scolded.

As Tomoe stiffened from being yelled at, Inugami lifted her up by the back of her hood. Tomoe was as helpless as a kitten suspended in midair.

Inugami put on a fake smile and bowed repeatedly to the shopkeeper. "I'm sorry, sir. We've got some business in the Republic of Turgis, but it's a first for my daughter and she's gotten all excited. Every time she sees something, it's 'What's this?' 'What's that?' She just won't be quiet."

"Oh... Ha ha ha, it's good seein' a child so full of curiosity."

"You really think so? Oh, I'll have some of those preserved fruits."

"Thank you! Come again!"

With Tomoe still held up in the air, Inugami paid for the goods, then received a neatly cut melon preserved in honey and left the stall behind with a smile.

Once they were in a place the shopkeeper couldn't see, Inugami put Tomoe down, crossed his arms, and looked her straight in the eye. "I ask you to forgive me for shouting at you. But, Little Sister..."

"Y-yes...?"

"Why did you ask a question like that?" Inugami maintained as calm a tone as he could manage, so as to not intimidate her.

Tomoe looked at him with upturned eyes, then hesitantly confessed, “I thought if I wanted to be able to help Big Brother and the others, I’d need to study up on other countries. That’s why...um...I wanted to ask him...”

Tomoe’s voice gradually shrank quieter as she spoke.

Inugami sighed. “There are spies who disguise themselves as merchants. If he were one of them, you might be marked for special attention because you wanted that information. It’s very dangerous.”

“I-I’m sorry...” Tomoe seemed genuinely contrite, and her wolf ears drooped.

Seeing her thoroughly discouraged, Inugami plopped a hand on Tomoe’s shoulder. “So, if you want to know about other countries, ask me. I’ll teach you everything I can. Naturally, I can’t tell you anything classified, though.”

Then Inugami extended the bowl containing fruits preserved in honey to Tomoe. She accepted one, took a bite, and smiled.

“This is so sweet, ‘Dad.’”

“I can’t help but be sweet. Especially to my ‘daughter.’”

After that exchange, though they might or might not have been on the same page, the two both smiled. To any who looked, they seemed just like a close father and daughter.

On the next day, Souma and the rest met up with them.

HOW A REALIST HERO REBUILT THE KINGDOM

CHAPTER 1
From the New City, Venetinova

THIS IS A STORY from around the time Souma left for the Republic.

The stage is Venetinova, a coastal city in the east of the Kingdom of Friedonia.

The Kingdom's coast was sharp and angular, as if a chunk of land had been cut away like a slice of cake. To encourage more active distribution of goods throughout the country, King Souma had sponsored the construction of Venetinova at the corner of that shape.

If there was one thing unique about this city, it was the two-level layout. In the lower level, facing the sea, there was a fishing port, a plaza, parks, and more. The residential quarter, governor's mansion, and other similar buildings were concentrated in the upper level.

Nearly all of the shopping areas lined the hill road between those two levels. This layout was in preparation for a great earthquake that was said to strike the region once every hundred years.

In one of the clinics along the hill road in Venetinova, an eight-month-old baby boy swung his legs as his mother held him.

"Goo goo!" the baby cooed.

This healthy baby was named Fuku. During Souma's visit to the refugee camp, Hilde Norg, a female doctor belonging to the three-eyed race, and Brad Joker, a surgeon, had delivered him by cesarean section. Incidentally, Souma himself had given the boy his name.

Today, little Fuku had come in with his mother for a regular checkup.

Hilde was the doctor examining him. "Hm...I don't see anything out of the ordinary. He's full of energy."

Until just recently, she had been at Ginger's Vocational School in the capital of Parnam, training doctors. Once the School was on track, Hilde—who preferred to visit homes to treat the common people over hiding away in a lab to study—left her duties to her juniors at the school. Because she was concerned about the former refugees, she followed them to this new city and opened a clinic.

That said, Hilde was considered one of the two greatest minds in the medical world. The other one was Brad Joker, the surgeon. They were both frequently called to the medical school in Parnam, but recently, she had been staying in Venetinova for a certain reason.

Hearing from Hilde that her child was okay, Fuku's mother bowed her head. "Thank you so much. It's all thanks to you and Dr. Joker that Fuku and I are both still here."

"No need to thank me," said Hilde. "It's my job, you know. More importantly, like the king told you, you should really be thanking your child for being born when both of us were there."

Perhaps to hide her shyness, Hilde turned to look the other way as she brushed Fuku's hair, which now grew evenly.

Fuku clapped his hands in glee.

Fuku's mother watched with a slight smile. "I guess you're right. Now we can wait together for my husband to return."

"Oh, that's right, they found your husband, didn't they?"

"Yes," said another woman, stepping forward. "I received word from my elder brother."

The one who responded to this question was an eighteen-year-old girl who wore an outfit similar to that of a stereotypical Native American, and paint on her cheeks that seemed magical.

Her name was Komain. She had originally been left in charge of handling the refugees by her brother, Jirukoma, and was now a community leader for the former refugees putting down roots in Venetinova.

Komain was here today to give support to Fuku and his mother during their routine checkup. "According to the messenger kui my brother sent, he should be on his way here now."

Jirukoma had returned north, leading all of those who refused to become members of this country, and who insisted on attempting to retake their homelands. He was now staying as a volunteer soldier in the Kingdom of Lastania, one of the smaller countries inside the Union of Eastern Nations, having responded to their call for troops.

In that land, he was also gathering information on those who had been scattered while being driven from the north. Fuku's father was just one of the lost he had found that way.

"He said your husband was searching for you in one of Lastania's neighboring countries," said Komain. "When my brother told him you were safe, and your child had been born, he dropped everything to rush here and be at your side."

"Honestly... That man's always been in such a hurry," Fuku's mother said, but she looked really happy.

Hilde gave an exasperated shrug. "Well, it's good to have the family together. Just...let me caution you on one thing."

"Huh? Uh, sure."

"Your belly's already been opened once for the delivery. The procedure went perfectly, and you can probably have a second, but... once the belly has been cut once, it's weaker, and a natural birth becomes more difficult. So, the next time you give birth, it would be safer for both you and the baby to cut you open and take it out."

Fuku's mother and Komain both gulped.

Hilde grinned at both of them. "When your husband gets back, you're going to have some romantic time together, right? If that makes you decide you really want a second, you'd better consult a doctor approved by either me or the country."

"Right!" Fuku's mother nodded enthusiastically.

Hearing that, Fuku let out a confident cry, too, which caused all three of the others to look at one another and smile.

"Is the checkup finished?" Brad poked his head out from deeper inside the clinic. He was a man whose expression was usually more subdued, but he was glancing worriedly at Hilde now. "Um...is it okay?"

"They're fine," said Hilde. "Both mother and child are healthy."

"No, that's not what I meant..."

"Honestly... You're more nervous than I'd have expected." Hilde stood up and shooed Brad into the back of the clinic. "For starters, there are no men allowed in here while I'm seeing a female patient!"

"No, you're seeing the baby... I just..."

"Enough. You go over there and get ready for tomorrow! You'll need to head out to the capital and look at the princess. They say she's gotten sick."

Having forcibly made Brad leave, Hilde returned to her seat. "Good grief," she muttered.

After seeing that interaction between the two of them, Komain tilted her head quizzically. "Dr. Brad is here, too, huh? I heard he'd gotten a case of wanderlust and was seeing patients all around the country."

Brad was, indeed, prone to wanderlust. He was the sort who would tell King Souma to his face, "I want to heal the poor, not the rich." To put it in flattering terms, he was a solitary sort; in less flattering terms, he still had a mild case of savior complex.

Even though he had received a request from Souma to hold lectures, he was still traveling around the country to see patients and treat them. Technically, he did take apprentices with him and call it training in the field, though.

That was why Komain had been surprised to see Brad here.

However, Hilde snorted. "What's there to be surprised about? Men are so simple," she said, rubbing her abdomen.

That gesture told Komain everything she needed to know. "You too, Doctor?!"

"Wow, congratulations!" cried Fuku's mother.

"Hmph..." Hilde turned to look away in embarrassment. But still, in a vanishingly small voice she replied, "Yeah, yeah... Thanks."

Despite themselves, the way she said it made Komain and Fuku's mother erupt in laughter.

"Komain, thank you for coming with me today," Fuku's mother said, bowing her head.

"Dooo," her little son agreed.

The time was a little past three o'clock in the afternoon. On the hill road outside Hilde's clinic, Komain rolled up her sleeves and said, "Oh, it's no big deal. Brother asked me to look after everyone. If there's anything I can do, please, go ahead and tell me."

"Thank you. Are you going home now?"

"No, I have some documents to submit to the governor, so I plan to head there next."

"Oh, is that right? Well, keep up the good work."

"I sure will! See you later, Fuku."

Taking Fuku's hand and shaking it, Komain said her goodbyes to the two of them and raced up the hill. The governor's mansion was at the highest point in the city. While Komain raced through the shopping street, the lady running one of the fruit shops called out to her.

"Komain, you always look so busy. Are you eating right?"

"Huh? Uh, now that you mention it, I may have missed lunch today."

"That's no good. Even if you're busy, you've gotta eat!" The lady threw one of the apples she was selling over to Komain.

"Whoa... Thanks, ma'am!" Komain caught the apple, waved vigorously to the lady, then went on her way.

People often waved at Komain when she was running through the streets.

She had been doing a lot of jobs lately—everything from cleaning, washing laundry, and babysitting, to making deliveries and removing bee nests. Though she was a young girl, she'd firmly taken on her role as a community organizer for the refugees. Because she had the guts to give the local men a piece of her mind, even though they were hard workers and could be a bit rough, it was little wonder she was so popular. She didn't know it, but she was already considered the poster girl of Venetinova.

But...I can't keep doing this forever, Komain thought as she ran through the streets of Venetinova. *The refugees are starting to put down roots in this new city. If we're going to assimilate into this country, it's better if there's no "wall" between those who were formerly refugees and those who weren't. My role as an organizer for the community is emblematic of that wall, so if everything goes well, eventually they won't need me anymore. That in itself is a good thing, but...*

Komain bit into the apple she'd been given and let out a little sigh.

It may be about time I began looking for a way of living for myself, like Brother did when he went north.

Komain thought about it as she ran through the streets. While she was still thinking, she arrived at her destination: the mansion where the governor who ran the city lived.

It wasn't the "lord's" mansion because Venetinova was part of the royal demesne, and therefore the lord of this city was King Souma. However, King Souma was based out of the capital, so he'd needed to dispatch someone to manage this city.

There were times when the administration of major cities was left to the nobles and knights working in the government office, but considering the importance of this city, a mere magistrate wouldn't have been sufficient.

The title created for the post of running this city was "governor." It was a new post, created for the person who would rule this important city on Souma's behalf, and the place where this governor lived and worked was called the governor's mansion.

Now, as for who the city's current governor was...

"Excuse me. Is Governor Poncho in at the moment?"

Indeed, it was the former Minister for the Food Crisis and current Minister of Agriculture and Forestry: Poncho Ishizuka Panacotta.

Because this important city couldn't be left in the hands of anyone less competent, the king's close associate Poncho was tapped, albeit temporarily, to handle the job. Because of that, Poncho's days now went by blindingly fast, with him going to work in the castle every morning and returning to Venetinova every afternoon.

Technically, his replacement was already chosen—it was the Lord of Altomura, Weist Garreau, who distinguished himself in the war—but until Weist was prepared to take over, Poncho's busy days were set to continue.

What was more, another batch of troubles was coming Poncho's way.

"The governor is present, but you're looking at a long wait if you want an audience with him," the guard said to Komain with a forced smile, and in a way that seemed to imply something.

"I understand," said Komain. "I have some documents to submit, so do you mind if I wait?"

"I understand. Go ahead, Madam Komain. You can stay in the waiting room."

Thanks in part to her being a familiar face, the guard readily let Komain inside.

The maid standing by in the front entrance to the building, who was tasked with guiding guests, led Komain to the waiting room where four women were already waiting.

The women seemed to be gathered in one corner of the room and were talking about something. They all wore gaudy outfits, and Komain inferred that they were young ladies of good parentage. The women glanced over at her as she entered the room, then huddled close and began whispering to each other.

Komain, feeling awkward, sat at a distance from the women. When she did...

"What's with that outfit? Is that girl aiming to become Sir Poncho's wife?"

"What a common girl. Does she think that if it's Sir Poncho, even a girl like her could seduce him?"

Komain could hear their whispering perfectly. She was from a tribe of hunters from the north, and they were sensitive to the presence of their prey and other noises. She could hear lowered voices like theirs whether she wanted to or not.

Komain sighed. *I knew it... They're women who've come to discuss a potential marriage to Sir Poncho, just as I thought.*

There had already been a public announcement that King Souma would be holding a ceremony to celebrate his marriage to Princess Liscia and his other queens-in-waiting. In response, there was now a rush of marriage offers from those who wanted to secure a position as a queen for themselves, too. Not only that, these offers of marriage were coming en masse to any unwed men among Souma's vassals who seemed to have a promising future.

The intelligent and attractive Prime Minister Hakuya, as well as Ludwin, the handsome Captain of the Royal Guard, were both popular, but the person these offers were most concentrated on was Poncho.

Being an upstart noble, Poncho was from a family of low status, providing a low barrier of entry for such proposals. On top of that, there was his pudgy body; those with confidence in their appearance thought he would be easy to seduce. In addition, many had an honest affection for him as one of the people who helped end the food crisis.

In short, Poncho was visited by those of high and low status, those interested out of ambition and those whose desires were pure... It was a truly diverse group of women proposing to him. The group here currently was no doubt full of women from ambitious houses.

"Just you watch," said one. "I'll make that pudgy man mine with this beautiful face."

"He seems like a timid sort, so if I push hard enough, he should submit easily."

"The way he looks, he can't be used to beautiful women."

The women continued talking in hushed voices.

This is kind of unpleasant, thought Komain. *I don't care what they say about me, but Sir Poncho worked with His Majesty to provide food relief to us refugees when things were hard for us. I want him to be happy, and I'd rather not see anyone too weird become his wife.*

However, as these women were saying, Poncho had a somewhat unreliable side to him. If the women pushed hard enough, given his personality, he may not be able to decline. Komain was worried for Poncho, but then a question came to mind.

Huh...then why hasn't he gotten married yet?

It was true Poncho was easy to push into things. However, despite that, she hadn't heard anything about him being engaged. And this was despite so many offers pouring in.

He's rebuffing all those offers from women like these? The Sir Poncho I know?

While Komain was still wondering about this, the maid came for the women and they were led off one by one.

The next thing Komain knew, she was alone.

At last the maid came for her, informing Komain that her turn had come.

"I'm sorry for the wait. Madam Komain, come this way, please."

As she followed the maid down the corridor, Komain saw one of the women who had been in the waiting room before walking quickly toward them from the opposite direction. Her face was tense, and she passed by Komain without seeming to take note of her.

Wh-what was that? She looked like she was on edge. Did her meeting not go so well?

While she wondered, they arrived at the reception room. The maid knocked lightly on the door, then waited for a response from inside before opening it and announcing Komain's arrival.

"Please do come in, yes."

Hearing Poncho's voice, Komain responded, "Excuse me," and entered the room.

Inside the reception room, a somewhat tired Poncho was seated on a sofa with a maid standing behind him.

Komain's eyes went wide despite herself as soon as she saw that maid. For a moment, she was overwhelmed by this woman who looked to be a little over the age of twenty, with a beautiful face and a poise that spoke to her great intellect.

Little wonder that woman outside looked so pressured...

With a beauty like that behind Poncho, it would no doubt destroy whatever confidence the visiting women had in their own looks. Had it been solely thanks to her that, despite all of the marriage offers, no woman had been able to push one through? In that case...

Huh?! Is she glaring at me?! Komain felt as if the maid standing behind Poncho had shot a glare at her.

When a beautiful person did the glaring, the impact was multiplied. Komain felt a chill down her spine, but this was the same Komain who spent her days openly speaking her mind to burly men.

She glared back, as if to say, *I won't lose.*

At Komain's return glare, the maid turned up the intensity.

Their gazes collided. It was as if an image of a wolf and a hawk could be seen behind them.

"Um, is something the matter, you two?" Poncho asked hesitantly, sensing the abnormal atmosphere between them.

Komain was the first to come back to her senses. "Oh, that's right. Poncho, I've brought the list of newly arrived refugees."

"Well, well. Thank you for your hard work, yes."

When Komain turned over the papers to Poncho, the oppressive vibe she had been getting from the maid vanished. In fact, the maid bowed to her and said, "I'll go prepare tea now," then left the room.

While there was still a question mark floating over Komain's head at the maid's sudden change in attitude, Poncho spoke.

"I'm sorry it seems we kept you waiting, yes," he apologized as he perused the documents.

"Oh, no. Um...do you have a lot of people expressing interest in marrying you?"

"Y-yes. Let's see. From what I hear, many of the unmarried men among His Majesty's vassals have been receiving such offers, yes. Even I have received a fair number. If Madam Serina, who is the head maid at the castle, hadn't handled them for me, I'm sure things would have gotten even worse, yes."

Serina... Is that the incredibly beautiful maid from before? If she's the head maid in the castle, she must be highly capable.

Poncho put on a troubled smile. "Of course, maybe it's because of the way I look. I've received an awful lot of offers to discuss the prospect, but not one of them has worked out, yes. I'm often told, 'Actually, let's call the whole thing off,' the moment they see my face at the interview."

Huh? Does that mean...

Komain recalled the moment of first entering the room. She'd seen the kindly Poncho, and the super beautiful maid Serina standing behind him.

Yeah... That was the first barrier. For those who had a little confidence in their appearance and thought they could easily seduce Poncho, when they saw Serina's beautiful face, they were likely to beat a hasty retreat. Even if they held their ground, the next thing to hit them would be that wave of intimidation from Serina. The average woman probably couldn't withstand that pressure.

Even Komain had felt something akin to the kind of shudder she would feel if she encountered a large wolf.

"Serina has been kind enough to manage things, so I feel bad for her, yes," Poncho said apologetically.

Wait, isn't it Serina's fault that none of these offers have worked out?! Komain nearly said that out loud, but the maid interrupted.

"Pardon me. I've brought the tea." Serina brought in the tea with what felt like carefully planned timing, so the words never left Komain's mouth.

While she drank the delicious tea, Komain's mind spun in confused circles. *Madam Serina is getting in the way of Sir Poncho's marriage offers? But why? Since she was sent from the castle, is that under His Majesty's orders? No, that can't be right. I can't see the king doing anything so nasty. Then is it her own will? Does she have something against Sir Poncho, maybe?*

While Komain was thinking, Poncho began gently talking to her. "How are the former refugees these days? Is there anything troubling them?"

"Oh, right," Komain said. "Everyone is getting used to life here. It's a gradual process, but I'm getting fewer requests for mediation than before."

"That's good, yes. Peace is the most important thing."

"It is. From my standpoint as a community organizer, I feel it's a load off my shoulders and I'm relieved. At the same time, I have less and less to do, so I've been thinking of starting up something new. Sir Poncho...you're as busy as ever, aren't you?"

"Yes. In addition to my work as governor, I also have to meet all the people making proposals, and His Majesty has instructed me to study something new, too. So I'm busy, yes."

Poncho looked at the mountain of books beside his desk and sighed.

"Study...? Study what, exactly?" Komain asked.

"The transportation of provisions. According to His Majesty, whether my name is listed among the people managing our soldier's food or not will make a large difference in the entire military's morale. That's why, even if just for show, he apparently wants to place me in an important post, so I'm in the middle of having the bare minimum of base knowledge pounded into me, yes."

Poncho was so widely regarded as a specialist on food that the common people referred to him as "Ishizuka, the God of Food." Even just having his name listed as a manager of military provisions would be enough to convince the troops they were going to eat something good, and it would raise their morale.

That's a trouble you run into when you're famous, I guess, thought Komain.

Serina leaned in to whisper something in Poncho's ear. "Madam Komain is your last visitor for the day. Thank you for your hard work."

"Oh, she is? Thank you, too, Madam Serina, yes."

"Oh, no, I was ordered by His Majesty to support you, after all."

"Still, I'm always grateful, yes."

Komain's far-too-sensitive ears picked up their whispered conversation.

Hearing their voices, Komain quickly struck down her earlier theory. There was no trace of hostility in Serina's voice. More than that, there was an excited "sweetness" in it. It was amazing Poncho could keep a level head while she whispered to him like that.

"If you're that grateful, then do it again tonight," Serina whispered.

"You really do like it, huh, Madam Serina?" Poncho whispered back.

Komain nearly spewed her tea.

Tonight?! She likes it?! Huh? What?! What are the two of them talking about?!

While pretending to drink, Komain glanced at the two of them over the rim of her teacup.

D-do the two of them have that *kind of relationship, maybe?! Oh! That explains why Madam Serina was being so intimidating! To keep anyone from taking Sir Poncho from her... Huh, that's a surprise. I wonder why a beauty like her is so deeply infatuated with Sir Poncho?*

Komain's head was filled with a different confusion than before, and it worried her.

"Oh, that's right," said Poncho. "Madam Komain."

"Huh?! Uh, yes...?!" Komain unintentionally let her voice go a little shrill.

"Do you have some work after this, Madam Komain?"

"No, this was the last thing for today... Um, why do you ask?"

Poncho put on a happy smile and said, "Oh, it's no big deal. I just thought I'd invite you to dinner, yes."

H-how did it turn out like this...?

Komain didn't understand the situation she now found herself in.

She was in the governor's private dining room at the governor's mansion. There, Serina and Komain were seated across from one another. Poncho was away cooking, so Komain felt indescribably awkward.

Serina suddenly bowed her head. "Madam Komain, I must apologize for earlier."

"Huh? Um, why is that?"

"For looking at you with appraising eyes. I thought you were another one of those women who think they can so easily seduce Sir Poncho."

It seemed that look hadn't been a glare, but one of appraisal. Komain was relieved to realize Serina had been protecting Poncho from the venomous fangs of women with ambitions.

"Um, I was wondering... Are a lot of the people who seek to meet Poncho and talk about marriage like that?" Komain ventured.

"Yes. Like you've seen, he's a man with many weaknesses. I've been asked by His Majesty to make sure Sir Poncho isn't ensnared by any strange women, but many of them run away at the first sight of my eyes. I do wish they would at least pay us the most basic level of respect."

Well, yeah, of course they'd be scared, Komain nearly said, but managed to swallow the words just before they left her mouth.

Serina may have only intended her looks to be probing, but even those with no ill intentions might get scared and run away at the sight of her.

"But you didn't run away, did you, Madam Komain?" Serina asked.

"I come from a tribe of hunters. I felt like I was being glared at by a large wolf. But you can't be a hunter if you let fear get the best of you."

Komain's words seemed to have left Serina a little shocked. "My look was on the level of a large wolf's?"

At that moment, Poncho came back carrying a substantial pot. "Sorry to keep you waiting. This is our experimental dish for the day, yes."

Poncho went on to serve portions from the pot onto each of their plates. When she saw what was being served, Komain winced for a moment. Her entire plate was covered in brown. What was more, it looked unappetizing.

Is this...the rice the mystic wolf people were cultivating? But I can see bits that look like thinly cut pasta here and there. On top of that, the whole thing's brown, too...

"Ohhh, this is wonderful, Sir Poncho." Unlike Komain, Serina was entranced by the sight of this dish. "This is like the 'yakisoba sauce' you served before, but you've mixed in rice this time, too. The noodles are thin, making them easy to eat together with the rice. This sinful sight of a staple food cooked together with another staple food, combined with the scent of the sauce, is simply the best."

Serina praised the dish like she was a young maiden in love. The gap between this and the intellectual beauty she had seemed like earlier was so great Komain found it a little off-putting. However, Poncho seemed reasonably used to this reaction and went on smoothly explaining the dish.

"In His Majesty's world, this is apparently called 'soba meshi.' First, you make yakisoba sauce, then add rice. From there, you add things like tendon and mix it all together. I'm thinking of serving it at my experimental restaurant in the castle soon, yes."

"I'll dig right in."

Serina scooped up some of the soba meshi with a spoon and carried it to her mouth. The moment she put it in her mouth, she broke into a smile of ecstasy, as if she had just received a revelation from on high.

Poncho watched her with a smile on his face. "I must say...you really do like it, Madam Serina."

Hearing those words, Komain recalled their earlier whispers. It seemed this was the thing she "liked" that they'd be doing "tonight."

Feeling a little embarrassed by what she had imagined, Komain took a bite of the soba meshi on her plate without hesitating, and...

Ohhh! Komain felt like she'd also just had a revelation from heaven. *What is this?! It looks awful, but it's so delicious!*

The sweet and spicy sauce stimulated her appetite, and her spoon went back for scoop after scoop of soba meshi. What an alluring flavor. She could see why Serina's face had melted like that. While she was satisfied with her explanation, she remembered what Serina had said.

"If you're that grateful, then do it again tonight..."

"Again," she'd said. In other words, didn't that mean Serina was eating delicious meals like this with Poncho nearly every night?

The moment that thought occurred to her, Komain couldn't restrain herself. She kicked back her chair and stood up, then kneeled on the floor in front of Poncho.

"Sir Poncho!"

"Y-yes! Um, Madam Komain? What are you doing, suddenly kneeling like that?"

"Madam Komain?" Serina asked, startled.

Seeing the dubious looks on their faces, Komain spilled forth the feelings she could no longer keep inside. "If I can eat food like this, I want to serve you, Sir Poncho! Please, keep me at your side!"

Komain was suddenly offering to serve under him.

While Poncho was still at a loss for words at the sudden turn of events, Serina rose from her seat to stand in front of the kneeling Komain. Her eyes had that same intensity in them which had driven away the women looking to discuss marriage with Sir Poncho.

While laying a gaze meant to make those it fell on shrink away on Komain, she said, "Is that...something you truly feel?"

Komain looked straight back at her, eyes unswerving. "Yes! I swear it on the honor of my people."

Serina and Komain were ignoring the man who, normally, should have been the center of this conversation, in order to stare each other down.

Poncho, as usual, was just flustered.

Shortly, Serina slumped her shoulders in resignation. "It seems you're serious... Very well." With that said, Serina extended a hand to Komain. "I accept you. Welcome to the Ishizuka family table."

"Madam Serina!"

The two exchanged a firm handshake. Their hearts had both been stolen by the same thing.

On this day, the two who were entranced with B-grade gourmet dishes were bound by a tie stronger than any plate.

Incidentally, Poncho, who had been left out of this, continued quietly eating soba meshi by himself.

Furthermore, though this is but a side note, from the next day onward, there were two women standing behind Poncho when women came to talk marriage with him.

HOW A REALIST HERO REBUILT THE KINGDOM

CHAPTER 2

Urgent News and a Meeting

THE REPUBLIC OF TURGIS was a state situated on the southern edge of the continent Landia.

On that continent, the average temperature dropped the further you went south. The southern edge of the continent, where the Republic of Turgis lay, was a land of ice and snow.

It was a mountainous country, but compared to the Amidonia region, it had more flatlands and a greater amount of arable land. However, because the winters were long and the summers short, the period in which the land could be worked was limited, and crop farming wasn't very prosperous.

The people of this country were supported by livestock farming. They lived off of free-range animals that could survive in cold regions, like yaks, woolly rhinosauruses, and mammoths.

In this land, the majority of the population were beastmen belonging to what were called the Five Races of the Snowy Plains. The five races included the snow monkey, white rabbit, white eagle, snow bear, and walrus.

In those five races, as with other beastmen, the women looked like humans with animal ears, wings, and tails, but the men had faces that were fairly close to the actual animals. Interracial marriage was allowed, but it seemed the children born from such a union always took after just one of the parents, so there was no mixing of their unique features.

The most common race were the white rabbits, known for their high birth rate. The least common race was the walruses, known for having an average height of over two meters.

Those races intermixed to form tribes inside the country, but their distribution across the land reflected the different abilities each race possessed.

The walrus and snow bear races, who could dive into icy waters to catch fish, made up a large percentage of the population along the coast. The tribes living in the mountains, on the other hand, had a higher percentage of members of the snow monkey and white eagle races, who could easily handle the terrain. Finally, many of those who lived in the flatlands, working the fields in the short summer season, were members of the white rabbit race.

There were human merchants and members of other races present, too, but the harsh winters made it difficult for the other races to live in the country. With the exception of slaves, they generally left the country before the roads were closed off by the snow.

Almost like Snu*kin.

Because the climate was so harsh, this country had never been destroyed by a foreign enemy. The air currents in the sky were always violent, and the temperature was chilly even in the summer.

Those facts kept air power such as wyverns away, and the icy seas prevented the use of sea power.

Because of that, the only avenue of attack was by land, and if the country put up a strong defense and held out through the summer, General Winter would come and sever the enemy's supply lines, forcing them to retreat.

In addition, there was little to gain by seizing this country.

It was said that, in its heyday, the Gran Chaos Empire could have gone toe to toe with the Star Dragon Mountain Range, but even then, the Empire had never once considered an invasion.

The Republic of Turgis was governed under a primitive iteration on a republic.

First, the chiefs, who were the representatives of each tribe, gathered in a Council of Chiefs. Then, the Council of Chiefs voted to select the nominal representative of the country, their head of state.

Matters of internal affairs were decided by discussion between the head of state and the Council of Chiefs, but foreign affairs (diplomacy, wars, and such) were controlled by the head of state.

This head of state was usually a position that lasted for one generation, but with the approval of the Council of Chiefs, the title could be inherited. The current head of state in the 1,547th year of the Continental Calendar was of just such a second generation.

Now then, having said all this about the Republic of Turgis, if we recall their relations with the Kingdom of Friedonia, they couldn't really be called cordial.

In search of unfrozen land and warm water ports, the Republic was always looking to the north for any opportunity to expand. Even during the recent war between the Elfrieden Kingdom and the Principality of Amidonia, they had moved their troops close to the kingdom's southern border looking for an opening to intervene.

I had deployed Excel and the navy close to the border, and that intimidation had been just barely enough to keep them from invading. If the war with the principality had bogged down, they surely would have attacked.

There was no letting our guard down with them. Still, I didn't want to quarrel with this country.

If we attacked them, there was nothing for us to gain. Even if we occupied their territory, the ways people lived in the Kingdom of Friedonia and Republic of Turgis were too different. The kingdom was pretty cold in the south, but the Republic's winter was even harsher. The people of the Republic had adjusted their way of life to that climate, and no matter how capable a magistrate I might send, they wouldn't be able to properly rule a country with such a different culture, set of values, and way of life. What's more, if we needlessly tried forcing our ways on them, it would just end in a rebellion.

A country we didn't want to attack us, but would be too troublesome to attack ourselves—that was the Republic of Turgis.

This was precisely why I, as the King of Friedonia, wanted to build cordial relations with the Republic of Turgis. Fortunately, during the recent war, our forces hadn't clashed directly with theirs. The sentiment of each of our peoples toward the other wasn't especially bad, either.

Now, if I could just experience their culture and way of thinking, and find a reasonable way to give them what they wanted, I suspected I could build cordial relations.

I knew this was a naïve hope. Still, a needless war would exhaust the country. Wars like the one we'd fought against the principality should be a last resort, not something that was the norm.

That cube-like thing which transcended human reckoning at the Star Dragon Mountain Range was as an element of uncertainty, too. I never knew what might happen or when, so I wanted to avoid needlessly expending the power of my country.

We were coming to the Republic of Turgis to see if that wish could be granted.

We arrived at a town in the eastern part of the Republic of Turgis, Noblebeppu. This place, which was close to the border of the Kingdom of Friedonia, was a quiet inn town surrounded by mountains in the north and the sea to the south.

It was toward the end of May, and the ice and snow blocking the roads had melted at last. The cold had lessened slightly, and it was a period that was, relative to the standards of this country, comfortable to live in. Because of that, there were many merchants from other countries, and the town was bustling as we walked through it.

Our group consisted of Aisha, Juna, Roroa, Tomoe, Hal, Kaede, and me, making for a total of seven people. Tomoe's bodyguard, Inugami, had come with us as well, but he was currently elsewhere along with the rest of the Black Cats, patrolling and guarding us.

To be completely honest, I had wanted Naden and Liscia to come, too, but Naden, as was typical of ryuus and dragons, couldn't stand the cold, and Liscia had fallen ill after returning from the Star Dragon Mountain Range, so she was resting back in the kingdom.

I was really worried for Liscia, but she herself told me, *"I'll be fine, so go see the world like a king should."* I couldn't have stuck around to tend to her after that.

I was worried, but I had arranged for the best doctors in the country, Hilde and Brad, to look after her, so she'd probably be fine. If anything happened, Naden would come notify me. In order to respect Liscia's feelings, I had to make a proper trip to the Republic.

"I'd heard it was cold, so I was expectin' nothing but snow, but it's not that bad," Roroa commented.

"It's late in May, after all," Juna said. "It still feels plenty cold, though." Roroa and Juna were both dressed more heavily than they had been in the kingdom.

For this trip, I was playing the role of a young merchant's son looking for prospective trade goods. Tomoe was my little sister, and Aisha, Hal, and Kaede were adventurers we had hired. As for the remaining two, Roroa was an employee who worked for my family's store, and Juna was my wife.

Juna leaned in and asked me a question. "Um, is this okay? Having me play the wife over the primary queens...?"

"It was a choice made with safety in mind," I answered. "You're skilled with both pen and sword, Juna, so I want you to keep your fighting abilities hidden in case something happens."

Even if we were attacked by ruffians, they'd probably have their eyes on Aisha, Hal, and Kaede, who were dressed as adventurers. They'd assume Juna was just a pretty girl. Then Juna would get them from behind because they'd let their guards down.

It's a bit late to say this now, but my fiancées were a little *too* combat-capable. Now that Naden had joined them, their average power level had massively increased.

"And, well, with that in mind, there were a limited number of people we might theoretically take with us on our trip who didn't have any combat ability," I said. "You don't seem like someone we'd employ, Juna, and I'm not sure about forcing you into the maid role like Carla."

"I wouldn't mind that," she said. "Give me any order you wish, Master."

She brought her hands to her chest, smiled, and tilted her head a little, so my heart skipped a beat.

"When did Lorelei turn into a maid café?!" I exclaimed.

She was going to get me in the mood, so I wished she'd stop.

"Well, Juna, you're his fiancée, too, so I figure it ain't a big deal," Roroa said.

"Is that right?"

"Darn tootin'. And you're the one playin' the wife, so why not have him spoil ya rotten?" Roroa wrapped herself around my arm.

"And you're the employee, aren't you?" Juna replied. "Is it really okay for you to hug the young master like that?"

"Sure is," she declared. "I'm an employee, sure, but I'm 'the employee who's aimin' to become the second wife by supportin' the young master, and maybe knock the first wife out of the picture if things go well.'"

"Don't go changing our backstory!" I objected. "And come on, that's a weirdly messy narrative."

"So Juna's gonna be callin' me 'you vixen.'"

"I-Is that the sort of role I'm playing?"

"Don't take her so seriously, Juna," I said. "Besides, in her case, Roroa should be a tanuki instead..."

"Ponpokopon!" Roroa mimed slapping her belly.

"Yeah, yeah. Real cute."

When I patted Roroa on the head, she grinned. Did tanuki in this world drum on their bellies...? Well, it wasn't like the ones in my original world did that in real life.

"Hee hee! When I see Roroa, it seems silly to hold myself back at all." Juna hooked herself around my other open arm. "We don't get the opportunity often enough, so spoil me, too, darling."

"Erm...sure. I'll do my best to escort you."

Kaede, who belonged to a fox beastman race, was watching us from a little ways away with her head tilted to the side. "'Vixen'? Is that something Ruby will call me, too?"

"In your case, she wouldn't even be wrong," Halbert said wearily. "Please, just try to get along."

"Well, we'll have to bring a gift back for her, then. But before you tell me that, try being that considerate yourself, Hal."

"Yes, ma'am..." Hal's shoulders slumped.

Ever since he'd taken Ruby as his second wife, he'd completely lost control of the situation. Well, not that I was one to talk.

Next to Hal and Kaede, Tomoe was riding on Aisha's shoulders. "Look, Aisha! There's a place selling steamed potatoes over there!"

"Oh, you're right. They look delicious," Aisha replied, drooling.

Having been unable to go to the Star Dragon Mountain Range, if you excluded the no doubt difficult time she'd spent as a refugee, this was Tomoe's first time traveling outside the country. She was eleven now, so she was as excited as an elementary school student on her first overnight field trip to the forest or sea. She stood out a little, but it looked like she was enjoying herself, so I let it slide.

"Ah! Hey, Darlin'—er, no, young master. C'mere a minute." Suddenly, Roroa pulled me over in front of a certain merchant's stall.

I looked, wondering what it could be about, and it appeared to be a place selling apparel. "Is there something you want? If it's not that expensive, I could buy it for you..."

"That's not it. No, if you wanna buy me somethin', I'm glad, but that's not it. Take a look at what they're sellin' here." Roroa lifted up one of the items on sale and held it out to me.

When I took it from her, it turned out to be an ornate metal hair pin. It was designed with a tree motif, but... it was incredible.

The designs were highly intricate. The details of each leaf were carved, and I could even make out a bird sitting in the branches.

"This fish earring over here has every scale carefully carved, too," Juna said.

"This donkey broach, too," Aisha said, setting down Tomoe. "The reins are done with a chain, but they're really detailed."

They continued voicing how impressed they were. It was true; each of the products was finely detailed.

The bunny-eared old lady who ran the shop spoke up. "Why, hello there, young'un. Those're some fine young ladies ya've got with ya there. Why don'tcha buy 'em some of my wares as a present? It'll show 'em what a man you are, y'know?"

The bunny-eared old lady laughed heartily and spoke in that merchant slang I always heard as Kansai dialect. If she had rabbit ears, did that mean she belonged to the white rabbit race? When I first heard about rabbit beastmen, I had imagined anime-style bunny girls, but... Well, there was a whole race of them, so of course there would be people of her age, too.

I picked up one of her products and said, "I like this one and want to buy it, but is it a work by a famous craftsman?"

"Nah, they make 'em at workshops everywhere. It's nothin' that expensive."

"Huh? At the workshop over there?"

Could something so intricate be made so easily? I had my doubts.

Roroa puffed up her chest and proudly explained. "The accessories made in the Republic of Turgis are famous for their detailed ornamentation. A whole lotta merchants'll come here in the summer lookin' to get their hands on 'em."

"Turgis ends up gettin' buried in snow durin' the winter, after all," the bunny-eared old lady put in. "We can't go out very far, so many of us stay in our houses, doin' work there. We've been livin' that way for a few centuries, so we Turgish people are good at workin' with our hands."

I see...so that's how it is. While I was busy being impressed, Roroa grinned boldly.

"Hey, young master. If Turgish craftsmen can do such detailed work, don'tcha think they'd be able to help with makin' *those things* you've been thinkin' about for a while?"

"Those things...? Oh, those!"

It was true, there was a thing I had been thinking of making for a while, but the development project hadn't made much headway, given the skill-level of the craftsmen in our country. But maybe the craftsmen of this country would be able to make them. If what the old lady said was true, there were highly capable artisans everywhere in this country. We might be able to not only develop what I had in mind, but also push them into mass production.

The Republic of Turgis... I'd thought they had nothing, but they were hiding immense potential. I turned to the old lady who ran the shop.

"Ma'am, I'm going to buy a number of these, so could you introduce me to a craftsperson who lives near here and is good at their work?"

"Thanks for your business. Well, why don't ya try goin' to the Ozumi Workshop? Taru's young, but capable. The kid's a little shy, and can be stubborn when it comes to her work, but if I write ya a letter of introduction, you'll be treated well."

"Please do. Oh! Roroa, Juna, Aisha, Tomoe, if there's something here you'd like, you can buy it."

Roroa reacted immediately. "That's my Dar—er, no, my young master! Whew, so generous!"

"Thank you, darling," Juna added. "Tomoe, would you like to choose ours together?"

"Huh...? Oh, sure!"

Juna, who knew it made a man look better if she didn't hesitate at times like this, bowed once, then invited Tomoe, who tended to hold back, to look at the lady's wares with her.

These were women with complicated backgrounds, but when you saw them giggling this way in front of an accessories shop, it was reassuring how like any other young girls the two of them were.

"This is perfect, Hal," Kaede said. "You should buy your gift for Ruby here."

"Sure. Oh! But can you help me pick one out? I'll buy one for you, too, of course, Kaede."

"I guess I'll have to. But I expect you to choose mine yourself, you know?"

"Uh, right."

It looked like Kaede and Hal were planning to buy something here, too.

"I think gold will go nicely with Ruby's red hair, you know," Kaede suggested.

"Yeah, you could be right. I feel like silver'd be a match for your golden hair."

"Hee hee. I think you have good taste, Hal."

The two of them had that sort of sweet conversation while looking at the shop's wares.

Wait, huh...? Where did Aisha go?

Come to think of it, I hadn't seen Aisha for a while now.

I looked around the area and spotted her a little ways away with two messenger kuis perched on her shoulders. It looked like she'd received a letter.

For some reason, I recalled the day when she'd received word of a natural disaster striking the God-Protected Forest. Try as I might to forget the look of anguish on Aisha's face from that time, I couldn't.

I waited tensely, wondering what sort of news had come, but there was no change in Aisha's expression. Then, having finished reading the letter, Aisha came over to me.

"Was there a message for us?" I asked.

"Yes. Two letters from Lady Liscia."

"From Liscia?"

"Yes. The first was addressed to me, and the second to you, Sire."

With that, Aisha passed a single unsealed letter to me. While accepting it, I tilted my head questioningly. She'd sent separate letters to Aisha and me? "Did something happen in the capital?" I asked.

"Well...in my letter, she asked me to do something specific."

"Something specific?"

"I'm sorry. She wrote not to tell you what the letter said, Sire." Aisha bowed her head apologetically.

I had even less of an idea what was going on now. I'd have to look at what my own letter said.

Let's see...

"Dear Souma,

I think this letter will arrive together with another for Aisha, so have Aisha read hers first. Make sure you read this letter after that."

That was how the letter started.

I didn't really get it, but she seemed insistent. Aisha seemed to have read hers already, so I could probably continue. I kept reading, and...

"Huh...?"

When I spotted a certain passage, I suddenly felt like I'd been hit in the head.

Wha...? Was this for real? Was she serious? No... She had to be. There was no point in telling a lie like this. Which meant... Whaaaaaaaaaaaaaaaaaaaaaaaaaaaaa?!

"Wh-what's wrong?!"

I must have had quite the look on my face, because Aisha started shaking my shoulder. That snapped me back to my senses, but there was still a cold sweat running down my back and my knees were shaking.

Seriously? I mean, seriously?

I turned my head towards Aisha like a broken tin robot. "I'm going home."

"Huh?"

"I'm going back to the kingdom right now!" I declared to everyone with bloodshot eyes.

Thinking back later, I don't think I was quite sane at the time. Every plan I'd had in my head up until that point slipped away. After all, my entire mind was now completely occupied by a certain thing written in Liscia's letter.

That one sentence sent me into a confused state of shock and delight. It said...

"I'm pregnant.

"I called Dr. Hilde to come and look at me, so I'm certain of it. Oh! Dr. Hilde was pregnant, too. I felt bad for calling her in. She says it's Dr. Brad's. They didn't seem to get along that well, so it's kind of surprising, huh?"

It was true, I was surprised, but I didn't care about that now!

While reading the letter, I wanted to poke fun at Liscia. The letter continued, *"But anyhow..."*

It was an awfully roundabout way of writing things. Maybe Liscia had been feeling tense herself while writing it.

"This is our child. Are you happy? You're happy, right?"

Damn straight I was! No, it wasn't like my mind had fully processed that fact yet, but I was just as happy as I was surprised. If Liscia were here now, I would have hugged her, without a doubt. The hands I held the letter with were shaking.

"By the way, the one most ecstatic about the news was our

chamberlain, Marx, who's been pressuring us to produce an heir. He shed a flood of tears, then stood up and declared, 'I must prepare a room and clothing for the young prince at once!' and went straight to work. Even though we don't know if it's a boy or a girl yet."

What're you doing, Marx? I thought. I was glad he was happy, though.

"I'm very happy," the letter said, *"to be able to bear your child. I can say this now that I'm pregnant, but I was a little worried. You know, because you're from another world, right? Lady Tiamat was saying that while we were both human, our origins were different, so I wondered if we could have kids, and what I was going to do if we couldn't. It looks like I worried in vain, though."*

Liscia...

I couldn't bear to sit still any longer. I wanted to fly to Liscia's side right away. I was dominated by that feeling, and tried to one-sidedly declare to everyone that we would be turning back to the Kingdom before taking off running.

However...

"F-forgive me!" Aisha suddenly jumped on me from behind, forcing me to the ground.

"Ack!"

With her arms wrapped around my back, I was like a fugitive being restrained by the authorities.

Underneath Aisha, I struggled to break free from her hold. "L-Let go, Aisha! I have to go to Liscia..."

"I don't know why, but Lady Liscia asked me to do this!"

Huh? Liscia did?

When I stopped resisting, Aisha thrust her own letter in my face.

"Dear Aisha," it said, *"If Souma says he's going home after reading my letter to him, restrain him. Then tell him to read his letter carefully, and do as it says. Also, until you've restrained him, keep what this letter says a secret."*

It looked like Liscia had predicted my response to reading the letter. I gave up, and, standing up, I continued reading.

"You can be overprotective when it comes to family, so I'm sure you'll want to come home when you read this, but...you can't, okay? You won't have many chances to look around another country freely, so make sure you do it this time.

"You don't need to worry about me. I have Serina and Carla, who both rushed here when they heard, waiting on me hand and foot, and I'm thinking of going to stay with my parents until the baby is born. My father's old domain is quieter than the capital, and it's in the rustic countryside. I'll go ask them all sorts of questions about how to raise a child. So, Souma, you do what you need to be doing now, too."

It seemed Liscia had carefully planned out things on her own end. And it didn't seem like I had anything to worry about, but... Even with that said, it was in my nature as a man to worry anyway, you know?

Still, with Liscia telling me all that, I guessed I couldn't abandon what I was doing and turn back now.

When my shoulders slumped, the last line of the letter caught my eye.

"P.S. You can start putting your hands on your other fiancées now."

Liscia... At the very end, that was what she'd decided to write? Maybe it was her way of masking her embarrassment.

Whatever the case, I decided to show everyone else the letter. The old lady minding the shop looked at us dubiously when we all moved away for a minute to whisper about it, but right now our family issues took priority.

When they saw the letter, everyone was surprised for a moment, but they all congratulated me.

"My word!" Aisha exclaimed. "This is a happy occasion indeed!"

"How wonderful," Juna smiled. "Congratulations, Sire."

"I'd say the succession's secure for now, huh?" Roroa smirked. "He he he! Ya think it'll be one of our turns next?"

"Congratulations, Big Brother!" Tomoe cried.

"Congratulations," Kaede agreed. "Now your house is secure. If this weren't a foreign country, I'd want to cry out, 'Glory to Friedonia,' you know."

"Congrats," said Halbert. "Souma a father, huh... It's kind of moving, as a guy from the same generation."

"Does this get you in the mood to finally make an heir for the House of Magna?" Kaede asked him.

"My old man's still the current head of the house. But...it makes me think it might be good to, yeah."

Hal and Kaede seemed to have a good mood going. They were going to use another house's good news to start flirting, huh? Well, not that I minded.

I stuffed the letter in my pocket and beckoned to Roroa. "Roroa, come here a minute."

"Hm? What's up...? Wait, whoa!"

I stuck my hands under Roroa's armpits and lifted her up high like a child.

Roroa was petite, so even with my weak arms, I was easily able to lift her. If I'd chosen the tall Aisha, or the shapely Juna, I doubt I could have done it.

With Roroa held up in the air, I spun around in place.

"What what what what?!" Roroa sounded uncharacteristically flustered.

After spinning around a good bit, I released my hands and caught her in my arms as she fell. Roroa's eyes were spinning.

"Wh-what are you doin' to me...out of nowhere?!"

"Sorry," I said. "I got kind of excited. Really, I wanted to do that to Liscia, but she's not here. I did it with you because you've got the closest figure to hers."

"Mrgh...I'm not so keen on bein' Big Sister Cia's substitute, but, well, it was fun for me, so I'll let ya get away with it. But, y'know, isn't it kinda rare for you to let loose like that, Darlin'?"

"Yeah... Well, it's just for today, so let it go."

I mean, I'd made a baby. A new member of the family. With Grandpa and Grandma's deaths, I'd lost the last people I could call family. That was why, feeling that Liscia and Tomoe were something like family, I wanted to protect them.

Now, with Liscia and me having conceived a child, we'd gone

from being something like family to an *actual* family. There was nothing that could make me happier.

"If we were at the castle now, I'd probably be proposing a system of childcare support!" I declared, gripping my fists and speaking passionately.

"Well, I can't see that bein' anythin' less than excessive," said Roroa, looking taken aback. "Maybe it's a good thing we've gotten you away from the castle for a while to cool down."

Yeah, I had to agree.

Exasperated, Hal asked, "So? In the end, what are we doing now?"

"Hrm..." I said. "I want to fly back now, but Liscia said not to yet."

"You're the king, so you should prioritize looking around this country, like Lady Liscia was saying," Juna advised.

"That's right," chided Roroa. "Ya need to keep the kingdom developin'. For the people in it now, and for the kid who's gonna be born, too."

For the kid who was going to be born, huh...? If she put it that way, I couldn't argue. "Fine," I said. "There's no change in plans. We'll start by going to that workshop we've got an introduction to."

Having settled that, we went back to the woman and her shop.

"What is it, young man?" the shopkeeper asked. "You're all done talkin' now?"

"Yeah. Now, where is this Ozumi Workshop you mentioned?"

"Ya can see it from this town. Look, it's up on that there hill," the woman said, pointing to the hill at the back end of town.

It was a grassy hill with a gentle slope. There were woods on both sides, and it looked like a skiing hill during the summer. Snow still speckled the woods here and there; even if we watched it all year, it probably wouldn't fully melt.

A red brick building sat halfway up that hill, adjacent to the woods. Was that the Ozumi Workshop?

We settled the bill for the things we were buying, had the old lady write us a letter of introduction, and headed for the building at once.

Leaving the town of Noblebeppu, we spent the next thirty minutes traveling on a rocking carriage. Soon we stood outside a building made of brick: the Ozumi Workshop.

That workshop, which stood in the middle of a field of tall grass with a forest behind it, had a chimney. It looked like they also handled blacksmithing, in addition to producing their own accessories. Convenient.

Having been told Taru was shy, it seemed likely I would surprise her if I dragged a bunch of folks decked out as adventurers in with me, so we left Aisha and the others by the carriage while Juna, Roroa, Tomoe, and I went inside.

From the looks of it, they didn't have a sales counter. The building was a ways out, so they probably sold their wares wholesale in town. I could hear the sound of something being pounded inside.

I knocked on the door, but no one came to answer. Had no one heard me? There seemed to be someone inside, so I tried knocking again, and after a little while, the door slowly opened.

A girl with a bandana wrapped around her head came out.

"Who is it...?"

The girl was petite and had a baby face. I put her at around fifteen to sixteen years old. Even though it was freezing out, she wore a short-sleeved shirt, long pants, and a blacksmith's apron. In her gloved hands, she held a hammer that seemed incongruous with her petite form. Could this be the craftsperson the old lady had been talking about?

"Erm, excuse me... Would you happen to be Madam Taru?" I asked, standing up straight.

The girl cocked her head to the side and looked at me with sleepy eyes. "Yes, I am. What is it?"

Dealing with you is tiring. If you have no business here, go home. That was what her general demeanor seemed to say.

Some people might have been offended at this point, but I was used to dealing with people like Genia, so I didn't think much of it. I bowed politely, then introduced myself. "I've come here with an introduction from a lady in Noblebeppu. My name is Kazuma Souya."

Naturally, I used a fake name. It would be a real hassle if my name got out, not to mention the names of all the other members of our group.

I then introduced the rest of us. "This is my wife, Juna; my younger sister, Tomoe; and my employee, Roroa."

"I'm Juna. It's a pleasure to meet you."

"I-I-I'm Tomoe."

"Roroa. Nice to meet ya."

"Taru Ozumi. Nice to meet you."

I felt like Taru relaxed her guard a little after the girls introduced themselves. Well, hearing Tomoe's stuttering introduction would warm anyone's heart.

When Taru took off her bandanna and introduced herself, I noticed two bear ears on top of her head. She was a bear beastman? I guessed that would make her a member of the snow bear race, one of the Five Races of the Snowy Plains. The atmosphere had lightened a little, so I immediately got to the point of our visit.

"I saw the accessories made by this country's craftspeople in Noblebeppu, and oh my, was I ever impressed! By the fine and detailed ornamentation, I could tell you must all be very skilled with your hands. It made me think that, if we commissioned this country's craftspeople, we might be able to make a certain thing that I've been planning to have manufactured. I asked if there were any good craftspeople around, and the lady I spoke to gave me an introduction to this place. Are you willing to listen to the rest of what I have to say?"

"Come in..." Taru gestured for us to come inside the workshop.

Phew... I thought. *I managed to speak smoothly, like the young son of a businessman, but...*

"Also, talk normally. I'm sure you're older than me. Besides, I doubt you're used to talking that way."

It looked like Taru saw through me completely.

Seeing me awkwardly scratch the back of my head, Roroa bit back a laugh.

Hey, no laughing! I'm embarrassed here!

When we were brought into the workshop, the roaring flame of the furnace made the place fairly warm. No wonder Taru dressed so lightly. We took off our coats, too, but when Tomoe removed her handmade white mage hood, Taru's eyes narrowed.

"You're a dog… No. A wolf beastman?"

"Oh, yes!" Tomoe beamed. "From the mystic wolf race."

Taru looked to me as if she wanted to ask something. "Wasn't she supposed to be your sister?"

Oh… That was what was bothering her, huh. Fair enough, since Tomoe and I weren't the same race, and our faces didn't look alike at all. We must not have looked like siblings.

"From another mother," I said. "It's a family matter, so I'd appreciate if you didn't pry too deeply."

"I see…"

I made it sound like there was a difficult story involved, and Taru didn't ask any more. When it came to topics like this, even if she was interested, it was best to let it slide, after all.

With that, Taru led the way, and just as we were about to take a seat at a table, I noticed something odd leaning against the wall in the corner of the room.

It was pole-shaped, but both ends bulged slightly. If this were an RPG, I'd probably call it a cudgel. It had a distinctive design with a long, thick centipede wrapped around it that continued down to where the wielder would hold it. I thought it looked cool, but I wasn't so sure about it as a weapon.

While I was looking at it dubiously, Taru asked, "Do you like it?"

"Oh, I mean, it's an impressive design, that's for sure, but..."

I didn't want to say anything weird about her products, so I avoided answering the question, but Taru just shrugged as if to say, *I know what you want to say.*

"It's fine. Your view is perfectly normal. What's abnormal is the taste of the idiot who ordered it."

"Idiot? Really? Um, this is your customer you're talking about, isn't it?"

"I know him well, and I call him that to his face."

Someone she'd call an "idiot with no taste" to his face? What was this person like, and what was Taru's relationship with him?

Well, setting aside the weird cudgel, it was time to get our business taken care of. Taru waited for everyone to be seated, then asked, "So, what is it you want me to make?"

"Could you make something like this?" I used a feather pen to draw on a pad of paper I had prepared in advance to explain exactly what sort of thing I wanted.

When she saw my drawing, Taru tilted her head to the side. "The shape itself is simple. But I think it would be incredibly difficult."

"I thought so," I sighed.

"The fact that you want it 'as thin as possible' but also 'sturdy' is especially hard. If it was one or the other, I could manage it, but balancing both is pretty difficult. Around how many will you want?"

"The more the better. I want them in the thousands or tens of thousands. I'm not saying I want to make them all here, of course. I'll be having this same conversation with other craftspeople, too."

"Tens of thousands?" Taru said in surprise, peering at me with her sleepy eyes.

"Wh-what?" I asked. "So, can you make them?"

"Before I answer, I want you to tell me one thing," Taru said in a serious tone. "How exactly will they be used?"

I was silent.

How they'd be used, huh? I was making a strange request, so it was only natural she'd be curious. But was it okay for me to say why in this place? It would be one thing inside my own country, but this was a foreign land. They were something I needed, but I honestly didn't want to reveal too much about the revolutionary new information my country had.

"Do I really have to say?" I asked.

"You do. Or I won't make them, and I won't refer you elsewhere."

She was being blunt about it, so I whispered to Roroa, "What do you think?"

"I know you don't wanna say why, Darlin', but lookin' at what she's made, I'm thinkin' this girl here can make what you're after."

"Then do you think it's okay to reveal how they'll be used?"

"I dunno. If we're gonna procure a whole load of 'em, that's more than this workshop's gonna be able to handle alone, so we've gotta hope whoever's in charge of this country ain't too hardheaded..."

"It all comes down to that, in the end..." I murmured.

While we whispered back and forth, Taru slowly pulled something out from between her apron and shirt. What she held out towards us was an obsidian arrowhead. It looked like she'd been wearing it as a necklace. The arrowhead was polished and had a dull shine to it.

While holding it, Taru said, "This arrowhead was a lesson from my grandfather, the blacksmith."

"It's from your grandpa?" I asked.

"'A bow and arrow can be used to hunt animals and fill people's stomachs, but it can also be used as a weapon to kill people. The arrowhead is a part of the bow and arrow. Even if it's just one part of a product we craftspeople are making, we must know how the things we make will be used.'"

Taru looked straight into my eyes as she spoke.

"For a craftsperson, it is their duty to know how what they make will be used. If something I made were used for evil, that would make me very sad. That's why I don't make things when I don't know how they'll be used. I can't."

"What happened to your grandpa?" I asked.

"He passed away last year."

"I see..."

This was a girl who took her grandpa's words to heart as she ran her workshop. I had lost my own grandfather just last year (though that year had switched to this world's calendar for me partway through), so I felt a strange kinship with her. I always had a weakness for hearing stories like hers. The human part inside me said, "Can't you just tell her?" while the part of me that was a ruler said, "Be cautious in all things."

While I was seriously agonizing over what to do, I suddenly felt something cold in my hand. When I looked, Juna, who was sitting next to me, had placed her left hand on top of my right. I looked at her in surprise, but Juna didn't say anything, just smiled quietly.

Please, do what you want.

I felt like she was telling me that. In that instant, my heart felt lighter, to the point that Juna's cold hand felt good to me.

Well...okay, then. Taru seemed to have thought hard on the matter, so it was probably safe to tell her.

Having decided that, I asked Taru a question. "Can I trust this will remain confidential?"

"Are these dangerous?" she asked.

"No, that's not it. Well, if they were misused, they could be, but the same could be said of a knife, right? This is one part of a tool that will save lives."

"A tool that will save lives?" Taru tilted her head to the side questioningly, and I firmly nodded in response.

"What I'm thinking of making is a hypodermic needle."

In persuading Brad and Hilde to become the two pillars of my medical reforms, I'd made two promises:

The first was to make a national health care system which would allow any citizen of the kingdom to receive medical treatment. The second was to have the top smiths in the country make scalpels, needles for suturing, and other medical equipment.

To secure the funding fulfilling the first promise, I had prioritized raising taxes. There was still a long way to go, but things were making steady progress.

As for the latter—the development of medical equipment—it was going well in some parts, and not so well in others.

The medicine in this world was mainly light elemental magic (recovery magic), and herbs brewed by a medicine man or woman (medicinal baths). Surgery was only practiced in a truly limited number of places. The tools made by one extremely rare example of a surgeon, Brad, were specially made for himself. While he had developed scalpels, stitches, and syringes on his own, there were limits to their functionality. He had been unable to make his scalpels small, and his syringes were considerably larger than what I was used to seeing.

His funds for research were limited, so it was hard to blame him, but it was still putting a lot of strain on the patients. That being the case, I wanted to set out on a national project to improve our medical equipment. I had been able to produce tools that satisfied Brad and Hilde for now, but I couldn't bring them into mass production yet.

Even if I had one craftsperson who could make thin hypodermic needles, there were limits to how many that one person could make. It was a given that they weren't being produced in a factory, and there weren't many craftspeople capable of manufacturing a thin needle. In the current situation, where we were trying to increase the number of doctors, we were obviously short on equipment. Because the medical equipment couldn't be immediately reused, and it had to be boiled again for each patient, the number required increased.

While we were having difficulty producing medical equipment, it seemed there were many talented craftspeople in this country who could do detailed ornamental work. That was why I thought it might be possible to set up mass production in this country.

Our country was currently studying many fields, and we were short-handed everywhere, so I thought it might be best to leave what could be left to other countries to those countries, while also protecting our existing smiths.

With that in mind, I explained the use of a hypodermic needle to Taru. Because surgery itself was unknown in the Republic of Turgis, I had to start with that, so it took a rather long time.

Once I had given her the rundown, Taru's eyes opened wide in surprise. "In the kingdom, you can heal people without light elemental magic? I think that's incredible."

"Y-you do?" I asked.

"In this country, the ground is covered with snow from October to March. Those with weak legs can't even go outside properly. If we had at least one doctor in every village, I think it would be a lot easier to live."

"Well, it's a real considerate policy the king's puttin' forward." Roroa grinned at me as she said that.

It was a compliment, so I didn't mind that much, but still.

Taru crossed her arms and frowned. "I understand these hypodermic needles are important. I think that, with our country's craftspeople, you should be able to mass-produce them, too. I want to take on the challenge. It's a job that'll set my heart dancing, I think."

"Oh! Then you'll..."

Take the job, I was about to say, but Taru held up two fingers.

"Still, even if I make them, there are two major problems with bringing them to the kingdom. First, exporting weapons to another country requires clearance from the state. If it's just adventurers buying weapons for personal use and carrying them out, they won't be accused of anything, but if we're exporting a product in large quantities, we need government clearance. It's the same in the Kingdom of Friedonia, too, right?"

"Well...yes, it is..."

It was true that our country also managed the import and export of weapons. It wasn't quite on the level of Edo Era prohibitions on guns coming into the city and women going out, but... excessive amounts of weapons being brought into the country from elsewhere could be a threat to peace. If the weapons were brought out of the country, that lowered our ability to defend ourselves. If they were brought in, that could foreshadow a rebellion. That was why, in any country, arbitrary importation and exportation of weapons was clamped down on.

"But needles aren't weapons, are they?" I said.

"If that's the case, you will need to prove that to the authorities. No country has had needles before this, so it will be difficult to tell at a glance whether they're weapons or not. If we try dealing them without a guarantee they aren't weapons, there's the risk of problems."

"If it's just needles, surely no one will think they're weapons, right?"

"Even if they aren't weapons themselves, it'll all be over if they're suspected of being weapon parts."

"I see your point..."

Unfortunately, Taru was right. If someone unfamiliar with syringes saw a hypodermic needle on its own, they wouldn't be fully confident it wasn't a weapon. If we had to explain their usage every time we were stopped at the entrance of a city or at the border, that would be a hassle, and there was no guarantee they'd believe us. It looked like I'd need to seek permission from this country to import and export them, after all.

But this country was a republic, right? They did, technically, have a head of state. But until I saw the balance of power between their head of state and the Council of Chiefs, I couldn't be sure who to persuade. It was a total drag.

I needed to think about this more carefully. "So, what's the other problem?" I asked.

"It's about shipping. The winters in this country are long. The land is closed off by snow, and the sea is coated with ice. You said you wanted tens of thousands, so that means there's a continuous need for them, right? That's one thing in the summer, but how do you mean to transport them in winter, when the land and sea routes are unusable?"

"I wonder..." I could only hold my head. Shipping would definitely be a problem.

Even in the Kingdom of Friedonia, the south was locked in

snow and ice in the winter. It seemed like it would be really difficult to secure shipments from the Republic of Turgis, where the winters were longer and harsher. This being a foreign country, I couldn't propose rolling out a transportation network, either.

I asked Roroa in a whisper, "Can we only trade with them in the summer for now? Even for that, we'd need to get official clearance, I'm sure. What do you think?"

Roroa brought a hand to her mouth and thought about it before quietly responding. "Yeah... But if you've decided on doin' it, Darlin', I think ya should negotiate directly with their top officials. If ya try to keep pushin' things forward as a merchant, it'll take time for reports of what's goin' on to filter upward."

"Don't negotiate under a fake name, but as Souma Kazuya, you're saying?"

"Ya can't very well meet the people in charge while wearin' a mask, now can ya?"

"Fair enough," I said. "Well, I guess we need to take this matter back home with us, then. Just when it looked like we could mass-produce them, too..."

While my shoulders slumped in resignation, Taru looked at us funnily. "I thought you were the young master and his employee? You look like you're acting as equals to me."

Oops... That had been unnatural just now, hadn't it? Roroa always felt like my partner when it came to business like this.

"Mwa ha ha, ya think so?" Roroa snickered. "Well, I'm not just any ol' employee, I'm his mistress with his wife Juna's approval, after all!"

With that, Roroa hugged my arm tight. Wait, a mistress my wife approved of?!

What kind of ridiculous backstory is that?! Now I have to play along with it!

I wanted to complain, but we were in front of Taru, so I held back.

Roroa was smiling happily as she looked at me. *Why, that little...* She knew I couldn't correct her here, so she was laying it on even thicker.

The air seemed to have frozen over. While Juna was smiling, there was a strange intensity to it, and Tomoe panicked when she saw her face.

Sensing the unease in the air, Taru backed away a little. "Is this...your family situation, too?"

"I'd appreciate if you didn't pry..." That was all I could manage to say.

Suddenly, Juna stood up. "Darling, we will be excusing ourselves for a moment."

"Huh? Juna?"

She had the same plastered-on smile as before. Then she stood behind Roroa and planted her hands on her shoulders.

Roroa's expression instantly stiffened. This was a cool country, but she was obviously sweating buckets.

"U-um, Ju—Madam, is somethin' the matter?" Roroa turned just her neck to look at Juna.

She smiled as she said, "Why don't the two of us go get a breath of fresh air together?"

"No... I wanna stay here...y'know..."

"Don't be like that. Come with me, Miss Roroa, 'the mistress I personally approve of.'"

There was a weight to those words that brooked no argument.

It was said "the quieter the person, the scarier they are once mad," and it looked like Juna was that type.

Roroa shot a look in my direction. Her eyes cried, *H-help me!*

But I simply shook my head in silence. *You joked around too much, Roroa. Deal with it.*

I-I just got a lil' carried away!

Make your excuses to Juna...

Noooooo...

"Hee hee! Shall we be on our...hm?"

Just as Juna was preparing to drag Roroa off, it happened.

Thump... Thump... There was an earthshaking sound off in the distance. At the same time, the room shook. It was a low-magnitude quake.

The tools hanging on the walls rattled. The sound and shaking were getting louder and louder.

"What's goin' on? Is this an earthquake?" Roroa asked.

"It seems...a little strange for that to be the case," Juna said.

"Tomoe, if the shaking gets any stronger, you take shelter under the table," I ordered.

"R-right!"

While we were panicking, Taru's expression didn't change in the slightest. Not only that, it seemed a little cold, and she sighed as she said, "This isn't an earthquake. It's just an incoming idiot."

"An idiot?" I asked.

Then the shaking subsided and Hal rushed into the workshop. "Hey! There's this huge thing outside!"

Huge thing?

When we all went outside, there was a huge, hairy thing just standing there. It was there right when we opened the door, so I let out a, "Whoa..." despite myself, and my head jerked back in shock. In that moment, I saw the hairy thing's face.

Its long, fat nose.

Its four big, tough tusks.

The surprisingly beady eyes that peeked out from beneath its bushy hair. If I were to describe the creature looming in front of me...

A four-tusked mammoth?!

Its body hair was long enough to touch the ground, and its legs were pretty short, but that seemed like an apt description of the creature. I knew the people of this country kept long-haired creatures as free-range cattle. However, it was too much for me to instantly recognize this thing in front of me as a mammoth.

One time, when Grandpa had taken me to an event at the science museum, I'd seen a reproduction of a mammoth's skeleton. Its height from the ground to its shoulder blades had been four, maybe five meters.

The one in front of me looked to be about ten meters.

I was used to seeing massive creatures like the rhinosauruses and dragons, but that felt a little different from seeing an upsized version of a creature from my old world.

Then the four-tusked mammoth bent its front legs and sat down. In that instant, its hair touched the ground and spread out. Even seated, it was still huge. It was probably only two or three meters shorter.

A voice that sounded like it belonged to a young man came down from above. “Hm? That’s unusual. Don’t usually see so many people at this workshop.”

The mammoth spoke!

Yeah...no. That couldn’t be right. It sounded like a young man’s voice, so he was probably riding on top of this mammoth.

“Sire, get behind me.” Aisha rushed over to stand in front of me.

Hal and Kaede were tensed and ready for action, too, while Juna subtly waited by my side.

Maybe because such a massive animal had shown up all of a sudden, everyone had gone into battle mode.

Roroa, being a noncombatant, had taken Tomoe and evacuated to a spot a little further away. Probably sensing our unease, the voice up top turned threatening.

“Who’re you guys? You’re not planning to attack this workshop, are you?”

“Huh?! No, we’re not! We’re—”

“Ooh ha ha!” Before I could explain, someone jumped down from the mammoth.

The one who flipped in midair before landing was a white monkey beastman. A white monkey... Did he belong to the snow monkey race, one of the Five Races of the Snowy Plains?

He stood around 160 centimeters high and appeared at a glance to be fifteen, maybe sixteen years old. Rather than having a full monkey face, he had large ears and long sideburns, and what you'd call monkey-like features.

Even in this cool climate, he wore a short-sleeved shirt and half-length pants, and the arms and legs sprouting from them had thick hair the same color as the hair on his head. He had a long tail like a lemur's growing out of his half-length pants, and if I were to quickly describe him, he looked like a live-action version of Sun Wukong (white-monkey version) from *Journey to the West*. That white Sun Wukong thrust his hand out as if striking a pose.

"Ooh ha ha! You've got real nerve, trying to force your way into Taru's workshop! I, the great Kuu Taisei, show no mercy in the face of such insolence! I hope you're ready to—"

"Master Kuu!" a weak voice called from on top of his mammoth. A girl with rabbit ears poked her head out and shouted, "Please, don't suddenly pick fights with people!"

This girl of about seventeen was apparently a member of the white rabbit race, like the lady running the shop in town. Now this one looked more like a bunny girl, although she was wearing a thick duffle coat that didn't show much skin.

The girl hopped down to stand beside Kuu. "If you cause a scene, your father will get mad again, you know?"

"Ooh ha? But, Leporina, these guys are armed, so they're bandits, right? You think I can stand by when Taru's workshop's about to be attacked?"

Bandits...? It looked like we'd been badly misunderstood.

The girl called Leporina put a hand on her hip and said, "Come on, that's clearly not the case. Look over there. You see the little girl, right? What bandit brings a child with them on a raid? They're just ordinary adventurers who were startled by your numoth, right?"

Having said that, Leporina stroked the...numoth's?...trunk with one hand while pointing to Roroa and Tomoe with the other.

Kuu's eyes opened wide in surprise. "Ooh ooh? You're right, there is a cute girl."

Before I could stop him, Kuu headed towards Roroa. Hiding Tomoe behind her, Roroa put her hands on her hips and glared at Kuu.

"Ah! Hey..." I began.

"What? I can't have ya fallin' for my pretty face," Roroa said. "I've already got a man I've set my heart on."

"Huh? I don't have any business with someone like you who doesn't have any."

"Doesn't have any...?" Roroa's gaze drifted down to her own chest, then her eyes went wide.

While Roroa was letting out a silent exclamation of surprise, Kuu peeked around behind her.

He was after Tomoe?!

"You're a cutie! What's your name?"

"T-Tomoe..."

"Tomoe, huh? That's a good name! Hey, Tomoe..."

"Y-yes...?"

"Will you be my bride?"

With those words, the atmosphere froze over. The climate was already cold to begin with, but now it felt even more frigid.

Tomoe...his bride? They'd only just met, and this man was already trying to lay his hands on our cute little sister? Before I knew it, I could feel the anger emanating from Aisha beside me.

This was...a challenge to us, right?

We had to put him in his place. "Aisha," I said heatedly.

"What is it, Sire? I feel like cutting up a monkey right now, you know."

"I'll allow it."

The blood had risen to my head because he'd mocked Roroa, a member of my family, and tried to make a move on my little sister, Tomoe. Like, there was a story in my old world, wasn't there? Slaying a demon monkey was a job for the dog named Shippeitarou. Just when I was about to sic the fierce dog Aisha on that insolent monkey...

"Both of you, calm down," Juna ordered.

"Ack!"

Juna grabbed both of us by the back of our necks. Unable to breathe, I turned back to look at her, and Juna rebuked me, anger seeping into her smile.

"You two... You realize this is another country? You both have your positions to consider, so please refrain from doing anything to cause trouble."

"Uh, right..."

"S-sorry."

"Honestly... Now listen, Sire, Madam Aisha." Juna pressed a

finger into my chest. Then, with a powerful smile, she put her face between Aisha's and mine and whispered in our ears, "In times like this, you have to dispose of him in a way that won't be discovered."

"Wha?!" Aisha and I ended up staring at Juna despite ourselves.

Then Juna said, "Hee hee, just joking," and gave us a charming smile.

While I was relieved it was a joke, having just witnessed how scary she was when she was angry, I doubted whether it really was one.

Maybe the anger seeping into her smile before hadn't been directed at the two of us, and Juna was angry at Kuu's behavior, too? I looked at Juna, considering that.

"If I say it's a joke, it's a joke," she insisted with a smile.

Yeah. Best not to think too much about it. No matter what, it would be provoking trouble I didn't need to. Thanks to her, I had managed to mostly cool my head. For now, I was more worried about Tomoe and Roroa.

I looked over to see Roroa picking a fight with Kuu. "Hey, you! Ya said I 'don't have any,' so what are ya doin' tryin' to seduce a little girl like her for, huh?!"

"Huh? Are you misunderstanding me? I was saying you don't have fur, okay?"

"Huh? Fur?"

Seeing Roroa so taken aback, Kuu snickered. "I like girls like her who have furry ears and tails. That, and this girl looks like she'll be a total knockout in ten years. I figured I'd make her an offer now. So, how about it? Will you be my wife?"

Tomoe silently but vigorously shook her head back and forth.

From behind me, I felt an intense stare. When I turned back, Inugami, her bodyguard, was staring hard in Kuu's direction. He seemed to be hiding his bloodlust so his target wouldn't notice, but the glint in his eyes said, *Please, allow me to take out this trash.*

Yeah... When there's someone madder than you, don't you find that you suddenly calm down?

Having settled down, I approached Kuu. If nothing else, I had to acknowledge he had a keen eye to have recognized Tomoe's cuteness. However, as her older brother, I wasn't giving my little sister to a man she'd just met.

"You're bothering my sister, so could I ask you to stop?" I asked coldly.

Kuu's eyes went wide. "Huh? You're this girl's big brother? You don't look like it."

"We have a complicated family situation."

"Hmm...well, it looks like she's shot me down anyway, so I don't have much choice. Ooh ooh ha ha." With that said, Kuu laced his fingers behind his head and grinned.

Seeing how he didn't seem all that disappointed, the proposal just now must have been almost entirely a joke. Well, of course it had been. He'd only just met her, and Tomoe was still just a child. Unless he had that sort of predilection, there was no way he would propose to her seriously. It looked like we'd been the ones who needed to calm down.

Thinking about it, I realized we hadn't exchanged greetings yet, and, after taking a breath, I extended my hand to him.

"I'm Kazuma Souya, a merchant from the Kingdom of Friedonia, here to investigate possible trade goods. These people here are my family and employees."

"Oh, that's all. Should told me that in the first place." Kuu accepted my hand and shook it vigorously. It kind of hurt. "I'm Kuu Taisei. Taru and I are childhood friends. I came because I figured the thing I ordered ought to be about finished, but then I saw there were these tough-looking guys with weapons surrounding the workshop. I figured you were getting ready to attack the place, so that put me on guard."

"We could say the same," I said. "When you rode in on this huge creature, it was only natural we'd be on our guard until we figured out what was up."

"Ooh ha ha. No kidding. But my numoth is more docile than he looks."

As if responding to Kuu, the numoth trumpeted loudly.

Hearing its voice, Tomoe came over to me and whispered in my ear, "Um, Mr. Numoth said, 'I'm sorry for startling you, young lady.'"

"He's surprisingly gentlemanly?!"

Maybe this numoth was a better person than his master...? I mean, he wasn't a person, he was a pseudo-mammoth thing, but still.

Then Kuu asked a question. "So, why did you people come to this workshop? It's outside town, isn't it?"

"We came to visit because we heard there was a talented craftsperson here," I said. "I thought maybe the person here could create the item I was thinking of as a trade good."

"Oh! If you discovered Taru's talent, you've got good taste. Taru may have no curves, but she's got skills like no other blacksm—ow, that hurt!"

Kuu suddenly grabbed his head and squatted down. Standing behind him was Taru, brandishing the cudgel with the golden centipede design that had been leaning against the wall inside her workshop. It made a good sound, so she must have hit Kuu upside the head with it.

Taru looked irritated. "Don't say I have no curves. And don't hit on girls in front of my business."

"Oho? You jealous?"

"Do you want me to hit you again?"

"He he, I'll pass... Wait, is that the thing I ordered?"

Kuu jumped up, snatched the cudgel from Taru's hands, then spun it around like a windmill. He looked just like Sun Wukong swinging the Ruyi Bang. After swinging the cudgel vertically and horizontally, and jumping around himself, Kuu suddenly stopped.

Ohhh, he really was kind of like a Chinese martial artist.

"It feels good. That's my Taru. You do good work. I love you."

"I don't need your love," Taru said. "I just want to be paid for my work."

"I'll pay. Jeez...you always play so hard to get," Kuu said, pouting a little.

Huh? He had been just fine when Tomoe rejected him before, but he made this sort of face when Taru was cold to him?

Oh, I get it... So that's how it is.

He was a really easy guy to figure out.

"Ah..." Taru said, seeming to have realized something. "This may be a good opportunity. Can we tell the dumb master about what we were talking about before? It might resolve one of our problems."

"Erm...what were we talking about again?" I asked.

"The part about needing permission from this country to make a deal. The dumb master has connections to the higher-ups in this country. After all...for all his shortcomings, he's the current head of state's son."

HOW A REALIST HERO REBUILT THE KINGDOM

CHAPTER 3

A Great Man Still in the Making

THERE WASN'T MUCH POINT in our continuing this discussion outside, so we relocated to inside the workshop.

In addition to those who had been in the workshop before, this time Aisha came inside, too, as a bodyguard.

Having seen him swing that cudgel around, I could tell that Kuu kid was pretty experienced. That was why, in preparation for the unlikely event that things went badly, I wanted Aisha at our side.

While drinking the coffee Taru provided, I explained to Kuu my request to this workshop.

"And, well, that's the gist of it," I finished at last.

There were medical reforms underway in the Kingdom of Friedonia, there would be a shortage of medical equipment in the future, and we were going to need to get the craftspeople in this country to mass-produce that equipment for us to import. We would also need to secure permission from the government so the medical equipment wouldn't be misunderstood as weapons when exported.

Because Kuu was the son of the Republic's head of state, and it was unclear if the two countries could form cordial ties, I was hesitant to show too much of my hand. But I had already discussed all of this with Taru, so I decided we couldn't trick him.

Incidentally, when I tried taking a formal tone in the discussions...

"Let's do away with all the stuffy formality!" Kuu declared cheerfully. "Yeah, I'm the son of our head of state, but we don't know if the Council of Chiefs will let me inherit the position. Having people get all polite with me just makes my butt feel all itchy."

So I opted to talk casually with him. He was awfully open, considering his position, but, well, who was I to talk?

Hearing what I had to say, Kuu thought for a moment, then let out a sigh. "Whew... Medical reforms, huh? That's awesome. Is that what our neighbor's doing? We don't get much news from outside around here. Our access to information is so bad we have to get our updates from the merchants who come in the summer. Like, it was only after the snow melted that we heard the Elfrieden Kingdom had absorbed the Principality of Amidonia to become the Kingdom of Friedonia."

Oh, he was right, that might be a bit slow.

The annexation of Amidonia had taken place from late fall to early winter last year. If he was saying the information hadn't reached here until the spring of this year, then yeah, that was pretty bad. It just showed how intense the snow was in this region. In a way, it was like having the evening and morning edition of the paper arrive at the same time.

"From what I hear, the king who was installed next door is pretty young, yeah?" Kuu added.

"He'll be twenty this year," I said.

Oh, but by the reckoning of this world's calendar, I was twenty already, right? Well...whatever.

When Kuu heard the (provisional) king was twenty, he let out an abrasive laugh. "Twenty, huh! I'll be sixteen this year, so he's not much older than me!"

"Isn't a four-year gap between humans and beastmen pretty big?"

Back when I was entering my first year of high school, this guy still would have been in elementary school, wouldn't he?

"Nah." Kuu shook his head with a laugh. "It's a rounding error, nothing more. If it's just four years, that's still well within my strike zone."

"What are you talking about?!"

"Women, of course," he said. "I'm down with anybody from twelve to thirty."

"I don't care! You're not laying a hand on Tomoe, got it?"

"That's a darn sha—ow! Hey, Taru, don't hit me with that thing!"

Taru had whacked Kuu in the head with the tray she'd used to bring in the coffee. It made a pretty loud *bong* sound. This girl didn't hold back when taking shots at the son of their head of state.

Taru held on to the tray and snorted. "Dumb master, your vulgarity shames our country. You ought to work on fixing that."

"Y-yeah, she's right," said the bunny-eared girl, Leporina. "I-Isn't your father always getting upset with you over it? For a start, you keep acting like you're loose with women, but you're not actually okay with just anybody, right? Pretending to have feelings for other women just to get the one you're interested in to pay attention is—ow, ow, ow! Don't pull my ears!"

"It's because you keep running your mouth!" Kuu shouted.

Ahhh, I think that exchange told me a little about who Kuu is as a person.

So that was it... If he was going to turn sixteen this year, that meant he was fifteen now. By the reckoning of my old world, he'd be in his third and final year of junior high. When I remembered what I was like at that age, I felt like I could understand how he was acting.

I would be spinning my wheels with eagerness and self-consciousness, and when I came to my senses, I'd often mistake the means for the ends, and the means I chose often wouldn't even match the ends I was pursuing.

"What's up, Darlin'? Why the frowny face?" Roroa asked while I was indulging in sentimentality.

"No, it's just... I was looking at how Kuu was acting, and I saw a bit of myself in him."

"Hm? Ya did?"

"Hee hee. Grandmother told me men are like that," Juna said with a smile full of charm, and I could offer no rebuttal.

Then, to mask his awkwardness, Kuu cleared his throat loudly and got back on topic.

"So, what's the young king like? I hear he annexed Amidonia not long after he got into power, so is he that great a warrior?"

"No, it's nothing like that," I said. "He didn't absorb Amidonia because he wanted to. The flow of events just made it a necessity... or so I hear."

Hmm...it was hard explaining myself while pretending not to be me.

"But, well, even if the king himself isn't a military man, he's assembled a talented group of subordinates," I added. "Their support lets him keep the country going somehow, you could say."

"Capable subordinates, huh... That's something to be envied. The only person I get to order around now is Leporina. I wanna hurry up and get some house vassals for myself."

"I-I'm not your subordinate! I'm your attendant, you know?! Don't order me around!" Leporina protested, but Kuu wasn't even listening to her.

"So..." Kuu said, looking straight into my eyes and trying to appraise me. "You're one of those capable subordinates that supports the king, aren't you?"

"I'm just a merchant, you know...?"

"Ooh ha ha, lying's not good. Those medical reforms are sponsored by the king, right? The equipment for them isn't something a single merchant, let alone the young son of one who hasn't even inherited the business, can handle the negotiations for. You're playing at being a merchant, but you're really acting according to the will of that king. Am I wrong?"

"..."

He'd hit the nail on the head, so I couldn't come up with a good response. It looked like he didn't think I was the king himself, at least, but acting on behalf of the king was equivalent to acting on my own behalf, so he wasn't wrong.

Taru had called Kuu the "dumb master," but he might be surprisingly sharp. If I underestimated him, I was going to get hurt.

"What if I am?" I asked. "Would you call off this deal?"

"I wouldn't say that," he said. "For our country's part, mass-producing that medical equipment or whatever would be a new industry. It's just...there's one point that bothers me."

"What would that be?"

He leaned over with his elbows on the table with his cheeks resting on his hands as he responded. "I think the neighboring king's medical reforms sound awesome. Those...doctors, was it? They don't rely on light magic, and even treat diseases that're hard to heal with magic."

I nodded.

"Basically, I want those doctors here, too. Exporting the equipment is fine, but if it's being produced in mass quantities, I can't accept not being able to use it ourselves. There are a large number of sick and wounded in every country. If there are tools that may be able to treat them, it'd be a waste not to have people on hand who can use them, right? That's why, if you want medical equipment from us, you'll give us doctors in return."

Kuu spoke in a strong tone. I felt an intensity in his eyes that he had every right to be proud of, as the son of their head of state.

Even though he was only turning sixteen this year, he could pick the fights needed to carry his country and people.

This was a man who might do great things in the future. Half-impressed, half-cautious, I accepted Kuu's stare, and he suddenly grinned and let the tension out of his shoulders.

"And, well, that's what I figure my old man would have said."

"Your father, huh?"

Even though those were clearly his own words, Kuu had brought up his father now to blur that distinction. He was a shrewd one, all right.

"I've thought this over," I said at last. "If your people will export the equipment to us, I will provide doctors...is what our king would say."

"Well, that's nice. But the winters in this country are harsh, you know? Can an outsider take them?"

"In that case, we can make doctors out of the people in this country."

"Our people?" Kuu asked.

I nodded. "To be more specific, what the kingdom will provide is the study of medicine. When it comes to the training of doctors, we are confident we are well ahead of other countries. So, if anyone in this country wishes to become a doctor, they can come to our kingdom to study. If those people return home after acquiring knowledge of medicine, you will have doctors who can stay here."

Kuu slapped his knee as if he got it now. "I see... That sounds like it'd work. That's how we'll trade doctors and medical equipment, huh?"

"Fundamentally, that's about right," I said. "What do you think?"

Kuu pounded his chest with one hand. "Sounds good! I'll talk to my old man. I mean, I insist you meet with him and discuss it now," he added with a happy smile.

I didn't have a bad feeling about this. If we could expect the backing of Kuu, the son of their head of state, that was going to be a great help.

Oh, wait.

"In regards to that, there's a person I want to have handle the negotiations with your head of state."

"You want to leave it to someone? You're not doing it yourself?"

"Yeah. I think negotiations should be handled not by me, Kazuma, but by His Majesty, King Souma."

"Ooh ooh?! A meeting between heads of state, huh!"

"Yeah. That'd be faster, right?"

"Well, yeah, but...can you get King Souma to come here?"

"I'm thinkin' it'll be fine, y'know? The king likes doin' the legwork." Roroa looked to me with a grin as she spoke.

Well, I *was* here, after all...

"Ooh ooh ah ha ha ha!" Kuu laughed heartily. "Okay! I'll talk to my old man. It'll be up to him what happens, but you people talk to your King Souma!"

"Got it."

"Now things are getting interesting! This'll be a huge deal!" Kuu seemed deeply entertained. "Hey, Leporina! You run over to the old man now, and let him know what's up!"

"N-now?!" she protested. "It's already evening, so let me set out tomorrow!"

"You dolt!" he yelled. "You've gotta make immediate decisions and act fast when it comes to business opportunities!"

"G-give me a break, please."

Kuu was hyped up and he was running Leporina ragged. Watching this boisterous master and servant, Taru, who had to this point been listening and not saying anything, let a few words slip out.

"I knew it... The dumb master really is dumb."

Her tone was cold, but the corners of her lips looked as if they had turned upward just slightly.

This unplanned meeting with Kuu resulted in the decision to arrange a sudden meeting with the head of the Republic.

To prepare, I dispatched a messenger kui to Hakuya in the kingdom, and Kuu dispatched one to his father, to arrange a time and place for the meeting. Then, when those arrangements were complete, it was decided we would stay in the country until the day of the meeting.

Taking the speed of messenger kui communication into account, the meeting would be in one week (eight days in this world) at the soonest.

However, I explained to Kuu I would be staying as a liaison.

Because there were issues of security and such when a king stayed in another country, I chose to keep my identity a secret for a while longer. Because I had, technically, entered the country on false pretenses, I also decided to have Hakuya subtly inform their head of state of that fact before the meeting.

That being the case, I thought I would use the time left before the meeting to continue deepening my understanding of the country, as originally planned. But Kuu said he wanted to accompany me.

"If you want to learn about our country, you'll need a guide, right? Being Turgish-born and Turgish-raised, I'd say I fit the bill, wouldn't you?"

"Oh, uh...I appreciate the offer, but I couldn't make the son of the Republic's head of state be my guide..."

I tried letting him down lightly, but Kuu laughed.

"Hey, don't sweat it. I may be his son, but I don't have any power. Besides, Kazuma, now that I know you're a foreign VIP, I can't let you out of my sight." Kuu sent a sharp, slightly provocative glance in my direction. "Sightseeing is fine, but I don't want you going anywhere too unusual. If you try going to military installations, for instance, I think we may have a little trouble."

That made sense... He'd be doubling as our handler, it seemed. The air got a little tense, but I shrugged and let the look Kuu was giving me slide. "I never planned on that, anyway."

"Ooh ah, just playing it safe," he said. "You people wouldn't want to be suspected of anything you aren't doing, right?"

"Fair enough."

Right now, we weren't in the country to gather intelligence. Our visit was purely to deepen our understanding of the country. There was no need to seek out their critical facilities. If Kuu was going to accompany us, we wouldn't have to worry about any undue trouble with the locals, so it was a convenient arrangement.

I offered Kuu my right hand. "If that's how it is, then please, come along."

"Sure!" Kuu took my hand and shook it firmly. "By the way, do you guys have lodgings booked for the night?"

"Yeah. We booked lodgings at the White Bird Inn in the town of Noblebeppu."

"The White Bird Inn! That's a good place. Now, if you're wondering why it's so good, that'd be the hot springs."

Hot springs!

I'd heard there were many hot springs in the Republic. The town of Noblebeppu was one of the few hot spring areas in the country, which was also one of the reasons we chose it for our base of operations in this country. We apparently had a decent number of hot springs in the Amidonia Region of our own kingdom, but there were few in the former territories of Elfrieden, and none of those were in the vicinity of Parnam.

I definitely wanted to take the opportunity to enjoy Noblebeppu's springs while learning more about the Republic.

The White Bird Inn, where we would be staying for a while, was a travelers' inn operated by a member of the white eagle race. What was more, for an additional charge, we could reserve the open-air baths for an hour a day for exclusive use by our family.

When Roroa's sharp eyes had picked up that detail during check-in...

"Hey, hey, Darlin'. We don't get the chance often, so how's about we reserve the bath and go in as a family? By 'we' I mean me, you, Big Sis Ai, and Big Sis Juna, of course," she'd said with a grin.

Being a man, it was a tempting proposal, but I had no idea how to explain our family situation to the innkeeper, and I felt it would be a poor influence on Tomoe, who was traveling with us. More than anything, I felt incredibly embarrassed, so I gave Roroa a firm but non-painful karate chop to the head.

Kuu suddenly slapped his knee. "Okay! I'll stay at the White Bird Inn tonight, too, then!"

Leporina let out a strange cry. "Whoa, what are you saying, young master?! You have a villa here, don't you?!"

But Kuu tut-tutted and waggled a finger at her. "Kazuma and his folks want to understand our country better, right? In that case, we've gotta let them experience our traditional culture."

"Traditional culture?" I asked.

"Ooh ooh ha ha!" Kuu cackled with glee. "In this country, when friends come from far away to visit you, it's customary to slaughter an animal and hold a feast. You and I are already like friends, after all! Let's ask the inn to hold a feast!"

With that said, Kuu threw his arm around my shoulder. It should have felt a little too chummy coming from a younger guy, but for some reason, it didn't bother me so much. There was no malice behind it, and I could tell this was just how he was, so I couldn't even bring myself to feel like, "Well, I guess there's no helping it..." It seemed this was his sort of charisma.

"I appreciate the offer, but wouldn't it be trouble for the inn, receiving a sudden request like that?" I asked.

"Oh, don't worry, I know the owner. If I pay money and provide the ingredients myself, it won't be an issue. Leporina, run over to the innkeeper's place and get the necessary materials together."

"Ugh... I understand, but... Young master, you're such a slave driver," Leporina complained. "You're already sending me to your father's place tomorrow."

Kuu heartily laughed it off. "While you're out shopping, you can buy that expensive cherry wine you like, too."

"I'll get right on it!" With a salute, Leporina took off and dashed out of the workshop.

Kuu was surprisingly good at handling his subordinate.

Kuu turned to the woman near him. "Taru, you come party, too. The more the merrier, after all."

"Honestly, dumb master, you're such a handful." Taru resignedly accepted. However, her white bear ears were twitching a little.

Could it be the snow bear race's ears functioned similarly to the mystic wolf race's tails? If so, despite how coldly she presented herself, she may have been unexpectedly enthusiastic.

Anyway, the impromptu feast had been arranged.

The sun went down, and a large carpet in the great hall of the White Bird Inn was packed tightly with plates bearing various dishes. The majority of it was meat, meat, meat... A smorgasbord of meat dishes. The white eagle innkeeper laid down platter after platter with new meat dishes.

The white eagle race was, as the name suggested, made up of eagle beastmen with wings on their backs, but their wings turned brown from the middle outward, so they didn't give off the impression of being angels. The men's faces were actual eagle faces, making them resemble the half-man, half-beast depictions of gods from ancient Egyptian murals.

While watching the innkeeper lay out the food, I spoke to Kuu beside me. "I'm seeing an awful lot of meat dishes."

"That's how our feasts are. We generally butcher our livestock, then eat the meat."

"This is party food, right? What is your normal diet like?"

"Aside from meat, we eat shellfish, fish, and dairy. We do have potatoes, but fruits and vegetables can only be harvested in parts of the north, so they're rare and expensive."

"Hmm..."

If he was saying there was demand for vegetables, we could probably develop a trade route and export them here. How were they getting their vitamin C and such? I'd read in some manga that, long ago, sailors had suffered from scurvy due to vitamin C deficiency, and it was really hard on them.

"You don't get sick from lack of vegetables?" I asked.

"Huh? Never heard of that happening. Like, we don't get sick much at all. We don't really have reason to be afraid of death by sickness. We're more afraid of death by freezing."

"Hmm..." Did they have some special way of taking in those nutrients?

Meanwhile, the preparations for the feast seemed to be completed. Present for the occasion on the Friedonian side of things were Aisha, Juna, Roroa, Tomoe, Hal, Kaede, and me; on the Turgish side was Kuu, Taru, and Leporina, for a total of ten people.

Some wooden goblets were passed around, one to each of us. When I looked, the goblet had a white liquid inside. Giving it a swirl, I could see it was just a little thick. Rather than milk, it seemed more like unrefined sake.

"A mysterious white liquid...?" I murmured.

"This? It's our famous fermented milk," Kuu answered.

"Fermented milk?"

"It's a drink made by fermenting snow yak milk."

Snow yaks were apparently a hairy bovine animal that lived in Turgis.

"It's got a strong taste, but once you get used to it, it's good, y'know?" said Kuu.

"Fermentation..." I murmured. "If it's yak milk, then...lactic acid bacteria?"

Come to think of it, didn't lactic acid bacteria produce vitamin C? If I recalled, it was part of the fermentation process... I only vaguely remembered it, though. Could it be the people of this country were supplementing their otherwise insufficient intake of vitamin C with this drink?

That aside, once everyone received their goblet, it was decided that Kuu and I would offer a toast. With everyone gathered around, he and I stood up.

"Long-winded speeches before a feast are so uncouth. That's why I'll keep this brief." With that said, Kuu turned to me and raised his goblet. "To our guests from Friedonia!"

In response to those words, I raised my goblet to Kuu. "To the people of Turgis!"

Then we clacked our goblets together.

"Cheers!" we both said.

"Cheers!" everybody else called.

Then the feast began.

"Now, go on and knock it back," Kuu urged me.

"R-right..."

I tried drinking the fermented snow yak milk. It had a strange taste. It was smoother than its appearance may suggest, but... How can I describe it? It was like drinkable plain yogurt, maybe. But it had that alcoholic flavor to it, too. It was better than I had expected, even this way, but I felt like it might taste better with honey.

Everyone but Tomoe smacked their lips over this fermented milk.

Incidentally, in this country, just like ours, there was no law dictating a minimum age for drinking. It seemed the custom was that, as of fifteen or sixteen, children could openly drink in public. I'd considered putting a proper law in place, but in some ways it was part of the local culture, so I let it be for now. If I meddled unnecessarily, it could invite a backlash from the public, after all.

Well, if the people became health-conscious, voices calling for a minimum drinking age would emerge naturally. I could wait to roll out a law until then.

While drinking my fermented milk, I looked around. In the most boisterous spot in the room, Aisha and Kuu were seated in front of big plates stacked high with food, competing over who could eat the most and the fastest for some reason. It seemed like Kuu, influenced by seeing the way Aisha ate, had challenged her.

The competition was apparently to see who could clear a plate stacked high with food first. They were both desperately piling food into their mouths.

In a simple contest to eat the most, I wouldn't have thought it possible for Aisha to lose, but with the speed element added in, who knew? From the look of it, the food was disappearing from their plates at about the same rate.

"Ooh ooh ha ha, you're not bad, for someone so slim."

"You, too. I'm impressed."

Their eyes crossed every once in a while, and when they did, they seemed to be having an exchange like that.

They were being watched by an exasperated Roroa and a bewildered Tomoe.

"Honestly… Big Sis Ai, what're you havin' a speed-eatin' contest for?" Roroa asked.

"Aisha's eating as fast as ever," Tomoe commented.

"Tomoe, don't ya let her beat ya. Eat up. Ya won't grow otherwise, y'know?"

"If I eat a lot, can I grow up big like Aisha?"

"It must be nice, havin' room for growth…"

I was pretty sure Tomoe was talking about height, but Roroa was looking down at her chest with eyes like a dead fish. She must have gotten depressed when she imagined our little sister growing larger than her in the future. I think she'd just chosen a poor person for comparison, and it wasn't as if she didn't have any, but… Broaching the topic with her too deeply would be suicidal, so I opted not to do it.

In another spot, Hal and Kaede were drinking with Taru and talking. Hal asked a question as he poured Kaede another drink.

"Taru, you're a blacksmith, right? Do you know what sort of weapon would suit me?"

"What kind of weapon do you want?" Taru asked.

"I specialize in wreathing my weapons in fire and then throwing them, but with ordinary spears, they burn up after I throw them. Meanwhile, magically enchanted spears are expensive, so I can't throw them away, and on the battlefield it's a lot of trouble going to retrieve them."

"That, and Hal often rides on Ru—uh, a large creature," Kaede added. "So he'd be best with a weapon he can use from on top of a creature like that, you know."

The large creature Hal often rode on was Ruby, but Kaede didn't mention that. If people learned Hal had a contract with a dragon without being from the Star Dragon Mountain Range, they were going to wonder just who he was, so she kept that part vague.

Taru seemed to think a little before she spoke. "In that case, there's a weapon called a Twin Snake Spear."

"Twin Snake Spear?" Hal asked. "What kind of weapon is that?"

"Like a twin-headed snake that has a second head on the end of its tail. It's a weapon with two spears connected at the base. They're connected with a thin chain, and if you use one as a throwing spear, you can pull on the other to retrieve it. It was originally made so someone riding a large beast like the dumb master's numoth could attack soldiers at its feet."

"Hmm, sounds like an awesome weapon."

Hal seemed impressed, but Taru shook her head quietly.

"It's just...it's incredibly hard to use. The length of the chain can be adjusted with enchantment magic, but the longer it gets, the more technique and strength it takes to use it. It's not widely used, even in our country."

"I think that should be fine, you know," Kaede put in. "If there's one thing Hal can be confident in, it's his strength."

"That's harsh… Couldn't you have found a more loving way to say that?"

"It's love that's making me look for a weapon to keep you two from dying on the battlefield, you know?"

"Urgh…"

Seeing Hal get verbally bested by Kaede, Taru giggled. "If I recall, we have one in stock in the workshop. I think it would be a good idea to test how it works for you first. If you like it, I'll accept an order for one."

"Oh! Thanks, I'll be counting on you," Hal said.

"We'll take you up on that offer, you know," Kaede added.

The three clacked their goblets together. Had a deal been struck? I hoped Hal would find a good weapon.

As for those of us who remained… Juna, who was playing the role of my wife, sat down, and the white rabbit Leporina poured the drinks. In part because we were seated directly on the floor and not in chairs, it reminded me of a Japanese-style reception in a tatami room.

"I'm sorry," Leporina said as she poured fermented milk into my goblet. "Normally, entertaining our guests would be Master Kuu's job..."

"No, no, I'm extremely grateful to have a welcome feast like this."

"It helps so much to hear you say that. Oh, let me take care of your wife, too."

"Hee hee. Thank you." Juna was having Leporina pour her drinks, too. She looked to be in somewhat of a good mood.

"You look like you're enjoying yourself, Juna," I said.

"Yes. We look so much like a husband and wife now."

"Y-you think...?"

That was kind of embarrassing. Leporina watched us with a big smile.

Juna scooped something that was in a nearby pot into a wooden bowl and offered it to me. "The dishes here are all so new to me, too. This soup is delicious."

"Oh, yeah? From the looks of it...it's like dumpling soup."

There were root vegetables and thin, white dumplings floating in a broth similar to miso soup made with red miso.

I took a sip and an unexpected flavor spread through my mouth. This wasn't miso soup—it was pumpkin stew. The dumplings were dumplings, but they were thin and stretched out. It was like... How should I put this? It was like a cross between houtou and pumpkin stew.

"It's not the taste I expected, but...it's good."

"Yes," Juna agreed. "It makes your body feel warm, somehow."

"Hee hee! That pumpkin stew is an old standard in our country, you know?" Leporina eagerly explained as Juna smacked her lips. "It's hard to get your hands on leafy vegetables in our country, but you can get a lot of pumpkins. That's why we have a wide variety of pumpkin dishes. Many of our sweets use pumpkin filling or pumpkin cream, too. They use sugar liberally, though, so they may taste too sweet to those from outside the country."

"Oh? You have a lot of sugar?" I asked.

"Yes. Like with the pumpkins, we have a lot of beets, too."

Beets. She was talking about sugar beets.

Like their name suggested, they were one of the plants from which sugar could be made. Most of the sugar circulating in our country was made from sugar beets, too. There was also maple sugar, which could be harvested from maple trees. Because sugar cane could only be grown in some places in the north of the kingdom, there wasn't much cane sugar in circulation.

But they could harvest a lot of beets in this country, huh...

"Food is one of the places where a land really shows its character," I commented.

"You're so right," Leporina agreed. "But it was only just recently that we began putting dumplings in pumpkin stew, you know? We started putting them in after we heard from an Amidonian merchant that you can eat the root of the beguiling lily plant."

"Wait, these were lily root dumplings?!"

"Yes. It seems a deity known as Lord Ishizuka, the God of Food, descended on Amidonia, and taught them they were edible. Thanks to that, we were able to eat a soup that was once a side dish as our main course. We have to give our thanks to that god."

We were all silent. To think the food culture we were spreading in Amidonia would reach this country, too!

What was more, Poncho was ascending to divinity as the God of Food; not just in Amidonia, but here, too... Rumors tended to blow things out of proportion, but at the rate things were going, I wondered if someone might actually build a temple to the god Ishizuka eventually.

Oh, Poncho, where are you going? Well, he probably didn't know it himself.

Kuu came over, patting his belly. "Hey, you two. Having fun?"

"We are, thanks," I said. "And you? Is the eating contest over?"

"Ooh ooh ha ha! That girl's tough. Speed eating is one thing, but I never stood a chance against her when it came to quantity. I'm shocked she can pack that much away and still eat more."

Aisha had won the contest? Well, in retrospect, that did seem like a foregone conclusion.

Kuu took Leporina's goblet from her and plopped himself down next to me. "I'll handle the rest, so you can go join the others, Leporina."

"Okay." Leporina waved and went over to where Aisha and the others were.

Juna said, "I'm going to go check in on Aisha and the rest, too," and vacated her seat.

It looked like it was going to be just us guys, drinking one-on-one from here. We poured out drinks for each other, then had a toast.

Kuu downed his drink in one gulp, then laughed cheerfully. "Whew! Booze you drink at a feast just tastes extra special."

"Isn't that line a little too old-man-ish for a fifteen-year-old?" I commented.

"Ooh ooh ha ha! Don't worry about it. Setting aside age and rank is the only way to party."

"Oh, yeah...?"

I poured Kuu another drink. Kuu sipped at his drink this time, and then slapped his hand down to rest on my shoulder. What? Was he looking to argue with me?

"So, how is it, Kazuma?"

"How is what?"

"This country, I mean. You enjoying it?"

I thought about that for a little bit before answering. "Yeah. I think it's a good country. There are hot springs, and the local dishes and fermented milk are delicious. You have capable craftspeople, too, so I think it's an attractive country."

"Ooh ooh ha ha! Yeah, you bet it is. I love this country, too." Kuu let out another cackling laugh, then took on a more serious expression. "I honestly think it's a good country, you know? We put our livestock out to pasture in the summer, and make excellent handicrafts indoors in the winter. It's cold, but the people huddle together to survive in this country. There're some hardheaded old folks who seem bent on expanding to the north, though."

I was silent.

I had heard the Republic of Turgis had a national policy of northward expansionism. In fact, during the time our country had been shaken by internal issues and a conflict with the Principality of Amidonia, this country had massed troops on the border showing their intent to invade us. While there was no direct conflict between our nations, I was surprised to find someone in the Republic of Turgis who thought like Kuu.

"Besides, even if we take land to the north, we can't hold it," Kuu continued, crossing his arms and nodding. "In the outside world, air power like wyverns is the most effective, right? A cold land like ours isn't suited to breeding wyverns. That's a plus when it makes it difficult for others to come invade us, but it's impossible to slice off part of a neighboring country's territory without wyverns. No matter how hard we tried, we'd take maybe a city or two at most. Besides, when winter came, the snow would shut down contact with the mainland, so it would be hard to maintain them."

Kuu's dumb behavior made it hard to see, but he had an incredibly precise grasp of his country's situation. Talking to him, I felt a charisma that would draw people to him, too. If Kuu had been born into the royal family of a kingdom with a better territorial situation, he might have become a rare hero.

Kuu gulped down his fermented milk in one gulp again. "Listen, Kazuma, I seriously think this country has its own way of becoming prosperous. We don't have to go north. This country has the underlying power to develop itself. That's how I feel."

"I feel like I understand," I said soberly.

"You do, huh?" he laughed. "I'm glad you get it! Here's hoping the negotiations between my old man and your king go well!"

"Yeah. I'm sure the meeting will be meaningful for both parties."

With that, we clacked our goblets together once more.

CHAPTER 4
To Know a Person

WHEN NEGOTIATIONS WERE FINISHED, it was decided that a meeting would be held ten days from now, with the utmost secrecy, at the inn where we were staying in Noblebeppu.

The reasons for the secrecy were the issue of security and the fact that to hold open talks would require the approval of the Council of Chiefs. If we took our time, that permission would likely be given, but we didn't want to go to the trouble.

Regardless, a date was set, and Kuu's father and Hakuya hashed out the rest of the details between themselves.

As for us, we had nothing in particular we needed to be doing until then, so we decided to explore the country as planned. Kuu had already volunteered himself as a guide, after all.

Today, we went to Moran, a fishing port near Noblebeppu. The seven members of the group included me, Aisha, Juna, Roroa, Tomoe, Kuu, and Leporina. Hal and Kaede said they would be at Taru's workshop checking out a weapon for Hal to use, and they went off on their own.

Now that he was a dragon knight, Hal was the ace of the Defense Force. Because there was great meaning in Hal having a weapon that would let him exercise his valor to its fullest, I was happy to give him permission to break off from the group.

"Wow..." Tomoe cried out as she walked through the town of Moran. "Big Brother! There's a really big person!"

It was true. As we walked through the town, we would occasionally see extremely large people. They might have been over two meters tall.

In addition to a height that would cause their head to burst through the roofs of the average house, they all had a roly-poly physique, like they were heavyweight sumo wrestlers. Even just walking around, they made a strong impression. It made me worry they might crush little Tomoe underfoot.

Seeing how startled we looked, Kuu laughed in amusement. "Ooh ha ha! It's a surprise, seeing them for the first time, huh? They're members of the walrus race."

The walrus race, huh...

Now that he mentioned it, the large people who happened to be men had two tusks growing out of their mouths. With the women, I only ended up thinking, *Their canines sure are long.*

"Members of the walrus race make their living in the fishing industry," said Kuu. "Members of the snow bear race like Taru are good swimmers, too, but they're no match for the walrus race. These are people who, when the water's frozen over in winter and they can't take the boats out, break through the ice to dive in and go fishing, after all."

Diving in the frozen sea?! That was incredible. Nobody had dry suits in this world, so it was amazing they didn't freeze to death.

Oh, wait, I get it. That's why they're built like that.

The blubber beneath their skin provided increased insulation, making them a race specialized for acting in frozen water. Was that a result of evolving to adapt to their environment, or did only races that were adapted to the environment manage to move forward? The question fascinated me.

When we followed Kuu over to the beach, we saw a group of walrus people gathered around a fire.

Kuu walked over and called out to them. "Hey, you guys! Having a cookout on the beach?"

"Oh! Young master," a man said. "Yeah. We brought in a big haul of shellfish, shrimp, and the like today, so we were gonna let loose and party the rest of the day."

On further inspection, a net was laid over the walrus men's campfire, and a variety of shellfish were roasting on it. There were clam-like bivalves that had opened wide, and bubbles escaping from the valves of a spiral-shelled variety that resembled the turban shell. Combined with the scent of the sea, they looked incredibly delicious.

Looking at them, Kuu laughed happily. "Ooh ha ha! That's nice! I'm actually showing some guests from abroad around right now. We'll provide the booze, so let us join you."

The men cheered when they heard Kuu's proposal.

"Oh, you mean it?"

"All right! We can drink lots now!"

Kuu turned back, pulled a pouch from his pocket, and tossed it to Leporina. It was apparently his wallet. "Leporina! Get us a barrel of potato vodka with that."

"Whaaaaaa?!" Leporina blinked at Kuu's order. "A barrel...? That's too much! It'll be too heavy for me to carry back by myself!"

"If it's too heavy, roll it."

"No faiiir..."

Leporina was at the mercy of Kuu's sudden ideas.

I felt bad seeing her run ragged by her boss, so I decided to offer a bit of help. "Aisha. Sorry, but could you go with Leporina and carry the barrel for her?"

I felt bad making someone else do it, but Aisha could probably lift a barrel or two with ease.

She pounded her breastplate proudly. "Leave it to me. Now, let's go, Madam Leporina."

"Whuh?!"

Aisha dragged off the still dumbfounded Leporina.

Watching them go, Kuu chuckled. "Yeah, I'm sure that dark elf girl can heft a barrel of liquor or two without any trouble."

"You can tell?" I asked.

"Well, yeah. I think even I could put up a good fight against your red-haired buddy, but...that girl feels like she's in a different dimension." Kuu spun his arm around in circles. "At the very least, that's not a level of power an ordinary adventurer has. Is she a military commander in the kingdom, or something?"

"No comment."

"I want her as a vassal myself"

"You can't have her."

"Ooh ha ha! Oh, yeah?"

While we were talking, the shells kept roasting. Then one of the walrus fishermen took something that was a milky white color out of a jar and put it on the seashells.

"What's that?" I asked.

"Butter made from the same yak milk we use to make fermented milk," the man said. "When we eat seafood around here, we pour alcohol over it as it cooks, then put this stuff on top when it's done."

That made sense. Butter, huh. Like with butter-fried scallops or short-necked clams. Shellfish and butter were a good match.

The fisherman went on to chop up some shellfish that were probably scallops with butter on them. He offered them to Kuu and me. "Go ahead, young master."

"You visitors, too," another man said. "Don't hold back. Eat your fill."

"Sure thing!" Kuu cried.

"Thank you," I added.

We thanked the fishermen and accepted the offerings. Immediately, the scent of the sea and the aroma of butter tickled my nostrils.

Oh, I don't know how to describe it… It was a very nostalgic experience. It reminded me of the whelk skewers they sold at little stalls at festivals. I'd never thought I wanted to eat them regularly, but when I passed by those stalls and smelled that aroma, I couldn't help but stop. That was the feeling I was getting now.

I used the fork I was given to eat them. Yeah, these were butter scallops. The taste of both the butter and the scallops were intact, and they were the best butter scallops I had ever had.

I let out an unintended groan of appreciation. "They're good..."

"I know, right?" Kuu happily agreed. "Frying them up on the beach and then eating them with butter is a proud part of our food culture."

"I see." Food culture, huh? Well, I wasn't going to let him outdo me.

I called out to Roroa, who was watching with great interest as one of the fishermen stabbed a metal skewer into a spiral shell, twisting it to extract the meat and organs.

"Hey, Roroa!"

"Hm? Whatcha need?" Roroa trotted on over.

"Do you have *that* on you now? You know, the thing you put in a metal container and brought from back home?"

"Ohhh, I think that's in the luggage I brought with me." Roroa rummaged through the bag of traveling equipment she had brought with her from the carriage. Producing a metal container about the size of a lunchbox, she inquired, "This it?" and offered it to me.

Kuu looked at it with curiosity. "Ooh ooh? What's that box?"

"It contains a seasoning we brought with us from our country."

When I opened the metal container, it was filled with a thick, yellowish-brown colored paste.

"Seasoning?"

"Yeah. It's called miso."

The container held the miso I'd had the mystic wolves back home make.

Like how Japanese people want to bring instant ramen or miso soup with them when they go abroad, I had brought miso and konbu for producing broth on this trip. With some water and whatever vegetables were on hand, I could make miso soup anywhere this way. If I had meat, I could add that in, too.

That being the case, I scooped up a spoonful of miso and put a small amount of it on my butter scallops. The butter scallops had now evolved into miso and butter scallops.

I stirred the toppings up a bit, then offered the result to Kuu. "Give me the benefit of the doubt and try them, okay?"

"S-sure..."

Kuu dubiously picked up one of the scallop chunks, throwing it into his mouth. In the next moment, Kuu's eyes opened in shock. "What is this?! The flavor's super complex now! No, it's delicious! It's delicious, but I can't help but want booze with it!"

"He he he," I grinned. "How's that? What do you think of my country's food culture?"

After a moment of being taken aback, Kuu let out an amused laugh. "Ooh ha ha! I see! You were feeling competitive because I mentioned food culture earlier! You've got me this time!"

"I'd say I only evened the score," I said. "I think frying them on the beach is a good culture to have."

"Ooh ha ha! No doubt about that! Ohhh, when's the booze gonna hurry up and get here?"

While we were talking, Leporina and Aisha came back. Leporina was carrying a small barrel and Aisha was shouldering two large ones.

After that, Hal, Kaede, and Taru rejoined us and we had a big party on the beach. The potato vodka Kuu provided was apparently strong stuff, and by the time the sun set, everyone was far past tipsy. Some started to let a little too loose.

The walrus men started dancing and chanting what was either an off-beat song or a cheer, I couldn't tell which. The way they contorted and wriggled, it was almost like they were belly dancers.

"How's a walrus man dance under the sea?"

"Oh! He dances wobble-wobble-wobblingly!"

Elsewhere, a no-doubt-drunken Hal was performing some sort of fire dance with two pieces of wood wreathed in flames.

"All right! I'm all fired up!" he cried.

An equally drunk Kaede was cackling and rolling around as she watched him.

"That's great, you know! Hal!"

Meanwhile, a drunk Kuu had a happy Tomoe riding on his shoulders.

"Ooh ha ha! C'mere."

"Aha ha ha! I'm so high up!"

From the high spirits she was in, Tomoe might have been drunk, too. Naturally, I hadn't let her have a sip of alcohol, but maybe she'd gotten drunk off the smell, or the alcohol used on the shellfish hadn't fully evaporated. Whatever the case, I'd failed in my role as her guardian. If Liscia heard about this, I was in for a lecture.

Next to them, possibly incited by Kuu, a drunk Aisha had Juna riding on her shoulders.

"Ha ha ha! What a jolly time we're having, Madam Juna!"

"H-hold on, Aisha! Put me down, please!"

Juna didn't seem all that inebriated, but her face was flushed red from embarrassment at all the attention she was getting.

I helped myself to another drink and just sort of watched as the chaos gradually unfolded on the beach.

"Hee hee hee, Darlin'." Roroa draped herself over me from behind. Resting her chin on my shoulder, she rubbed her cheek against me. It was a cute, cat-like gesture, but she smelled a little of alcohol. "You drinkin' like you should be, Darlin'?"

"I'm drinking, yes," I said. "But you, Roroa... You sure you haven't had one too many?"

"Hee hee hee." She had a glass in one hand and a shell in the other. They were both already empty, so the fact that she wasn't about to let either of them go was proof that she was already pretty drunk.

"Hey, Roroa..." I began.

"Zzz..."

"Wait, that was fast! We were in the middle of talking!"

Roroa was snoring softly with her chin resting on my shoulder.

There was a little drool coming out of her mouth, but I decided to pretend I didn't see it. With no other choice, I got her down off my shoulder, and let her borrow my crossed legs as a pillow.

"Purr..."

"..."

Honestly... She looked so happy, sleeping. While patting Roroa's head, I looked over to the stupid ruckus Kuu and the others were still kicking up. They were drinking, eating, and partying together.

Having shared that fun time together, *a certain thing* began to take root in me.

I reflected on that silently.

Then, in order to wipe it away, I downed the glass I was holding. I did not, at this time, realize there were eyes looking at me with concern.

The party in Moran continued until late in the evening, and we ended up staying there overnight. That was because nearly everyone was totally sloshed, and while Noblebeppu was nearby, it was still far enough that we would have to use carriages to return.

In the end, we all ended up sleeping on the floor in the great hall of an inn that Kuu used his reputation to get us into.

Those difficulties aside, the next day came.

Kuu, Juna, and I went for a walk and visited the fishing port near the beach where we'd had the cookout. The rest of the group was hungover and out of commission.

Roroa, Hal, and Kaede were hit especially badly, and Tomoe was working with Aisha and Leporina, whose symptoms were less severe, to nurse them. It seemed Kuu's potato vodka had caused those unused to drinking it to suffer a nasty hangover.

But why was I fine?

I could understand why Kuu, who was used to the stuff, was fine. And I could see why Juna, who'd started holding back at some point, was okay. But for some reason, I wasn't hungover, either.

I only drank when participating in the nobles' banquets, or while eating at Poncho's place on days that work kept me busy until late at night and I missed dinner. I mentioned that to the two of them in puzzlement.

"Maybe you just take your liquor well naturally?" Kuu suggested.

I take my liquor well, huh? Was it a genetic thing?

But thinking back, I recalled my grandpa could be a pretty bad drunk. I vaguely remembered several times when he'd gotten drunk after drinking heavily at a party with his buddies, hadn't made it home because of the police taking him into custody, and then received a thorough tongue-lashing from my grandma the next day.

"Is it really something natural about the way my body works?" I murmured.

"Ah..." Juna quickly looked away.

What was that about?

"Juna?"

"What is it...?" Juna showed me her usual calm smile. However, her cheeks looked like they were twitching just a little.

I peered at her face. "Is something the matter?"

Juna blatantly averted her eyes. For Juna, who rarely let her emotions show, she seemed unusually out of sorts.

Suspicious.

"Do you know something?" I prodded.

"Whatever do you mean?"

I stared down Juna, who was trying to dodge the question.

"It must be because of the *uwabami,*" she said finally, averting her eyes.

An uwabami... That meant a heavy drinker, right? Maybe it did have to do with my genetic makeup... Wait, huh? She'd said it was because of *the* uwabami, not that *I* was an uwabami, right? "Uwabami" was a word that also meant a large serpent, didn't it?

Hmm...there was something bugging me about this.

For a while we played a game of tag where I would try to look Juna in the eye and she would look away, but then Kuu pointed to the sea and started talking.

"Hey, Kazuma. Can you see that?"

"What?" I looked out to sea to see what he meant, and there was a white object spread out across the horizon.

Was it ice? This country was on the southern tip of the continent. That being the case, that might be the ice of this world's south pole. Because the maps were vague, there was no way to be sure if there was a continent beneath the ice, though.

Kuu looked directly below the ice as he spoke.

"Those are the ice islands. They gradually approach this country at the end of summer. When winter comes, that ice and this beach are connected, and once it snows, you can't tell what's land

and what isn't. This sea gets covered with ice so thick you could ride a carriage over it and it wouldn't break."

Kuu sat right down on the beach and crossed his legs.

Then, propping up his elbows on his lap, he rested his cheeks on his hands and looked resentfully out to sea. "Large sea creatures hate this frigid sea. That's why medium and small fish gather, and it's why our country has a wealth of places to fish. But that also means large shipping vessels can't come in."

"It's tough, huh," I nodded.

The large ships of this world had large sea creatures like sea dragons pulling them in the same way that horses would pull a carriage. If those sea dragons hated this sea, that was good in that Turgis wouldn't be invaded by foreign navies, but it was also bad in that large transport ships couldn't come here, either. The Republic could carry out trade by methods that didn't rely on sea creatures or the air, but that was only an option during summer. This world didn't have ice-breaking ships that could push through the frozen winter seas.

"There are limits to what shipping overland can do," Kuu said. "Traveling merchants only come in summer, and with the land locked in ice during the winter, it's hard to even walk around. If we use creatures like the numoth, we can transport things even in winter, but there aren't that many of them. The vast majority we do have were raised for military use, too."

"You can't transfer them to jobs in shipping instead?" I asked.

"They're our only means of mobility during the winter. If some monsters pour out of a dungeon, or brigands are attacking a village, or a small village has been isolated by an avalanche...we need their legs to carry us there at times like that, right?"

"I see..."

The numoths were already working at full capacity, then. They probably couldn't be reassigned for shipping.

Kuu was scratching his head vigorously. "So, well, it's not like I can't see why the old men would want to advance northward. If we could receive large transport ships in winter, too, it would do a lot to make this land more prosperous. But even if we invaded and took a warm water port, what would come of it? So long as the difficulties of shipping don't change, only the area around that port would benefit from trade. Invading land that's going to be hard to support like that seems like the equivalent of wooing a beautiful woman in your dreams."

Wooing a beautiful woman in your dreams. That seemed to be a local saying, equivalent to calling something a picture of rice cakes in Japanese. Basically, no matter how hard you worked to seduce a beautiful woman you met in your dreams, it was meaningless, and would only leave you feeling empty.

Hmm... Winter shipping methods, huh...

I wracked my brain.

That issue was a problem for our country, who wanted to trade with this country, too. If the period of trading was limited, that would put limitations on the potential trade goods. Vegetables seemed like they would be a good thing to export to this country, but many fresh foods didn't keep for long.

We have the Little Susumu Mark V (Maxwell-type Propulsion

Device), so we can send out large ships even during the winter, I reflected. However, it won't let us break through thick ice. I have people studying it, but who knows how long it will take to produce an ice breaker like the Garinko-go...

Could we manage with what we had now, somehow? How about stationing a mage on the ship and having them carve a path?

No... It was hard to use magic at sea, wasn't it? What's more, the frozen area was too wide, so no matter how many mages we had aboard, they'd eventually run out of steam. Meanwhile, if we tried to attempt transportation by air, the air currents would be too wild, so flying mounts wouldn't be usable. Also, because the land was covered with snow, if we didn't use creatures like the numoth, overland transportation would be difficult.

There are no snowplows, either. If there were something like sleds, we could slide over the top of the snow... Wait, wouldn't we need numoths to pull those sleds? ...Hm? Slide over the top of the snow?

That was when I remembered the existence of a certain thing.

Earlier, when thinking of uses for the Little Susumu Mark V, there was something I'd developed almost entirely as a joke. *Maybe with that... I pondered. Guess I'll try contacting Genia.*

I didn't know how it would go yet, so rather than give Kuu false hopes, I decided not to tell him and to contact the royal castle in secret.

When the afternoon rolled around, the hungover members of the group started to feel a lot better, so we decided to return to the town of Noblebeppu. It was already evening by the time the rocky carriage ride came to an end.

Kuu was saying we'd have another party tonight, but since most of us hadn't fully worked last night's alcohol out of their systems, we politely declined and decided to let our innards rest for the night.

The shaking of the carriage had aggravated Roroa's, Hal's, and Kaede's hangovers, so they went to their rooms as soon as we got to the inn and went to sleep without dinner.

Aisha took Tomoe out to walk around the town at night. They were apparently going to look at souvenirs. Left behind, Juna and I talked about nothing of real consequence and relaxed.

Eventually, while I was thinking that all there was left to do was take a bath in the hot springs and go to sleep, suddenly Juna said, "Oh, I just remembered something I need to do. Excuse me," and left the room.

She had business to attend to at this hour? Had she gone to look for Aisha and Tomoe, maybe?

Having been left behind all by myself, I had nothing to do, so I decided to take a bath. This inn had just one large open-air bath fed with free-flowing water that was partitioned into men's and women's sides.

I rinsed myself with hot water, then immediately went to soak in the tub.

Normally, I'd want to wash myself first, but the nights were cold here, and this being an open-air bath, if I didn't get in quickly, I'd catch a chill and bad things would happen.

As I sank into the steamy water from the cold outside air, my body felt like it was pleasurably melting.

We were the inn's only guests now, and Hal was about the only other person who might come into the men's side, so I was able to relax without having to be considerate of anyone else.

Whew, so warm.

The water seeped into my body, washing away the fatigue I'd built up while moving around.

Leaning on the edge of the bath, I was humming the hot springs song from Noboribetsu when I heard someone walking behind me.

That wasn't the direction of the women's bath. In that case, had Hal woken up and come to the bath?

I was thinking that as I turned around, but...

Whuh?!

There was Juna, naked.

In her right hand she had a tray, and in her left she held a towel that just barely covered her. Her slightly flushed skin and round, womanly figure burned themselves into my mind.

I was still dumbfounded by this sudden occurrence when Juna laid down the tray and began pouring hot water over herself.

"Excuse me while I get in beside you," she said as she got into the bath. Then she sat down so close to me that our shoulders were touching. Her soft, white flesh was right next to mine.

Once she had submerged up to her shoulders, she let out a breath. "Whew!"

That sexy sigh finally brought me back to my senses. "U-um... Juna? This is the men's bath, you realize?"

"I asked the innkeeper to reserve it for us for an hour or so. So it's fine."

Now that she mentioned it, Roroa had been saying there was a system like that.

"No, but it's still embarrassing..."

"Hee hee! Where's the harm? We're a couple, after all." With that said, Juna leaned against me. "So, please, feel free to call me by a pet name now, darling. We're all alone, so I don't want you to be so formal."

"With you, being polite just feels natural, though," I objected. Still, I tried to loosen up, like she wanted. Hmm...yeah, this was embarrassing. "I actually have to actively try to speak less formally."

"I think, in terms of our positions, it's only natural for you to speak informally," she told me. "I know you said you feel tense around older women, but you call my grandmother Excel, don't you?"

"That's because I have a stronger sense of Excel being my vassal. I need to make it clear who's the master at all times, or that woman will run me ragged. But with you, I just feel like being extra polite. Naturally, that's not an attempt to set you aside from my other fiancées or anything like that. You're like my reliable older wife."

"Hee hee! Am I?" Juna watched me with a calm smile as I did my best to explain myself.

Juna pulled over the tray she had brought. The tray had two small glasses and a pale yellow bottle on it.

She passed me one of the glasses and held up the bottle for me to see. "First, a drink."

"Is it alcoholic?"

"No. Considering last night, I decided on juice instead. This juice is made by almost the exact same process as a cherry wine that Leporina said she likes. It seems the only difference is whether you add water or alcohol to the syrup produced."

With that explanation, Juna poured me a glass.

While it was juice, it still felt like we were sharing alcohol, so I poured Juna's drink for her in return, as was common courtesy.

Finally, having gotten used to the sight of Juna's white skin—well, I wasn't tired of seeing it, of course, I just was able to keep myself under control a little better—we had a toast.

Then, soaking in the bath together, we drank together, with juice taking the place of wine. During that time, I couldn't help but glance at those swells which were larger than Liscia's. Juna's wet skin had a glossy shine to it.

She noticed, of course. "Hee hee! You can go right ahead and look."

"Please...spare me," I murmured.

The juice shouldn't have had any alcohol in it, but I was feeling woozy. I was going to get dizzy from the heat in no time. There was an epic battle between lust and reason being waged inside my head.

"Is there something you're thinking about?" Juna asked suddenly.

I was on edge, thinking she'd realized how full of lustful thoughts my head was right now, but Juna had a serious look in her eyes.

"Ever since the cookout on the beach, you've had something on your mind. Today, too...your mind seemed to be somewhere else."

"You noticed that, huh?"

It was true; there was something I'd had on my mind since the cookout. No...it might be more appropriate to say I was confused about it.

Juna leaned her head on my shoulder and spoke to me with downturned eyes. "It may not do any good to tell me what it is. Still, if telling someone will lessen your worries at all, please, darling, do not bear the burden alone. You have partners, including myself, with whom you can share anything."

"Juna..."

Among all my fiancées, Juna was the one who was always taking a step back to look at the big picture. It was fair to say that she was the best of all of them when it came to showing careful concern. *That's why she easily detected the worries I thought I was hiding.*

Then Juna took on a tone like a sullen girl. "I thought you would tell me on your own once we were alone, you know? Despite that, you've said nothing. That's why I arranged for us to be together like this. In a place where nothing is hidden, I thought you might bare your heart to me as well."

"You did it all with that in mind, huh?" I commented. "I really am no match for you..."

"Hee hee."

She looked cute when she was sulking, so I stroked her face, and she gave me a happy smile. She had seen through me, but Juna's smile wiped away any frustration I had over that.

That's why I revealed what was concerning me. "Juna...what do you think about Kuu?"

"Sir Kuu? He seems a bit boisterous, but I find him to be an affable young man."

"Yeah," I nodded. "He's got a mysterious ability to attract people, too. He'll be a good ruler someday, I'm sure. If he were an expansionist, he'd be an enemy we couldn't afford to underestimate, but Kuu is satisfied with internal development. He's the kind of ruler I'd want to see in a neighbor."

"None of this sounds bad, though." Juna tilted her head to the side.

It was true; it wasn't bad.

"If he'll become my sworn friend, there's no one more reliable," I said. "Having the illegal fishing problem with the Nine-Headed Dragon Archipelago Union to our east, the Union of Eastern Nations struggling with the Demon Lord's Domain to our north, and the unpredictable Mercenary State Zem and the theocratic Lunarian Orthodox Papal State to our west, it would make things a lot easier if we could have amicable relations with the Republic of Turgis to our southwest, at least. It'd give us a land connection to our secret ally, the Gran Chaos Empire, too."

She listened silently.

"However, we haven't formed an alliance yet. I learned too much about Kuu before that happened."

I stared into the glass in my hand.

"When we were drinking with Kuu, Taru, Leporina, and the other people in this country, and acting like idiots, it was fun, but I had another thought then, too: If it came down to it, could I make enemies of these people?"

"Enemies...?" Juna's expression grew clouded. *Why would that come up?* her face seemed to ask.

"I think Kuu is a likable guy," I said. "But in addition to being myself, I'm the representative of a nation. I have to think about my preferences as a person and my preferences as a country separately."

"Because we haven't formed cordial relations with the Republic of Turgis yet?"

"Yeah. If the Republic of Turgis were to become hostile to us in the future, could I fight the country where Kuu and his people live...?"

That was the vague worry I'd been feeling.

"When I resolved to open hostilities with Amidonia, the enemy's plans were already in motion, and it was a kill-or-be-killed situation. That was why I decided to go to war. But if I had known there were people like Roroa, Colbert, and Margarita there before the war started, would I have been able to make that decision? Even when it might mean losing Roroa and the others?"

She was silent.

"It's the same this time," I said. "If the Republic opposes me, it's my vassals and my people who will suffer if I'm too slow to decide. Knowing that, can I still resolve to do it? I may have grown too attached to Kuu and his friends. I felt worried, thinking that."

Juna placed her hand on my cheek.

"Juna?"

"I am sure you will make the right decision, darling." Her voice was endlessly calm and gentle.

Then Juna wrapped her arm around my neck and held me close. Surprised by the suddenness of it, I dropped my glass into the bath. My left arm was cushioned by a soft sensation.

"Whoa, Juna?!"

"I'm sure you'll struggle with the decision. You may even regret it afterward," Juna whispered gently in my ear. "However, even with the hesitation and regret, you are the kind of man who does what he needs to do. I've been watching you all this time. I know your strengths and weaknesses. No matter how your heart screams out that you don't want to fight, you are the kind of person who can resist when necessary."

I was silent.

"If the choice tears your heart to pieces, then tell us. We will carry your hesitation, regrets, and sins together as a family. Hee hee! You have five future wives, so let's split your troubles into six equal parts!" Juna said the last part teasingly.

My heart lightened. "Thanks, Juna."

"Hee hee! Also, thinking about fighting the Republic of Turgis now is like worrying if a boulder might roll down a distant mountain. If you do that, you may trip over the rocks at your feet, you know?"

"Aha ha ha, true."

While looking into the distance, I'd trip on what was already at my feet, huh? She was so right.

Rather than consider what to do if the Republic became hostile to our kingdom, it was better for now to think about how to prevent that from happening. If I didn't want to fight Turgis, that was even more true. Yeah… I had a direction, now.

"In order to forge a formal alliance, I need to show a gain to be had from forming amicable relations with us, and a threat to make them hesitate to oppose us," I said. "I have to impress upon Kuu's old man that our country could be a valuable ally, and a terrifying foe."

"Gain and threat, is it?" she said. "But how will you do that? You can't be planning to bring our military into the meeting, right?"

"Don't worry. I have a number of ideas."

Unlike before, my mind was working properly now. Instead of fearing what would happen if Turgis became hostile, I could now focus on figuring out how to keep them from becoming that way. That was thanks to Juna.

"You have my gratitude, Juna," I said. "Thanks to you, I think the path… Huh?"

Suddenly my vision blurred. The world was spinning. Oh, damn, this was bad.

"D-darling?"

It looked like I'd gotten dizzy from the heat. Now that I thought about it, I'd been in the bath since before Juna's arrival.

The last thing I saw in the spinning world was Juna's white skin, and then I lost consciousness.

When I came to, I was on top of the bed in the room where I was staying.

Erm...I passed out in the hot springs, didn't I?

I was...not naked now. Had Juna carried me back and dressed me?

I felt a gentle breeze on my face. Looking next to me, Juna was sitting on the edge of the bed and fanning me. "Juna?" I asked.

"Oh, you've come to?" Juna said with a look of relief. "You passed out in the hot spring, so I had the inn staff help me carry you back to your room. The outside air was too cold to pull you out of the spring and treat you there, after all."

"Sorry. How embarrassing."

"Don't worry about it. It gave me the chance to look over your body." Juna brought a hand to her cheek and smiled mischievously.

Oof... Even though it had been in the hot spring, I was really embarrassed to think she'd seen so much of me while I was unconscious.

As if she saw through to my innermost feelings, Juna giggled. "By the way, are we already back to you being so polite with me?"

"Ahh... Yeah, this just feels more natural."

"I see," she said. "Then let's have you loosen up with me when it's just the two of us alone."

"It's embarrassing to have you put it that way, but...let's do that."

Talking differently when we were alone together... I thought that might be okay.

"By the way, are Aisha and the others back yet?" she asked.

"No, not yet. You were only out for about ten minutes."

"I was...?"

"Yes. So we can do things like this."

Juna leaned in, brushing back her beautiful blue hair, and pressed her lips against mine. Then she pulled her face back and giggled. "Shall we keep the fact that we took a bath together our little secret for a while?"

"Huh?"

"If Aisha and Roroa hear, I'm sure they'll get jealous and want to join you for one, too. I want you to be able to rest, darling."

I understood her meaning. So, for now at least, let it be our secret.

HOW A REALIST HERO REBUILT THE KINGDOM

CHAPTER 5

Fighting Together

THERE WERE STILL a few days until my meeting with Turgis' head of state, so we had Kuu show us around the nearby cities.

Going to unfamiliar places, seeing how the locals lived, and identifying the similarities and differences between them and our own people was fun. Whenever we found something new, we met the discoveries with excitement.

"Oh, what's this?" I commented. "I've never seen this kind of fruit before."

"Big Brother, they're selling some weird animals over here!" Tomoe called. "They're small and cute."

"Let me see... Wait, Tomoe, doesn't it say there that they're for eating?"

"People eat them?!"

Tomoe and I looked around with great enthusiasm, while Juna and Roroa smiled.

Those easygoing days continued, but today was different.

Today, there were two days left before the meeting with the head of the Republic.

It was still early in the morning, but Kuu rushed over to the room where we were staying. He was out of breath and looked like he'd been in a hurry. Behind him was Leporina, looking just as winded.

"Haaah... Haaah... K-Kazuma..." he panted.

"What's wrong?" I asked. "You're totally out of breath."

When I invited them into the room and asked Aisha to fetch some water, Kuu raised a hand to stop me, and tried to get his breathing under control as he said, "It's fine... I don't need water. Before that, I have a favor to ask."

"A favor?"

"For now, can you get all of your people together in this room?"

Seeing a serious expression on Kuu that I'd never seen him make before, I gathered my traveling companions, despite some misgivings.

There were nine of us gathered in the four-person room: me, Aisha, Juna, Roroa, Tomoe, Hal, and Kaede, along with Kuu and Leporina. Having nine people made it awfully cramped, but he had said "everyone," so there was no helping it.

"So, Kuuie. What'd ya have in mind, gatherin' us all here?" Roroa asked suspiciously.

He was the son of their head of state, so I thought it was a bit much to be calling him "Kuuie"... but given the tense situation, I decided to pretend I hadn't heard it.

Kuu stood up and bowed his head to all of us. While we were all still taken aback by the suddenness of it, Kuu desperately said, "I'll keep this brief! Please! Lend me your bodyguards!"

"P-please do." Leporina hurriedly stood up as well, then bowed her head like Kuu.

"I'm sorry to get foreigners caught up in this! But still!" he cried.

"Calm down, Kuu," I said. "Just what happened?"

"Ah...r-right." Kuu finally calmed himself. With a big, deep breath, he slapped his own cheeks, maybe as a way of psyching himself up. "The thing is, a previously undiscovered dungeon has been confirmed to exist near a mountain village that's around two hours north of here by carriage. It seems it was a rocky mountain, and when there was a landslide, the entrance to the dungeon appeared."

A dungeon... I was used to them being a thing in RPGs, but in this world, a dungeon was understood as a labyrinthine place with its own ecology. They were also the only place outside the Demon Lord's Domain where monsters could be found. But the monsters found in such places all had intelligence on the level of wild beasts, and they were nothing like the sentient demons found in the Demon Lord's Domain. There were a fair number of these dungeons on this continent.

This was what I knew about dungeons so far:

- They came in a wide variety of types and were inhabited by low-intelligence monsters.
- The deepest point contained what was called a dungeon core.
- For as long as the core existed, monsters would continue to appear, no matter how many were defeated.
- If the core was destroyed, the monsters stopped appearing... And so on.

The connection between monsters and dungeon cores was still unknown. However, the destroyed dungeon cores could be used as jewels for a Jewel Voice Broadcast.

In addition to the cores, there were also cases where other out-of-place artifacts and over-technology could be found. The existence of such artifacts had boosted progress in this world's technology to a truly insane degree.

There were even groups that made it their life's work to study such artifacts. The House of Maxwell, to which Genia the "over-scientist" belonged, was one of them.

In addition, there were adventurers like Dece and Juno, who made their living exploring the dungeons; and nearby towns that profited off such adventurers gathering. With these various demands overlapping, dungeons were considered dangerous, but also potentially profitable.

With a look on his face like he had bitten into something unpleasant, Kuu told us about the dungeon that had just been discovered.

"Now, I'm sure there are things to be gained from a dungeon," he said. "However, that's something we can only discuss once the safety of the people in the villages near the entrance is secured. You never know what's in a newly discovered dungeon, after all."

"So something came out, then?" I asked.

"Yeah. I hear ten ogres, or something like that."

Ogres "or something like that," huh...

Ogres were oni. In Japanese mythology, oni were a symbolic representation of those who didn't conform to the system. They were depicted as powerful and terrifying, but somehow tragic. However, in Western mythology, ogres were man-eating humanoid monsters, and were often barbarians or demi-humans. From what I was hearing, these ogres sounded like the latter.

"Around the same time that the guys from the village who found the dungeon rushed to the capital to report their discovery, a little over ten ogre-like creatures crawled out of the dungeon and attacked the village," said Kuu. "From what the guys who got away said...the ogres were eating people indiscriminately."

"Eating people..." I murmured.

If the ogres were attacking people indiscriminately—and eating them, at that—it was no different from an attack by dangerous beasts. Unlike a war waged for a purpose, there was no room for negotiation, and we could only exterminate them like we would animals.

"Naturally, we're putting a force together to put them down ourselves, and we've put in a request with the guild for adventurers to slay the monsters that came out of the dungeon, but...time is of the essence," Kuu said. "Once a beast has a taste for human flesh, it's sure to attack people again. These things are going to be the same. We don't know when they'll attack another village. I dunno if they're ogres or what, but I'm not letting them do what they want any longer."

Kuu looked more serious and heroic than I had ever seen him before. He was completely different from the aloof Kuu who was always laughing. This was his anger over the people of his country being attacked. Kuu had acted like being the son of their head of state meant nothing to him, but in that anger, I felt like I could see the pride of one who stands above others.

"I see," I said, nodding. "You have to prevent any further casualties."

"Yeah. That's it, Kazuma. I want you guys to help!" Kuu said and bowed his head once more. "We can travel to the village quickly from here. Also, I know you've got capable bodyguards on hand. Particularly the dark elf girl and the red-headed guy. If they'd come, it'd be reassuring. Do you think you could ask them to?"

Emotionally, I wanted to help, but...I'd be risking the safety of my family, so I couldn't say yes so easily. I wanted a little more information.

"Aisha?" I asked. "Just how strong are ogres?"

"Well, they have the strength to crush boulders with their bare hands, but even ordinary soldiers could defeat one if they surrounded it with ten men. I could do it alone," Aisha added with a confident snort.

"It sounds like there are more than ten of them," I said. "Can we fight that with the strength we have on hand?"

"If it's around ten, I don't see us failing. Madam Juna, Sir Halbert, and Madam Kaede are all superb combatants, and Sir Kuu is quite skilled himself."

"I see..." In that case, if we could confirm the situation on the ground, we could help. "Got it," I said. "Let us help."

"You mean it?!" Kuu cried.

"This is a problem that could happen in any country. It's practically a natural disaster. Now isn't the time to be worrying about whether it's Friedonia or Turgis."

"Thanks! I owe you one!" Kuu seemed relieved to have our help.

"However, I want you to bring me, too," I added.

"Darling?!" Juna shouted.

"Darlin'?!" Roroa cried.

Before they could say any more, I raised my hand to stop them. "I can't fight, but my magic is suited to scouting. Let me help."

"If that's how you want it... Okay," Kuu said. "I'm counting on you."

"Yeah. We'll get ready to go immediately, so wait outside for us."

Kuu said, "Be quick about it," and left the room with Leporina in tow. Once we could no longer hear the sound of their footsteps, Roroa confronted me.

"Hold on, Darlin'! Are you outta your mind?! Goin' to a dangerous place like that?!"

"I'm opposed to it, too," Juna objected. "If anything were to happen to you, Sire, I..."

From the fact she was referring to me as "Sire" and not "darling," I could see she was seriously concerned.

Roroa continued. "You're not strong like Big Sister Ai, now are ya?! Why can't ya just wait here?!"

"Listen, I'm well aware I'm not strong, but I want you to let me go." I plopped my hand down on top of Roroa's head. "I don't think Kuu was lying, but to prepare for the possibility of a trap or any other unplanned-for event, it'd be convenient for me to be next to our greatest combat asset. If I'm going to be loaning out my family and vassals, I need to make sure they're returned to me."

"Well, maybe, but..."

"Besides...I think this is a good opportunity for me to learn about what monsters are like."

"Learn about monsters?" Roroa asked.

"Yeah. Since coming to this world, I've seen vicious creatures through the eyes of a Little Musashibo that I made to work as an adventurer, but when it comes to monsters, I only have second-hand knowledge. Thinking about the future, I'd like to actually see them and gauge the threat they pose for myself."

There might eventually come a time when I would have to face demons from the Demon Lord's Domain. If that happened, I could get tripped up if I approached them with the naïve assumption that I'd be able to negotiate with another intelligence. In addition to the demons, there were apparently scads of monsters in the Demon Lord's Domain, too, after all. That's why I wanted to take this chance to learn about monsters.

"Of course, I'm going to secure my own safety as much as possible... Inugami?"

"I am here." Inugami suddenly appeared from the shadow of the door Kuu and Leporina had left through.

There were always more than ten members of the Black Cats posted nearby, watching over us unnoticed. It had been that way ever since our departure from the Star Dragon Mountain Range.

I handed something over to him and gave him an order. "You were listening to us, right? I want you to send some of the Black

Cats to scout out the site now and confirm that the situation and number of monsters matches what Kuu told us. I'll leave the choice of members to you. If there are more ogres than we can handle with our number, report back to me with this wooden mouse. If that turns out to be the case, I'll feel bad for Kuu, but we'll have to back out."

"By your will."

Inugami took the wooden mouse possessed by my Living Poltergeists, then vanished as suddenly as he had appeared. He was getting more and more like a ninja, wasn't he?

"Hrm... Well, if you're gonna be stayin' in a safe place, I guess it's fine..." Roroa murmured.

"We'll have to accept it," Juna agreed.

I smiled. My thorough safety measures had made Roroa and Juna reluctantly accept that I would be going along.

"Have no worries!" Aisha declared. "We'll wipe out those monsters immediately. We'll not let them lay one finger on His Majesty. Right, Sir Halbert? Madam Kaede?"

"Sure thing!" Hal agreed. "I was just thinking I wanted to test out my new weapon, too!"

"Jeez, Hal..." Kaede muttered. "But if it's a royal command, we'll follow it, you know."

Aisha proudly thumped her chest, and Hal and Kaede nodded. What a reliable fiancée and comrades I had.

Now that our plan was decided, I gave each of them their individual orders. "Roroa and Tomoe will stay in this town. We'll leave some members of the Black Cats to guard them."

"Well, even if we did go, we'd only end up bein' a hindrance," Roroa said.

"Stay safe, Big Brother," Tomoe added.

"Sure. I won't do anything dangerous, so just trust me and wait." I placed a hand on each of their worrying heads and patted them gently. "The rest of the group will go with Kuu to put down the monsters. I will keep in contact with the Black Cats and scout ahead from the rear. I'll ask Juna to be my bodyguard."

"Leave it to me," Juna said.

"Aisha, Hal, and Kaede, you'll put down the monsters with Kuu. But don't push yourselves. If you think it's dangerous, pull back immediately. That also goes for me, if I detect more enemies than anticipated during my scouting and give the order to retreat. I won't stand for us losing a single person here in another land!"

"Yes, sir!" Aisha exclaimed.

"Gotcha!" Hal said.

"You can leave it to us, you know," Kaede confirmed.

Hearing everyone's replies, I gave the order. "Now then, everyone... Let's go!"

"Yes, sir!"

In the carriage on the way there, I explained my magic to Kuu and Leporina.

Obviously, if I told him about the limitations or the area of effect in detail it would take a long time, so I only told him what he needed to know.

"My magic transfers my own consciousness into objects

modeled on living creatures, like mannequins, and allows me to control them freely. For instance, if I transfer my consciousness into this wooden mouse, I get an overhead view of...well, just assume I can see what the mouse sees."

"Wow, that's one hell of an ability!" Kuu said, impressed at seeing the wooden mouse moving around on my hand almost like it was the real thing. "Ooh ha ha, if I had an ability like that, I could peep on the women's bath all I want!"

"You had to go there immediately?!" I exclaimed.

"Young master, you're embarrassing me as your subordinate, so please show some self-control," Leporina protested with tears in her eyes.

Unlike the pensive look on his face when rushing into the inn, Kuu was already back to his usual self.

I ignored them and continued. "That's why, if I send this wooden mouse out to scout, I can get an accurate picture of the situation without the other side knowing. The problem is, if I don't know what direction the enemy is in, I can only send it to patrol the area around us."

I couldn't do something like sense the enemy's presence, although maybe Aisha could. If I knew the direction the enemy was in, I could send one out immediately, but until then, I'd have to have them spread out in the area around us to patrol.

That said, once sightings came in from the Black Cats we'd sent on ahead, I'd know the right direction immediately. However, I couldn't let Kuu and Leporina know about the clandestine unit operating under my orders.

"In that case, we can have Leporina look," Kuu said as if it was no big deal. "Leporina and her fellow white rabbits have good ears. Even in forests with poor visibility, she can sense in what direction things are moving by the sounds they make."

"I only know the direction of the sound, and whether it's a single source or many, though," Leporina added.

Oh, that paired well with my ability. Leporina could narrow down the direction, and then I just had to send out the mouse.

Then I received a message.

"Inugami reporting in. Target sighted."

The report from Inugami and his men came into my mind through the separated portion of my consciousness.

"We have visual confirmation of five from here. The targets are ogres. However, Your Majesty...their forms are somewhat warped."

Warped? I was able to see the dolls I was controlling from an overhead view, but that also meant I could only see the area around them. Because the Black Cats were monitoring the targets from a distance, I couldn't see them myself, so I could only imagine based on the report.

"Their faces and size match ogres, but their arms are massive and touch the ground, resulting in them walking on all fours," said Inugami. *"I hear many monsters are bizarre in form compared to those told of in legends. Most likely, this is one such sub-race."*

A sub-race of ogres...huh. I made the mouse he was carrying shake to indicate I understood.

The arrangement was that, for now, Inugami and his people would stake out the dungeon the ogres had appeared from. That was to prepare for a situation where more monsters crawled out of there, and because I couldn't have a unit of spies doing anything that stood out too much.

Even so, it caught my attention that many of the monsters that resided in dungeons had bizarre forms.

The large number of monsters and demons that showed up after the appearance of the Demon Lord's Domain were distinct from the many strangely shaped monsters that inhabited this continent's dungeons. What was the difference between them? Was there even one to begin with?

In order to get a full picture of this world, I may need to turn my eyes to that, too.

It was a vague feeling, but that was the sense I got.

While I was thinking that, we reached the mountain village said to have been attacked by the monsters. It was a hamlet with only about ten buildings, but it looked like it had been hit by a typhoon. None of the buildings were burned, but almost all of them were collapsed or had holes in the walls. If there was one difference from a typhoon, it was the splatters of blood.

The lines of blood that looked like someone had been dragged away were especially disturbing.

"Damn... First, we search to see if anyone's here!" Kuu said, gritting his teeth.

We all looked around to see if there were any survivors. However, we couldn't even find the bodies. Those who could escape had fled, and those who couldn't must have been devoured or dragged off.

Having confirmed there was no one left in this village, we gathered again and began our search.

"Leporina," I said. "Can you tell what direction the monsters are in?"

"I'll try." Leporina perked her rabbit ears up and twitched them. A few seconds later, she said, "There are five at two o'clock, seven at three o'clock, and noises indicating the presence of several others."

"I hear ogres move in groups," Aisha explained. "The five and seven are likely ogres."

The several others were probably the members of the Black Cats posted throughout the forest.

I sent the wooden mice in the directions Leporina indicated. When they had gone about eight hundred meters from the village, I confirmed five ogres, and another kilometer away were seven more.

Like in the report I had received from the Black Cats, the ogres did indeed have a bizarre form. Their arms were bizarrely fat and big, making their bodies extremely unbalanced.

From manga and games, I had an image of ogres as fat macho guys with horns, wearing straw skirts and swinging clubs around. But while these ogres definitely had ogre heads, they wore no clothing, carried no weapons, and their bodies were covered in long hair. They were like what you'd get if you crossed an oni with a gorilla, and resembled the ijuu I had seen in the youkai encyclopedia I had read as a child.

The wooden mice crept closer and confirmed both groups were sitting in a circle and feasting on something. I had a bad feeling, so I decided not to look closely, but I still caught a glimpse of one of the villag—no, best not to think about it.

The gorilla-like ogres with their bloodshot eyes were devouring their food with reckless abandon. The only thing I got from them was they were intensely hungry.

Good thing we didn't bring Tomoe...

If I were only considering my objective of learning about monsters, Tomoe's ability would have been useful. But I could tell just from looking that there was something different about these guys. They were only thinking about eating.

When it came to humans and animals, once their stomachs were full of food, they calmed down. However, these ogres were eating, but they didn't show any signs of satisfaction whatsoever. They were like starving ghouls out of hell. If Tomoe could understand what they said, she'd probably faint in shock. It was a pretty harsh sight.

While forcing down the nausea, I informed everyone of what I had just seen.

Hearing my report, Kuu slammed his fist into the ground as if to take his frustrations out on it. "Those bastards! I'll never forgive them!"

Hal crossed his arms and said, "Is there a distance between the two groups? It'd be a pain if they joined up."

"Defeating a divided force is basic strategy, you know," Kaede, who was Ludwin's staff officer in the National Defense Force, agreed. "If possible, I'd like to dispose of the smaller group quickly."

Kaede placed five and seven stones on the ground, then dug a trench between them with a stick.

"I'd like to lay a trap between these two groups. That will let us delay the seven if they notice something is wrong with the five and rush to their aid, and it might injure them if we're lucky."

"Do we have time to be laying traps?" I asked.

"I can easily use my magic to make pitfalls, if nothing else, you know. That's why I'd like to sit out the fight with the five, and instead focus keeping them separated. If possible, I'd like to have an archer who could aim to injure and weaken them."

"Then Leporina can go with you," said Kuu. "She acts like a moron, but she's a capable archer."

"You didn't have to call me a moron," Leporina protested, but she still followed the order.

That more or less gave us our battle plan. While Kaede and Leporina delayed the arrival of the seven, Aisha, Hal, and Kuu would wipe out the five with their full combat potential. I, myself, would only be in the way, so I'd be supporting them at range using the Little Musashibo (Small) I had brought, equipped with a bowgun. Juna was to be on standby as my bodyguard and strike commando.

When the operation started, Kuu gave an order. "I'm sorry to get you people from another country wrapped up in my country's problem. But for now, please, lend us your strength! Let's get this impromptu combined force going!"

"Yeah!"

Though we were a small, hastily thrown-together team, the first joint battle between the Kingdom of Friedonia and the Republic of Turgis had begun.

In order to defeat them all before the seven arrived from elsewhere, we decided we would first hit them with a surprise attack with the greatest power possible. The goal was to make sure at least one went down in the initial strike.

And among us, the one with the most power was…Aisha.

"Hahhhhhh!"

With a war cry, Aisha swung her greatsword.

Caught unaware by the assault, one of the ogres was bisected without being able to do anything about it. The other four panicked when they saw one of them had gone down.

Then Aisha, Hal, and Kuu sprang on them.

"I'm sure you know this, redhead, but we don't have much time!" Kuu shouted.

"I know, whitehead!" Hal shot back.

Wait, Hal! He's the son of their head of state, okay?

Kuu wielded the cudgel decorated with a golden centipede that we had seen in Taru's workshop. Hal held two short spears, but the bottoms of their shafts were bound by a thin chain. Was that the new weapon he said he'd bought at Taru's place? I believed it was called the Twin Snake Spear.

"You punks are gonna pay for what you did to our people!" Kuu spun his cudgel around like a windmill, then wove nimbly through his opponent's oncoming arms to whack the ogre's forehead, solar plexus, and other vital points. "Too slow! Here, you can eat this, too!"

Most likely, that cudgel was strengthened with an enchantment. Every time the cudgel struck flesh, there was thumping sound. The ogre held the places where it had been struck and winced in pain.

Compared to Kuu's style of melee fighting, Hal was working at medium range. He wreathed his right-hand spear in flames and threw it at the ogre. When the ogre evaded it, the spear stuck in the tree behind it. That same moment, the flames burst. There was a loud roar and the tree exploded into pieces.

The ogre closed in on Hal, unintimidated, and raised up its huge arms.

"Oh, crap!" Hal cried.

Before the ogre could swing down, Hal yanked on his remaining spear. That pulled on the chain connecting the spears at their base, and the other spear smoothly returned to his hand. Hal crossed the two spears and blocked the ogre's downwards blow.

"Urgh… Yeah, I'm not doing so hot, taking it into battle without any practice," he groaned.

While he slid his crossed spears and redirected the ogre's arms to the right, Hal spun his body, and landed a flaming backwards roundhouse kick on the ogre's flank. The ogre's body, which was easily over two meters tall, was thrown back about five meters.

Hal cracked his neck and looked at the ogre. "Sheesh… I'll have to train to be able to use it quickly."

Hal grinned, then threw his left spear at the ogre.

The ogre tried to dodge it again, but Hal used the remaining spear and chain to change its course. The ogre was unable to avoid the spear, and it struck the ogre's right shoulder.

"Blow up!" Hal shouted, and the flame-wreathed spear blew away the ogre's right arm.

While Kuu and Hal seemed to be holding the advantage in their battles, Aisha was fighting two ogres alone. Despite that, there was no sign whatsoever that Aisha was in trouble.

Warding off the ogres' heavy blows with her greatsword, she followed that up by slashing them. As time passed, the number of gashes carved into the two ogres' bodies increased.

"So inexperienced. This isn't even a warmup," Aisha said as she cut off one ogre's fat arm at the shoulder.

All three of them were doing an amazing job fighting.

For my part, I was watching them from a distance. That was so I could keep watch for the seven that were being delayed, as well as keep an eye out for any signs of further enemy activity in the surrounding area.

While I would occasionally see an opening and have my Little Musashibo take a shot, the ogres' thick muscles kept getting in the way, so my supporting fire wasn't doing much more than harassing them.

"Everyone's so strong," I murmured to myself.

"Of course," Juna said. She was standing beside me as my bodyguard. "Aisha and Sir Halbert are among the best warriors in our country. Sir Kuu is strong, too, I might add. I'm not sure I could beat him."

"Oh, yeah. Now that you mention it, you were one of them, huh?"

Juna used to be the commander of the marines in the former

navy. She was someone who had a strength she could compare against others.

"I know I can rely on you," I added.

"Hee hee." She seemed pleased. "But...don't let your guard down, okay?"

Juna suddenly pulled out a number of knives and threw them forward.

The water-wreathed knives left a trail as they flew forward. They stabbed into a large boulder that had flown our way at some point, and in the next instant, the boulder was pulverized. It seemed one of Aisha's ogres had gotten cornered and, in desperation, started throwing around anything that came to hand. One of those things must have ended up coming our way.

"Because the thing to truly be afraid of at a time like this is the stray arrow that comes at you without killing intent," she finished.

"Oh! Okay..."

As she brushed her hair back and said that, I felt myself falling for Juna all over again.

When there was only one ogre left, we learned there had been movement from the other seven.

"Ah! The seven are coming this way! Kaede and Leporina are coming, too!"

I reported that to everyone, then prepared myself for battle again.

Leporina and Kaede rushed in from the distance. They were moving as planned, but for some reason, Leporina looked flustered. She rushed straight over to me.

"Wh-what is it?" I asked.

"Haaah... Haaah... K-Kazuma! In addition to the seven, another group is coming in from eight o'clock! There are five of them!"

Another group?! Reinforcements, now?!

But I'd received no report from the Black Cats. Whatever the case might be, I sent a wooden mouse in the direction Leporina indicated. Then, when I confirmed the group...I was shocked.

Huh?! What are they *doing here?!*

I was so surprised, I was at a loss for words. When I came to my senses, I hid my Little Musashibo doll in the bushes. It'd be bad if those guys saw it.

"Wh-what is it?! Is it something bad?!"

Leporina had a worried look on her face, so I hurriedly shook my head.

"Oh...it's fine. They're not our enemies."

And then they came out from the other side of the bushes.

You could tell at a glance that they were five adventurers: the handsome swordsman; the green-haired, boyish female thief; the muscled martial artist man; the mild-mannered priest with the gentle face; and the quiet beauty who was a mage. I knew these people well.

"We've come to support you in response to a request from the adventurers' guild!" the handsome swordsman known as Dece shouted. "Is there someone in charge here?"

Whenever I had Little Musashibo go out and play adventurer, this was the party he often teamed up with.

The swordsman's name was Dece, the female thief was Juno, the mild-mannered guy in the priest's uniform was Febral, the female mage's name was Julia, and the muscled man's name was... Who was he again? He hadn't been there the first time I'd teamed up with the party... Oh! Augus. It was Augus.

"Hm?" Juno came over to me. "Hey, you. Haven't we met somewhere?" she asked while staring me in the face.

◇ ◇ ◇

This is just a reminder, but adventurers were people who made their living clearing the dungeons that existed all over this continent, slaying the dangerous creatures that sometimes spilled out of them, and performing tasks like defending merchants and subjugating bandits.

A group of adventurers' final goal was to clear a dungeon and earn wealth and glory by destroying and bringing back its dungeon core.

Among themselves, they had job names based on the roles they played.

If they specialized in close combat, they were a swordsman or brawler. If they specialized in long-range combat, they were an archer. And if they focused on magic, they were a mage. In addition, there were the scouting and commando roles played by the thief, and the healer role played by the priest. However, these were only job titles. It didn't mean they were actual thieves or priests.

They were like Jacks- and Jills-of-all-trades whose bodies were their primary assets, which meant their position in society was not particularly high. But if they managed to recover something useful from a dungeon, they could possibly strike it rich, so adventuring was a reasonably popular and romanticized profession.

Furthermore, due to the nature of their trade, adventurers often worked across borders, so registering with the adventurers' guild also had the benefit of simplified checks when entering or leaving a country.

You might think that would make them easy to use as spies, but it also meant that it was easy for them to draw attention. If an adventurer carelessly got too close to important secrets, they would surely be put down without question.

Still, it was true that it was a convenient way of getting someone into another country undercover, and that was why the Gran Chaos Empire's Little Sister General, Jeanne, had used it to make contact with Souma in past.

Now, returning to the story. We turn back to about half a day earlier...

On this day, the swordsman Dece, the thief Juno, the priest Febral, the mage Julia, and the martial artist Augus left their usual area of operations in Friedonia in order to visit the Republic of Turgis.

They were in the Republic to buy equipment. They needed to procure new arms and armor to replace the ones they had used up in their adventuring business, and they all agreed that if they had to buy them anyway, they should get Turgish equipment, which was noted for its high quality.

Being contractors who took jobs from others, they evaluated their equipment not only by function, but by appearance.

Because imports were relatively expensive, they had decided to go to the place where fine Turgish arms were made as a means of conserving money.

Dece and the others were all smiling after buying their new equipment, but then the adventurers' guild issued an emergency quest.

Apparently a dungeon had been discovered near a mountain village, and ogres had crawled out of it to attack that small settlement. The quest was to "cooperate in subjugating the ogres."

These sorts of emergency quests were issued in the names of both the guild and the country, and adventurers in the affected area were somewhat forced to accept them. They could refuse, but in the event they did, they would face harsh consequences—such as being stripped of their status as an adventurer.

"Well, if it's an emergency quest, we can't exactly refuse," Dece commented. "Let's go, everyone."

"Urgh... I *just* got this new equipment, and I need to get it dirty already?" Juno complained.

The adventurers' shoulders slumped as they realized they were getting dragged into some real trouble. Even so, they couldn't ignore an emergency quest.

There was nothing else they could do, so Dece and the others hurried into the mountains to join up with the group that was already on location and dealing with the issue.

◇ ◇ ◇

"Hey, you," Juno said. "Haven't we met somewhere?"

The female thief had distinctive green hair and was seventeen, maybe eighteen years of age. Her defiant eyes seemed a poor fit for her childish face as she stared hard at me.

Within her party, she specialized in scouting and ambushing, so she dressed lightly, with hot pants and a tank top with a breastplate over it. But because of this country's cold climate, she was now wearing a cape on top of that.

"Your face..." she went on. "I feel like I've seen it somewhere before?"

"Erm..." I said. I wasn't sure exactly which face she meant. Was it my face on the Jewel Voice Broadcast as the King of Friedonia, or my face from when we'd encountered each other in the former slums, or the face of the person inside the adventurer Little Musashibo...? Oh, wait, I had been controlling that Little Musashibo remotely. Well, no matter which of my alternate identities it was, it would be troublesome to explain.

Judging from the wrinkles on Juno's brow, it seemed Juno herself couldn't recall where she had seen me. In that case, my solution was decided.

I offered my right hand to Juno. "Nice to meet you. Would you people happen to be the adventurers coming to support us?"

"Huh? Uh...yeah, but..."

"Whew, it's a good thing you're here." I took Juno's right hand and shook it hard.

My plan was to move things along before she figured anything out. While I was still holding Juno's right hand, I pointed to the last of the five ogres which the others were working on defeating.

"We also came here to slay ogres and answer the request for aid that Sir Kuu issued."

"Y-you did?" Juno looked at me blankly.

Whew... It looked like I'd managed to play it off well enough.

"Darling?" Juna, who had been standing beside me, was looking at me with a smile.

Even though she hadn't said a word, I could tell what she was thinking...

"Oh my, just how long do you plan to hold her hand for? Just what sort of relationship do you have with her...?"

I felt like I was being interrogated. I was like a frog, paralyzed by a snake's glare. No, not just any snake; a giant sea snake. It was times like this when I could really sense that Juna was the granddaughter of Excel the sea serpent.

I let go of Juno's hand, then turned the conversation over to the party leader Dece, who had a look on his face like he was wondering what we had been talking about.

"We've finished slaying these five, but another seven ogres are coming this way," I said. "I'd like your assistance in subjugating them."

"S-sure," he said. "Got it. Let's go, everyone!"

"Yeah!" said Augus.

"Yes, sir!" Febral and Julia shouted.

Juno continued staring at my face, but thanks to Juna subtly inserting herself between us, we were able to break her line of sight.

Juno took on an irritated expression at someone getting between us. Juna didn't let her smile break, even as the other woman glared at her dubiously. Sparks flew between them.

Why was that? I felt a pain in my stomach.

Not long afterward, the seven ogres appeared, but with our original group of seven being bolstered by the five adventurers, there were now twelve of us.

Excluding myself, of course, because I was unable to use my Little Musashibo doll in front of Juno and her party. That meant I was reduced to a scouting role, with Juna guarding me. But we still had enough people to overwhelm the remaining monsters.

While Dece and Juno were way below Aisha or Hal in terms of ability, they and Augus kept the ogres under control on the front line. Febral healed their wounds, Juno disrupted the ogres and cut them with twin poison-coated swords, and Julia finished them with magic.

They took out two ogres that way, defeating enemies they couldn't beat alone with the power of teamwork. It was a style that differed from soldiers on the battlefield, and it suited them as adventurers.

Little Musashibo has been part of that...

The Little Musashibo I was making act as an adventurer had often formed a temporary party with them. His role was the sort of front-line fighting that Dece and Augus were doing. Even if it was temporary, he had joined them a number of times, so I was confident he could work in concert with them.

He had been asked to formally join the party, too, but I couldn't afford to let one of my consciousnesses be constantly devoted to adventuring, so I'd politely declined.

To think I'd encounter them in this country... I pondered. *Was this meant to be...?*

"Fate is a fickle mistress, and misery acquaints a man with strange bedfellows..." I murmured.

"Hm? Did you say something?" Juna asked.

"Nope, not a thing." I shook my head.

What had at some point become the last ogre took Hal's flaming spear in its flank, which gouge a massive hole in its flesh when it exploded. Now we'd exterminated all the ogres in this area.

There was no report of more enemies from the Black Cats watching the entrance to the dungeon, so this was mission accomplished.

"You all did great," Kuu said. "Kazuma and company, and you adventurers, too. I thank you on behalf of the people of this country."

Kuu and Leporina both bowed their heads. He was speaking formally, no doubt because he was the quest issuer.

Then Kuu raised his head and smiled at Dece and the others with a laugh. "You really saved us. We'll tell the guild the quest's complete. And about your part in it, too, of course. Go to them for your reward."

"R-right," said Dece. "Understood. We'll be going, then."

Dece and the others bowed and turned back down the road they came. When they were almost out of sight, Juno seemed to panic about something and raced back over on her own.

Oh, crap! Had she figured something out?

She stood in front of me and thrust a finger in my direction. "I remember now! You—you were the guy in Parnam's refugee camp!"

Oh, that's the one she remembers, huh?

It seemed she recognized me not as a king, or as the one inside Little Musashibo, but as the guy she'd happened to encounter in the refugee camp. I wondered how I was going to dodge the issue, but I had a feeling that trying to lie while she was staring at me so hard would backfire.

I put my hand on top of my head and bowed slightly. "Ohhh... thank you for that time..."

"I knew it! I've wanted to ask you all this time! Back then, I never gave my name, but you called me Juno! How'd you know my name?!"

"That's..."

What was the best way to answer that? I couldn't say it was because I was Little Musashibo and I had often worked with her party...right?

But...was there a need to keep that secret? It would be problematic if they learned I was the king right now, but if they found out I was connected to Little Musashibo…that wouldn't really be a problem, right?

"Well…the truth is—"

"Hey, Juno! We're leaving you behind!" Dece was calling her from off in the distance.

Juno ground her back teeth, then thrust her index finger towards me again. "Next time we meet, I'm getting answers out of you!"

Leaving those words behind, Juno ran over to the rest of her group.

"Next time we meet, huh?"

I was fine with telling her, but I ended up keeping the secret, after all. To be fair, I was always in the center of Parnam, and I didn't go out to the castle town that often, so was I ever actually going to meet Juno in the flesh again?

While I was wondering that, Kuu clapped his hands. "Now then… Leporina, Kazuma, there are no more ogres left outside, right?"

"Right," Leporina said. "I don't hear any more groups moving around."

I concurred. "I sent my wooden mice after the individual sound sources, and can confirm there are no ogres left near here."

Kuu nodded. "In that case, it should be fine now. The army should be getting here any time now, so we can leave guarding the dungeon to them. You were watching the entrance just in case, right?"

"Yeah," I said. "Looks like there's been no movement there."

Though, if I were to be wholly accurate, the ones watching it were the Black Cats. There had been no more reports, so it was probably fine.

Kuu considered that for a while. "Then can I get you to watch until the military arrives?" he asked finally. "If any more monsters come out, we'd have to deal with them."

It spoke well of him, as one who stood above others, that he was taking every precaution until things were fully secured. Naturally, I wholeheartedly agreed to do it.

"Roger that," I said. "I'll keep watch until the military arrives."

"I'm counting on you. Okay, shall we get going back, too, then? Man, I'm sorry. Getting you caught up in our problems like this," Kuu said with a grin. "I'm really grateful, you know? Let me pay you the same reward we'll be paying the adventurers."

But I shook my head. "No, this was within the realm of international cooperation. I don't need any compensation."

"Huh? I don't feel right leaving it like that..."

"You don't? Hm...if you insist, then could you ask your father to be willing to make all sorts of concessions to my country in the coming talks?" I asked jokingly.

Kuu laughed and threw his arm around my shoulder. "Ooh ha ha, that's not happening! When it comes to negotiations with other countries, my people's livelihoods are involved. I may be grateful, but we can't make concessions there."

"Ha ha ha, really? That's too bad, then."

"You don't mean that," Kuu grinned. "Or if you do, then try to look a little more disappointed."

We looked at one another and laughed.

Aisha and Juna watched us with smiles. “I don’t know how to say it, but they’re just so young when you look at them like this,” Aisha said.

“Hee hee,” Juna giggled. “It’s relaxing, somehow.”

I felt a little bit embarrassed.

CHAPTER 6
A Trump Card in Negotiations

AFTER WE TURNED OVER the handling of the dungeon to the Republic's military, we hurried back to the town of Noblebeppu, where Roroa and Tomoe were waiting, and where talks with Kuu's father, the head of the Republic of Turgis, were waiting for us.

It had been arranged that the talks would be held in a room at the inn where we were staying, with a very limited number of people attending. This was the result of taking the Turgish side's situation into consideration. A larger meeting would have required taking the time to go through a process with the Council of Chiefs.

We were able to make it back to Noblebeppu by noon on the day of the talks. We stayed in the mountain village near the dungeon for one night after the ogres were exterminated, then set out just before dawn, but it ultimately took us that long to arrive.

Though the situation was explained to the other side, we must have kept them waiting for a fair amount of time.

When I dismounted from the carriage in front of the inn, Roroa and Tomoe came out to greet us.

"Welcome back, Darlin'!" Roroa called. "Ya had me worried."

"Welcome back," Tomoe said. "I'm glad you're okay, Big Brother."

"I'm back, Roroa, Tomoe."

When I patted them on their heads, they cooed and smiled. Seeing them like that, I was relieved I had been able to come back safe.

Having had help from Dece, Juno, and the rest might make it seem like there ultimately hadn't been much danger, but seeing those ghoulish ogres that looked like they'd crawled out of hell, feasting on what looked to be human meat, may have made me feel a little weak at heart. That was a traumatic sight, after all.

"Whew, we're here, we're here!" Disembarking from the carriage, Kuu spun his arms in circles. "It's already noon, so have your king and my old man already started the talks?"

We Friedonians looked at him blankly, but...

Oh, right, everyone quickly realized. The only ones here who didn't know the truth were Kuu and Leporina.

I put on a strained smile and told Kuu, "No, not yet. One of the leaders only just arrived, after all."

"Huh? What's that supposed to—"

When Kuu was about to ask, a group of about five people walked towards us from across the way. The one leading them was a large-bodied, stern-faced snow monkey.

He was a mountain of muscle. His sideburns and beard had merged into something like a white lion's mane. If Kuu was Sun Wukong, this man was fit to be called the Monkey King. His white robe and white cape with shoulder pads made him look every bit the person of high station that he was.

With soldiers following behind him, the great man stood before us.

"Hm? Well, hey, if it isn't my old man," Kuu said to the snow monkey. "What happened to the talks?"

Just as I'd assumed, this great snow monkey was Kuu's father, and also the head of the Republic of Turgis.

The man ignored Kuu and stood in front of me. "It is good to meet you, King of Friedonia. Welcome to the Republic of Turgis. I am the head of state, Gouran Taisei." Sir Gouran smiled and extended his right hand. He had a stern face, but it wore a courteous smile.

I took his right hand. "It's good to meet you, too, Sir Gouran. I am King Souma Kazuya of the United Kingdom of Elfrieden and Amidonia."

We brought our left hands together with our clasped right hands for a two-handed handshake.

While watching us, Kuu's mouth hung open as if he didn't understand what was going on. Eventually he must have worked it out, because his eyes went wide.

"Whaaa?! Kazuma's a king?!"

"Now, Kuu, you're being rude to Sir Souma," his father scolded.

"No, it's my fault for not saying anything," I said. "Sorry for not telling you, Kuu. My real name is Souma Kazuya. I did, at least, contact your head of state about it."

Once I had apologized for keeping it a secret, Kuu let out a sigh. "To think...the guy I bumped into at Taru's workshop was the king of a neighboring country..."

"I could say the same," I said. "Who would have expected the son of this country's head of state to come riding in on a numoth while I talked business with Taru?"

Talk about serendipity. All either of us could do was laugh wryly.

Sir Gouran, who had been watching us, gave a hearty guffaw. "If we're keeping score, I'm the most confused of all. Who would have expected my own son was working with a foreign king? What's more, it seems you helped us subjugate the monsters that spilled out of a dungeon. I thank you cordially on behalf of my people."

Gouran bowed his head. I could feel he was related to Kuu from that forthright posture of his.

"Please, raise your head," I said. "The monsters in dungeons are a threat to all of mankind. They're like a natural disaster, so it's only right that I would offer help, irrespective of whether they happened upon citizens of the kingdom or the Republic."

"Well, I'm grateful to hear you say that... Oh?" Sir Gouran noticed Roroa, who was standing beside me, and blinked. "Pardon me. Would you happen to be Princess Roroa of Amidonia?"

"Yes, Lord Gouran. I am Roroa Amidonia." Roroa lifted the hem of her coat and curtsied.

For a moment, that gesture was so well refined I had to question if she was really Roroa. Had she suppressed her usual merchant slang and responded politely because he was the representative of a nation? For those of us who knew the usual Roroa, she looked like a little tanuki playing innocent.

"You know who I am, Lord Gouran?" she asked.

"We aren't directly acquainted, but you reminded me of your mother," he said.

"My mother?" Roroa tilted her head to the side.

If I recalled, Roroa's mother passed away when she was little, hadn't she? I remembered that because when we'd held a funeral for Gaius, he was interred in the royal family's tomb, where his wife had already been laid to rest.

With a hearty laugh, Gouran continued. "When I was young, there were only minor skirmishes, but I crossed blades with the Amidonian military on several occasions. In that process, I gathered information on Amidonia. You know, Sir Gaius made for a fearsome adversary. Nothing could have been more troublesome."

"I...I see..." Roroa struggled to give a proper response.

There had been a rift between Roroa and her father. When someone was laughing and telling her things about him that could be compliments or insults, she had no idea how to respond.

Sir Gouran continued despite Roroa's reaction. "I hear your mother was a person so cheerful, she could laugh Sir Gaius' stern face away. I've also heard talk about how you married yourself, and your country with you, to King Souma. You must have inherited her boldness."

"Th-thank you..." Roroa responded while shooting me a look that screamed, *Darlin', help me!*

It seemed she was troubled by Sir Gouran bringing up awkward topics it was hard for her to respond to, and apparently doing it with no ill intent, at that.

Unlike Roroa, though, I was impressed with Sir Gouran. Even though he lived in this closed-off land, he hadn't been lax in gathering information about the outside world.

Well, that aside, Roroa was tearing up, so I decided to help her. "Sir Gouran, should we start the talks now?"

"Oh, sorry. I've been rude," Sir Gouran said. He took on an extremely serious expression. "I know the talks were scheduled for today, but between subjugating the ogres and traveling, you must be tired. Please, relax for today, and we will hold the talks tomorrow."

"Well...okay," I said. "I'd be grateful if we could do it that way."

I didn't want to rush the negotiations; I wanted us to take our time. And it was true that I was tired. I decided to accept Sir Gouran's considerate offer.

We would stay in the inn, and Sir Gouran and his entourage would stay at the villa where Kuu had been staying near here. Then, tomorrow, we would reserve this entire inn to hold the meeting.

This was where it would all be decided.

That night, I used the jewel I had brought in secret to contact Hakuya back in the capital of Parnam. When I explained the situation in Turgis...

"Honestly... What were you thinking?" he asked in exasperation. "It should be unthinkable for the king of a nation to go out slaying ogres."

That was the first thing out of Hakuya's mouth.

"Well, I thought I had to—"

"It would seem a scolding from Lady Liscia is inevitable at this point," he went on.

"Erk...is Liscia there, too?" I asked hesitantly, but Hakuya shook his head.

"No. Lady Liscia has already gone to rest in Lord Albert's domain."

"Thank goodness... I wouldn't want to worry her now."

She was carrying our child in her womb. I couldn't afford to worry her unduly.

But it really was a shame to be unable to see Liscia's face or hear her voice. I wanted to thank her directly for having our child. This made me feel like a father living away from the family due to business.

Hakuya looked exasperated. "If you know that, I want you to be prudent. You will be a father soon, Your Majesty."

"I'll take that to heart..."

There was nothing else I could say in response. I had to be honest with myself and reflect. That said, if I encountered a similar situation in future, I didn't really know if I could play it safe.

"So, how is the plan going on your end?" I asked.

"I've already received assent from the other party. The preparations are complete, but... What are your thoughts on Sir Gouran, Sire?"

"How do you mean that, exactly?"

"Do you think the talks will be a success or not?"

I thought about that a little, recalling what I had seen of Sir Gouran today. "He seems abrasive, but there's a more sensitive side to him. He looks like a warrior, but that's not all there is to him. If we underestimate him, he'll take advantage of that. He's not the head of a nation for nothing."

"Sire...in order to make negotiations move smoothly, you wanted to demonstrate the power of our nation, correct?"

"In order to form friendly relations, I want to show them the merits of forming an alliance with us, and the demerits of making an enemy of us. But from the look of things, he's not going to be intimidated by just anything. That's all the more reason why the trick you've set up will be useful." I grinned.

"Please, do not go to the talks tomorrow with that look on your face." Hakuya sighed in exasperation.

◇ ◇ ◇

Meanwhile, around this time, Head of the Republic Gouran and his son Kuu were in the living room of their villa in Noblebeppu, talking about Souma and his companions over drinks.

"When you were working with that king, what was your view of him?" Gouran asked while tilting back a goblet of fermented milk.

"He's a weird one," Kuu chuckled. "He looks weak, but there's something about him you just can't figure out, I guess you could say?"

Gouran tilted his head to the side at his son's words. "So... which is he, in the end?"

"Like I said, I don't know. He's probably a king who rules by the pen, not the sword. Kazuma—no, *Souma* looks weak, and he really isn't strong, but he's got a good collection of subordinates around him. That dark elf especially. She's in a class of her own. And even if Souma looks like he's wide open, if you make the mistake of trying to lay a hand on him, his subordinates will leave piles of bodies lying around."

"Hm..." Gouran pondered. "He's a king who is loved and protected by his vassals, then?"

"Ooohaah...I feel like it's more than just that. He's a smart one, so he won't be reckless, but it's not like he's completely without courage. No matter how much he trusted his subordinates, a weak guy wouldn't decide to accompany me on a dangerous task like subjugating those ogres so easily, right? If he can place his own life on the scales, that's proof he's made it through his own share of trials."

"They say he defeated a military man like Gaius VIII, after all," Gouran nodded.

Triggered by Souma's ascension to the throne, a war had broken out between the Elfrieden Kingdom and the Principality of Amidonia. From the stories they had heard, the war had been a crushing victory for the kingdom, but Gaius VIII showed his pride as a warrior to the end.

Even with the war decided, his troops broken and scattered, and Crown Prince Julius on the run, Gaius himself had gone with his personal retainers and charged into a great army, coming within steps of wringing Souma's neck.

Even in defeat, Gaius maintained his pride as a warrior.

Those who lost a war were always vilified at first. The victors spread those stories to demonstrate the righteousness of their own actions.

However, in Gaius' case, because his daughter Roroa was going to marry Souma, and an attempt was being made to unify the two countries, Souma never spoke ill of him, and he did not have an undeserved reputation.

Setting aside people's views of his performance as a sovereign prince, Gaius' reputation as a warrior was being defended by a daughter who hadn't gotten along with him, and her fiancé who had fought him as an enemy. Whether this was a neat contrivance of history or an irony was up to the individual to decide.

Gouran thought that perhaps by confronting Gaius, Souma had gained a courage that did not match his own weak body. *If so...Gaius has left behind an incredible memento.*

Whether Gouran wished for it himself or not, the threads of fate continued to wrap themselves around him. While feeling the flow of time, he looked to Kuu, who was drinking fermented milk in front of him.

Will getting involved with Souma bring about some change in my idiot son? That may prove to have great meaning for the Republic...

Gouran downed the rest of his fermented milk, and made his decision.

◇ ◇ ◇

The night broke, and it was the day of the meeting.

We reserved the great hall of the inn where we were staying, and Gouran and I sat across from one another. It was the place we had used for the party before, so there were no tables or chairs. We sat cross-legged on brilliantly colored cushions laid out on the carpet.

On either side of me were Juna and Roroa, who no longer needed to hide their positions, and Kuu sat next to Gouran.

Behind us were Aisha and the rest of the members of our group, with the exception of Tomoe, and behind Sir Gouran and Kuu were a group of this country's soldiers led by Leporina.

Each of those groups stood at attention and guarded their respective leaders.

I bowed slightly, then looked Sir Gouran straight in the face. "First, allow me to thank you for arranging this meeting."

"Think nothing of it," he said. "It is not often one has the chance to speak with the king of a neighboring country. I would very much like to use this rare chance to speak openly about things that will be of benefit of both our lands." Sir Gouran returned my slight bow and looked me straight in the eye.

We were both the leaders of our respective countries, so neither could bow deeply in a way that implied one was higher or lower than the other.

Gouran turned to look to the side. "Still...I'm surprised. To think you would bring such a thing here..."

He was looking at a jewel for the Jewel Voice Broadcast. The massive crystal that I had also used to communicate with Hakuya yesterday was occupying a corner of the room.

Sir Gouran furrowed his brow. "That is a Jewel Voice Broadcast jewel, correct? Is this being broadcast somewhere?"

"No, this is only for communication purposes," I said. "I'm not broadcasting it to the people."

"I see."

"Do you have jewels in this country, too?" I asked.

"Just one. I would like to have more, but they're made from dungeon cores. Unfortunately, we've only cleared one dungeon in this country."

"I see..."

It sure was inconvenient that there was only one dungeon core. The country had a fairly large amount of land, so I would want them to have one for broadcasting and one for communication, at least.

If we'd had any to spare, I'd have been willing to sell or trade them, but of the five dungeon cores we currently had, one was used for broadcasts from the castle, one for communicating with the Empire, and three were for broadcast programs. Unfortunately, I had no way to help.

With the pleasantries set aside, I dove into the matter at hand. "Now then, Sir Gouran, I have a proposal for you."

"The 'medical alliance,' I believe." Before I could say it, Sir Gouran crossed his arms and grunted. "Treatments that don't rely on light magic... It really is fascinating. Doctors, were they? For this country, where it's hard to even walk around outside in winter, there would be great meaning in being able to permanently station one person who could perform treatments in every village. Besides that, you say they can treat diseases that light magic can't. I'd very much like to have that."

Sir Gouran sounded impressed. It felt like we weren't off to a bad start, but then his expression grew stern.

"However, there are things I don't understand here. Why would you bring this to us? Wouldn't studying the subject alone allow your country to grow more powerful?"

Suspicious eyes. He was trying to feel out if I had any ulterior motives.

When he asked me that, for a moment, I thought about how the empress of the Gran Chaos Empire might answer. She might say, "Medicine knows no borders."

That person, who was not a self-proclaimed saint, but had been proclaimed a saint by others, was the sort to think about what was best for the whole world, and so those kinds of words suited her.

For me, on the other hand, that sort of idealism was a poor fit. I always thought of my own country's benefit first. I didn't think that was a bad thing, but if someone like me said, "Medicine knows no borders," the words might sound hollow.

So I looked Sir Gouran in the eyes as I responded, "That's... for practicality."

"Practicality?"

"Yes. It's true; it would be best to study it with only my country. However, that would take too much time and funding. Medicine is not a subject one country can fully study on its own. If I were to try to do it all with one country, I wouldn't have enough time, personnel, or funding."

What I needed to demonstrate was the realistic benefit of dividing the research. If I could prove it would be of benefit to both the kingdom and the Republic, I could get things moving.

"That is why, like I proposed to Kuu, I want the Republic to produce medical equipment and to export it to us. We will dispatch the doctors who can use that equipment. If this can be realized, the field of medicine should progress greatly in both our countries."

"That's true. It does sound like both countries stand to profit." Gouran gave a big nod.

Was this going to work? "Well, then..."

"However..." It had looked like things were coming together, but then Sir Gouran fixed a stern look on me. "Can this truly be called an *equal* exchange?"

"What do you mean?"

"Hearing your proposal of a medical alliance, I did a fair amount of thinking about it for my own part. It may look advanced, but to make matters quick, I think it's really just a development in the way medicine men and women treat their patients."

"You're right..." I admitted.

He wasn't mistaken. We had managed to cut out a lot of the process because of the existence of the three-eyed race that could see microorganisms, but doctors were merely a further development of the medicine man or woman who brewed medicinal infusions.

"In that case, it is something we can understand, too," Sir Gouran said. "Basically, the kingdom trains incredible medicine men or women, and our country is expected to create the incredible tools they use, right? If that was all we were dealing with, I'm sure you could call it fair, but there's one more element: the medicinal infusions the medicine man or woman uses."

"Medicinal infusions… You mean drugs?"

"We each hold one card: the doctor and the medical equipment. However, the 'drugs' card is floating in midair. We can't take the drugs card for ourselves yet. If the kingdom takes that card, the balance of power will largely shift in your favor."

Drugs, huh.

It was true that, in the kingdom, the three-eyes race had developed three-eyedine (an antibiotic). Three-eyedine was extracted from a subspecies of gelin that could live even in poisonous swamps.

This country was very cold, and the liquid gelins would freeze solid, so they didn't live here. It wouldn't be possible for them to develop such a drug on their own.

Naturally, they'd be dependent on imports. If the kingdom had control of those imports, it would be easy for more funding to flow into the kingdom.

To be honest, I hadn't thought about that until it was pointed out.

Obviously, I had considered the element of drugs, but I hadn't expected Sir Gouran to deem it a cause for suspicion. Still, now that I thought about it, it was only natural he would. The

Republic was approaching these talks with a lot of determination of their own. They would think desperately about what could be disadvantageous to their country, and try to rub it out.

Sir Gouran must be a good ruler... Well, in this case, his fears are unwarranted.

I mentally shrugged my shoulders. It wasn't like I was deliberately avoiding the topic of drugs in order to make a profit down the line. I turned both of my palms towards Sir Gouran.

"There's no need to worry. That card is no longer in the kingdom's hands, you see."

"Hm? What do you mean?"

"Juna. Bring that thing out."

"Yes, Sire." Juna brought out a board-shaped thing that could fit in her arms, and placed it in front of the jewel so everyone could see it.

It was a simple Jewel Voice Broadcast receiver. Projected on that simple receiver was a single beautiful woman.

When they saw the woman, Sir Gouran and Kuu's eyes went wide.

"D-Dad!" Kuu cried.

"Yeah..."

"Hee hee, I'm sorry that I seem to have surprised you." The woman on screen smiled, then bowed slightly to Sir Gouran and the others. "It is a pleasure to meet you, Sir Gouran Taisei, head of the Republic of Turgis. I am Empress Maria Euphoria of the Gran Chaos Empire."

CHAPTER 7
The Tripartite Medical Alliance

SEVERAL DAYS before the meeting...

With the Jewel Voice Broadcast jewel and simple receiver that had been delivered, I contacted Hakuya in Parnam Castle and informed him that I wanted to demonstrate Friedonia's strength in order to ensure negotiations went smoothly. Demonstrating that our nation could be both a reliable friend and a troublesome enemy would make the alliance firmer.

When I asked Hakuya for his insight on the subject, the first idea he proposed was, "Would you be willing to deploy troops along the border?"

"Wait, we're suddenly resorting to open intimidation in our diplomacy?" I asked, taken aback.

"I believe it is an easily understandable show of force," Hakuya said with a cool look on his face.

Huh? Was it possible he was serious?

"You're joking, right? That would only make the other side needlessly wary, wouldn't it?"

"I jest, of course. I was merely presenting the quick and easy method. If you hope for a long-lasting friendship, a show of military might may not preclude that, but it's far from the best option."

"..."

He'd said all that completely deadpan. It must have been Hakuya's idea of a joke.

Way to make a joke that's hard to get... I thought as I glared at him.

The next proposal he offered was, "Let's get the Gran Chaos Empire involved in these talks."

Empress Maria of the Empire?

"If your negotiations go well on this occasion, you intend to bring up the medical alliance with the Empire, too, right?" he asked. "You can move the schedule up on that."

"That's... Well, yes, it's true I was thinking of it..."

If we were going to develop medical treatments and make them generally available, no single country could handle that alone.

If we forged ahead alone, we might be able to create a gap between ourselves and other countries, but our funding and manpower would have limits. If we tried to force just one country to do all the research, the progress would be slow.

In this world, external injuries, even serious ones, could be treated with light magic, but there were still many people suffering from ailments that magic didn't work on.

If someone close to me fell to disease while I was wasting time, I'd definitely regret it. It couldn't hurt to be quick about developing medical treatments.

For the sake of that, I wanted the Gran Chaos Empire—the largest nation of mankind, and the one with considerable budget and manpower—to handle one wing of that development. I had a diplomatic channel to the Empire, after all, and their leader, Empress Maria, was a woman I could talk to. She was sure to support the idea.

However, I had been meaning to get things in place with the Republic of Turgis before I brought this subject up with the Empire. Because the kingdom and Empire were distant, we needed a country to act as an intermediary between us, or this would be all pie in the sky.

And yet Hakuya wanted to involve the Empire...to involve Maria...in our current talks.

"There is more than one way to show strength," he said. "Our connections are another form of power. If we can introduce Empress Maria at the meeting, Sir Gouran will be shocked. It would inform him that the nations to the east and west of the Republic have their own independent line of communication."

"True... I'm sure that would shock him."

If the Empire and kingdom were coordinating in secret, the Republic could be caught in a pincer attack the moment it opposed either. Well, given their geographical situation (in winter they were completely isolated by ice), there would be hardly any benefit in invading them and occupying their territory, but it would still put pressure on them.

"But still..." I scratched my head hard. "It would be incredible if we could do that, but it's probably not realistic calling in

Madam Maria. There aren't many days left until the meeting. Isn't it impossible, considering security, the necessary processes, and everything else?"

"What are you saying, Sire?" Hakuya objected, looking exasperated. "Who is each of us talking to right now, and where is that person?"

"Oh." I finally realized what he meant.

If Maria attended the meeting remotely over the Jewel Voice Broadcast, there was no need to invite her to come to the Republic from the Empire. I'd been imagining them meeting in person, so I must have been a bit out of it to overlook something this simple.

I felt awkward, and cleared my throat loudly. "Ahem... With that in mind, even if the meeting is held over a Jewel Voice Broadcast, will Madam Maria take time out of her busy schedule to attend?"

"Almost beyond a doubt."

"You seem awfully sure of that."

"During my talks with Madam Maria's younger sister Jeanne, I made the request to put negotiation about medical technology on the table, and said that we are willing to compensate them appropriately."

"You already had your eye on this, huh?" I said. "Well done."

"We haven't decided on a policy for medical technology yet, so we've just been slowly feeling one another out on the issue."

Hakuya and Jeanne were feeling one another out, huh? They were both sharp, so their conversations were probably like laying down stones in a game of Go. But I doubted they were tense about it. With my and Maria's permission, Hakuya had even done things like exchange gifts with her while Piltory was making his temporary return to the country.

In regards to their relationship, Maria had once said to me during a broadcast meeting, "Lately, Jeanne feels so full of life. Hee hee, do you think she and your Prime Minister found something in common to talk about?"

She'd seemed so happy about it. The only thing I could imagine them having in common to talk about was complaining about their respective masters, though. I wasn't so sure it was a good thing if they were having a good time talking about that.

"Regardless," I said, "in short, if we bring up the negotiations on medical technology, we can call Madam Maria to the meeting with Sir Gouran, right? Then, by showing off our connection to them, we'll shock Sir Gouran, and we can take the negotiations in a direction that's beneficial to us?"

"Indeed."

"It feels like accomplishing two things at the same time, but… Aren't you saying that we should effectively convince two separate countries simultaneously?"

"I believe that will be up to your abilities, Sire."

"You make it sound so easy," I grumbled. Honestly…

But… Well, that was probably the most effective way to do it.

"Let's go forward with that," I said. "Hakuya, negotiate with the Empire and move the preparations along. Make sure there are no mistakes made with the other matter I asked you to address, too."

"Understood." Hakuya bowed respectfully.

◇ ◇ ◇

And that brings us to the present.

The heads of the Republic of Turgis, Gran Chaos Empire, and Kingdom of Friedonia were meeting, even if it was over a broadcast.

For a little while, Sir Gouran was left looking dumbfounded at Maria's sudden appearance, but his expression soon returned to normal. "Why, it's a pleasure to meet you. I am the head of the Republic, Gouran Taisei." He nodded to the empress on the simple receiver.

The jewel was on the opposite side of the simple receiver, so Maria could see he was nodding to her.

The Jewel Voice Broadcast of Maria giggled and smiled at Sir Gouran. "Please, forgive me for the rudeness of not informing you beforehand that I would be taking part in this meeting. I heard that a medical alliance was to be discussed here, and the Empire would very much like to participate."

"I'd like to apologize, too," I said. "It was decided on so suddenly, I didn't have time to contact you in advance."

Maria and I bowed our heads in unison.

Sir Gouran looked at us with a blank expression for a moment, then let out a hearty laugh. "Aha ha ha! It looks like Sir Souma's pulled one over on me! I never thought you were connected to the empress of the Empire!"

Even though he was laughing, his eyes were fixed on me. He was probably cautiously probing my intent.

I corrected my posture while making sure not to avert my eyes from his gaze. "I apologize for keeping quiet about this. However, I want to form this medical alliance between the Kingdom of Friedonia, the Republic of Turgis, and the Gran Chaos Empire: the three nations that make up the south of the continent."

I was stating it clearly for Sir Gouran and Maria.

"I believe knowledge in the fields of medicine and treatment should be shared equally with all of mankind. Sickness strikes all, irrespective of race or borders. If an epidemic runs loose in one country, the damage will definitely spread to its neighbors. When that happens, if only one nation had the knowledge, drugs, or equipment to address the issue, would we be able to protect our people? I say nay. Even if there is no discourse between countries, people such as merchants and adventurers move back and forth between them constantly. We can try to protect only our own people, but infectious diseases will spread regardless."

"That's true," Maria said. "Fortunately, I haven't experienced one myself, but history records occasional epidemics on this continent, and how seriously they shook up the countries who underwent them."

Yeah, history had recorded the same thing in my previous world, too.

In studying history for my entrance exams, I learned that the Black Death was transmitted from Asia to Europe along the

Silk Road, bringing chaos to many countries and then spreading onward to Africa, contributing to the fall of the Mameluke Sultanate.

In fighting epidemics, it was important to prevent the outbreak from spreading in its early stages. In order to do that, we needed to share medical knowledge.

"As long as our three countries share their medical knowledge, if an epidemic begins to spread in one country, we may be able to limit its spread to the minimum," I said. "Furthermore, if an outbreak occurs in a country other than our three, we can coordinate in order to limit the area of our borders we have to inspect people at."

"You're right," said Gouran. "For the Republic's part, not having to worry about our borders with the Empire and the kingdom would be appreciated."

"I agree," nodded Maria. "Our borders are unbearably long, so there's nothing we would appreciate more than even a slight reduction in the number of checkpoints."

Sir Gouran and Maria were both nodding. I could probably assume I had their support thus far.

"Having confirmed the need for sharing medical knowledge between our three countries, I will return to the conversation I was having with Sir Gouran before," I said. "The discussion was about how the kingdom will aim to train doctors and improve on their techniques, the Republic will produce and develop medical equipment, and we will trade our results. I've been thinking it best to divide the labor, and focused research would be effective in leading to the development of the field of medicine. By having the Empire join us in this, I am hoping to have them handle the mass production of drugs, and the improvement of them."

"Drugs...?" Maria asked.

I nodded. "In my country, the three-eyed race has developed three-eyedine, an antibiotic. That's a medicine that works well on infectious diseases, but the subspecies of gelin it's extracted from will require land and manpower to raise, so we have not yet gotten to the point of mass production. If we can't secure it in quantity, drugs will continue to be high-priced. For that reason, I want to request that the Empire—with its land, manpower, and funding—handle the production of the drug."

"That's wonderful," Maria said with a smile. "If you can tell us how it's produced, I would like to create a system for mass-producing it at once."

I could only imagine a dubbed-in voice saying "I want your technology" behind that smile, so I couldn't help but smile wryly.

"I'll tell you about how it's made..." I said. "However, I do want something in return."

"Of course. How much do you want us to pay you?"

I reflected on what I had been thinking about earlier. "I don't want money. I want something else from you."

"Something else? What might that be?"

"A Jewel Voice Broadcast jewel. In other words, a dungeon core. Looking at the scale of the Empire, don't you have a lot more than we do? I'd like you to let me have one."

"A dungeon core, is it...?" Maria got a pensive look on her face, but she must have felt there was no loss to her in the deal, because she soon nodded. "Very well. I accept those terms."

"Thank you," I said. "And Sir Gouran."

"Hm?"

This time, I looked at Sir Gouran. "It must be inconvenient to only have one jewel to use in domestic broadcasts. I am thinking of giving the jewel I receive from the Empire to you. How does your providing us with medical equipment at no cost for the time being sound as a payment for that?"

"Hm...it's certainly true that we can't simply acquire a jewel whenever we want." Gouran thought for a little while, then slapped his knee. "Very well! However, I will want to discuss the exact amounts to be provided further."

"Yes. That will be fine."

"This is some awfully indirect negotiating," Maria said, sounding a little exasperated.

I smiled wryly and shrugged my shoulders. "I did my best to make things work out for all three parties. If the Republic only has one jewel, that's inconvenient for coordination between the three countries. I thought they'd definitely want one."

"Ha ha ha!" Sir Gouran chuckled. "It seems you saw right through me."

"I see..." Maria had a serious look on her face. "By the way, Sir Souma, I have one question for you."

"What might that be?"

"In regards to the three countries each taking on a field of research, is it not allowed to research the other fields? In my country, for instance, would I not be able to research medical training or equipment?"

"No, you're free to research the other fields. In fact, I very much hope you will."

"It's fine, then?" Sir Gouran checked to confirm, and I nodded.

"The reason I say I want each of us to specialize is in the name of efficiency," I said. "However, if that's all we each do, the moment one of the three countries is lax in their duties, the whole thing falls apart. Besides, in order to improve our drugs and medical equipment, I'm sure the knowledge of doctors and their techniques will be needed. Please, I'd like both the Republic and the Empire to send anyone you want to master the study of medicine to our country. They will study with us, teach what they've learned in our country when they return home, and give birth to more doctors. If they do that, then the Empire and Republic should be able to educate their own doctors, too. On the other hand, I'd like the Republic to send a number of craftspeople who can produce medical equipment to us, too. I want to get a system in place that allows us to produce our own medical equipment if the situation calls for it, after all."

"However, if we do that, ultimately, won't we all end up studying every field?" Sir Gouran asked. "Doesn't that defeat the purpose of dividing the research among us?"

"No, Sir Gouran," I said. "This is insurance, and it's also a race. If we fully divide things, it will be over the moment one country decides to break off this relationship. By all of us studying each field, we can prepare for that situation should it arise. Furthermore, the fact that other countries are also studying it means that if you neglect your research, the other countries may get ahead of you."

"I see," Maria said thoughtfully. "In order to prevent that, you've introduced the element of a race into this."

You've thought into this quite deeply, she seemed to be implying.

Well, of course. I debated this to death with Hakuya. We'd spent almost the whole time in between this conference being called and my going out to slay the ogres discussing it.

Sir Gouran said, "Hm..." with a pensive look on his face.

"Was there some point that was unclear?" I asked.

"No, I think you've put a lot of thought into this, but...there remains one problem."

"A problem?"

"I'm sure you're aware, but in winter, our land is closed off by snow, and our seas by ice. In that period, means of shipping are limited, and we can only carry out trade in the summer."

In other words, Sir Gouran was concerned about trade.

In this world, when you tried to ship large volumes, it either meant land shipping using large creatures like rhinosauruses, or sea shipping using boats. Neither was suited to the Republic of Turgis' winter.

The seas froze in winter, preventing the ships from coming in, and the land was covered by snow, which forbade the entry of creatures that were susceptible to the cold like rhinosauruses. There were cold climate animals like the numoth, but the amount one of those could carry was limited, and they were slow, too.

That was exactly why merchants only came to this country in the summer.

I couldn't blame Sir Gouran for being concerned. However, I had already heard about this problem from Kuu.

"I have some ideas about that," I said. "Roroa?"

Roroa, who had been silent up until this point, pumped her arm as if to say, *I've been waitin' for this.*

"It's finally my turn! Let's get on with showin' 'em that thing, then!"

Maria and Sir Gouran were taken aback by her sudden enthusiasm, but it was too soon to be surprised.

We still had a card up our sleeve, after all.

I requested a temporary suspension of the meeting so I could prepare.

Having gained Maria and Sir Gouran's assent, I explained the situation to Sir Gouran, and received permission to bring *a certain thing* in from the kingdom.

I'd assumed that if I brought *that* in without clearance, it would cause a huge fuss. If things went badly, they might even think it was an invasion.

I had Sir Gouran write up a document to show at the border, and had a messenger kui carry that document to the border where *that thing* was supposed to be waiting.

"I've given my permission, but...I find it hard to believe," he said.

"Same here," Kuu added. "Not that I think Souma's lying."

The Taisei father and son gave their honest reactions as they watched the messenger kui fly away.

I shrugged with a wry smile. "You may find it hard to believe, but there is no lie or exaggeration in anything we've said, you know?"

"Yeah, you two just look forward to seein' it." Roroa had gone back to her less formal speech style at some point, but she spoke with confidence.

"Hmm...in that case, I find it all the harder to believe," Sir Gouran said.

"Ooh ha ha!" Kuu laughed. "If it's true, it'll be worth seeing, now won't it?"

Gouran was dubious, while Kuu laughed with enthusiasm. They were contrasting reactions.

Regardless, until *it* arrived, we decided to relax and drink tea.

About two hours later, maybe, there was suddenly a lot of hubbub outside, all but confirming *it* had arrived. When we all went outside the inn, *it* was already visible.

It was a large object, the bottom of which was black, the top of which was orange, and which was about the size of an elementary school's gym, standing at the entrance to town where nothing had been before.

When we approached, it became apparent that it had a two-layer structure. The top half, colored orange, was like a large ship, and it was supported by the lower half, which was made of a black, rubber-like substance. *It* also made a constant sound like air was being expelled from it.

"How do ya like 'er? This is the amphibious ship, *Roroa Maru!*" Roroa shouted loud enough that she could be heard over the sound it was making.

Gouran's and Kuu's mouths were agape at the majestic appearance of the *Roroa Maru.* It was an amphibious ship—one that could travel by land or sea.

I explained how it worked to Gouran and Kuu, who were still flabbergasted.

"Like Roroa said, this is a ship that can run on a water surface without waves, or on land. By constantly sending air into the black rubbery part, that large body floats, and even if there's water underneath, it's able to drive across it. In the world I came from, it would have been called a hovercraft."

"Hovercraft..." Gouran repeated the unfamiliar word.

This massive object was the hovercraft *Roroa Maru,* which I had sent for from the kingdom.

The *Roroa Maru* was one-of-a-kind, built as an experiment while we were looking for uses for the over-scientist Genia's invention, the Little Susumu Mark V.

The Little Susumu Mark V was a ring-shaped machine that created propulsion by pushing water or air that was in front of it out the back side. I'd thought it might be possible to create a hovercraft that floated off the ground if that ring was faced towards the ground, and the air was blown up into an enclosure made of the recently discovered rubber-like substance.

And so, with Genia's design, and with funding from Roroa and Sebastian's company, The Silver Deer, the *Roroa Maru* was now complete. Incidentally, when I'd asked Roroa what she wanted it named, since she had put up the money to develop it...

"Hey, hey, Darlin', in the world you came from, what were ships' names like?"

"Hmm...most of them used the names of people or places."

"Hmm, that ain't much different from how we do things here."

"Yeah. Oh, and for fishing ships, a lot of them had Maru on the ends of their names."

"Maru? Hey, that's got a cute sound to it... All righty then, I've decided! This ship's gonna be the Roroa Maru*!"*

*"*Roroa Maru*?! You're putting your own name on it?!"*

And that was how it had ended up with that name.

It was registered to The Silver Deer, which was the investor. Dealing in everything from apparel to the dishes from Earth that Poncho and I had recreated, The Silver Deer had its fingers in a lot of pies, but did they plan to enter the trade business as well now? They had clothing, food, transportation...almost everything at this point.

"A ship that runs on land..." Maria sighed with admiration on the other side of the simple receiver Aisha was carrying. "The kingdom can even make things like this, huh?"

We were having the jewel carried behind us so that she could see this scene clearly, too.

"Would you sell us this ship?" Maria asked. "I'm prepared to pay a handsome sum, you know?"

"It uses technologies that are a state secret, so I can't sell it."

"You can't? That's unfortunate." Maria looked like a child who had been told she couldn't buy a toy. She was as much of a quiet beauty as Juna, but her actions were a little childish.

"Well, it looks impressive, but it's hard to use," I said with a wry smile. "It's got a bad cost-to-performance ratio, and it takes a fair amount of labor to move it."

"Is that right?"

"Yes. Its top speed is only a little higher than a rhinosaurus going at full speed, and its carrying capacity isn't that high. Technically, it's an amphibious vehicle, but using rhinosauruses on land and ships at sea is a much lower cost option."

It had a Little Susumu installed, and it ran on magical power stored in curse ore. For the Little Susumu Mark V Light, which was loaded on wyverns, we had people charge it themselves, but the charging of the large model Little Susumu used on ships and such was carried out by multiple mages attached to the military.

Because of that, the amount of magic power that could be charged in a day was limited, so I had prioritized deploying the *Roroa Maru* on battleships or carriers over it being a substitute for the rhinoceros train on land.

These were also reasons why it was hard to apply the Little Susumu to civilian transport ships. To provide propulsion on civilian ships, we had to wait for the development of a motor as an alternate technology. Setting that aside, though, the *Roroa Maru* did have its benefits.

"It's not efficient enough as a means of transportation in peacetime, but because it doesn't make contact with the surface, it has the ability to ignore some effects of difficult terrain," I said. "Specifically, in places where it's normally hard to move around, such as marshes, sand, and even snowy plains, it moves ahead smoothly."

"Snowy plains... I see. So that's it." Sir Gouran seemed to realize what I was leading up to.

"Yes. This *Roroa Maru* is the only one we have for now, but I am sure it will serve as a viable means of transportation that links my country, the Republic, and the Empire—if only in winter."

"Certainly. If it can tie the three countries together as a means of winter transport that's faster than a rhinosaurus and has the same capacity as a ship, even if there is only one of them for the time being, it will create a valuable trade route." Sir Gouran crossed his arms and grunted.

Then, as might be expected from a head of state, he began thinking about the trade route created by the *Roroa Maru*.

"Even in winter, domestically we can use our military numoths and other such livestock to secure transportation. If we gather all our goods at a port town, can we use this amphibious ship to trade with other countries? It looks like we'll need to expand a port town like Moulin."

Maria giggled. "Hee hee! We'll need to open a port town near our border with the Republic of Turgis, too... I think I do want one of those ships, after all." She glanced sneakily in my direction.

"No can do," I told her with a shrug. "Please, don't do anything like seize her the moment she comes into port, either. It's hard to build one, and you'll force us to make it self-destruct just to keep our secrets."

I said that to casually indicate to the two of them that if they tried to steal it, we would destroy it ourselves. I wasn't bluffing, either. When we used the *Roroa Maru* for trade, I intended to have a mechanism in place that would cause it to self-destruct if seized.

I couldn't let the Little Susumu and other technologies fall into the hands of other countries yet. In order to send the one-of-a-kind *Roroa Maru* to other countries, I had to be prepared to destroy it, if necessary.

Maria gave a wry smile. "I know. I can't put the relationship between our nations in danger over one ship. I really do want it, though."

That was the third time she'd said she wanted it. Was this one of those '*It's important, so I said it three times*' things?

Whatever the case, I wanted to wrap this topic up now. "With the use of the *Roroa Maru,* I would like to affirm a medical alliance between our three countries, as I was saying before. How does that sound?"

Sir Gouran laughed heartily. "Ha ha ha! If you've gone this far, I'm not about to say no. I'll accept your alliance."

"We of the Gran Chaos Empire will accept, too."

With Gouran's and Maria's assent, the Tripartite Medical Alliance between the Kingdom of Friedonia, the Republic of Turgis, and the Gran Chaos Empire was formed.

The formation of this alliance not only promised that the field of medicine would develop by leaps and bounds, it was also significant in this era of uncertainty. With the Demon Lord's Domain sitting to the north, our alliance laid the groundwork for our three nations to coordinate.

While I silently breathed a sigh of relief at the successful conclusion of our negotiations for the medical alliance, Sir Gouran extended his hand to me.

"Sir Souma. We are now sworn friends. I look forward to working with you."

"Yes, Sir Gouran." I extended my own hand, and we exchanged a firm handshake. "I look forward to working with you, too."

Maria, who was watching us, said, "It's a shame. If I weren't on the other side of a receiver, I could have shaken hands with you, too."

That made Sir Gouran and I look at one another and laugh.

Once we had finished, Sir Gouran suddenly took on a serious expression. "Now then... Since you've become my sworn friend, there is a favor I'd like to ask of you." He had a pensive look on his face.

"A favor?" I asked.

"Indeed. The favor concerns my boy, Kuu. Could I ask you to keep Kuu with you in the kingdom for two to three years?"

"Huh?"

"Whaaa?!" Kuu exclaimed.

The look on his face was a mix of shock and bewilderment. He'd heard his name brought up, and now there was immediately talk of him being left in a foreign country, so it was hard to blame him.

Once Kuu returned to his senses, he rounded on Sir Gouran in anger. "What're you talking about out of nowhere, Dad?! You want me to be a hostage in the kingdom?!"

"That's not it," said Gouran with a serious look on his face. "I want you to go see what the kingdom is like now, for me." He paused. "I've been thinking about this since last night. When young Empress Maria of the Empire was invited to take part in our meeting today, that cemented it for me."

"Cemented it? What?" Kuu demanded.

"There's a new wind blowing across this continent," Sir Gouran said, then turned to me. "If you'll excuse my rudeness, Sir Souma, may I ask how old you are?"

"I'll be twenty this year."

Sir Gouran nodded in satisfaction. "From what I can see, Madam Maria must be about the same age." If I recalled, she was twenty-one. "The Empire in the west is ruled by a young queen, and a young king has arisen in the kingdom in the east. When you get old like me, you start to sense something akin to fate in these things."

Kuu, Maria, and I listened intently to what Sir Gouran, the only member of an older generation who was present, had to say.

Sir Gouran continued in a quiet voice, "In the world of man, there is something like a flow. Whether we want it or not, that flow affects all things. Some ride that flow, others struggle against it, and yet others drown in it. That is how one might become famous, and another might fall. How one country might prosper, and another might perish. The fierce warrior, Sir Gaius, fell, and Sir Souma, a man of culture, was victorious. With the help of Princess Roroa, he annexed Amidonia and created a new country."

It was hard to react to what he was saying. The look on Roroa's face said she didn't know what kind of expression she should be making, either.

However, hearing Sir Gouran's words, Machiavelli's words about preparing for the changes of fortune came to mind.

Gouran laid a hand on Kuu's shoulder. "That's what the times are like. No one can read where this world is headed. However, when the east and west are both led by the younger generation, our country may be left behind by the era if we are the only ones to cling to old ways. In order to avoid that, I want to raise a breath of youth of our own."

"A breath of youth… You mean me?" Kuu asked.

Gouran nodded firmly. "You are still inexperienced, but you have a flexible mindset. If you see how the kingdom changes under Sir Souma's reign, that will act as a compass for you when the time comes for you to be leader of this country."

"No…I haven't decided yet if I'll take over the headship or not…"

"You may not be head of state."

"Huh?"

Sir Gouran answered the question mark hovering over Kuu's head with a serious look on his face. "Depending on the flow of the times, our country may need to centralize power and abolish the Council of Chiefs in favor of a monarchy. In that event, you must become a king who can stand shoulder to shoulder with Souma and Maria. That may be the era that comes. That's all the more reason why I want you to broaden your horizons while you still can. While you're in the kingdom, I will bring the Council of Chiefs under control, and build the foundation for you to put your shrewdness to work."

This was some incredible stuff he was saying. The look on Sir Gouran's face right now resembled the face of the former king, Albert, when he'd entrusted Liscia to me and left the castle.

It was the face of one entrusting things to the next generation.

Even though I was awed by the atmosphere, I hesitantly raised my hand. "One question. You said you want to leave Kuu with us, but do you mean you want him to study abroad in our country?"

"No, not as a student. I want you to use him as a temporary vassal. I think that will be a better experience for Kuu."

"An uninvited vassal, then..." Kuu muttered.

In terms of position, he'd be like Aisha initially was. Basically, I could treat him as a vassal who doubled as a friend, like Hal. I could let him stay in a room in the castle.

"I don't mind, but does Kuu?" I asked.

"It doesn't matter if I mind or not... I don't have the right to refuse, do I?" Kuu glanced at his father, seeking confirmation.

Sir Gouran simply nodded without saying anything.

Kuu, sensing the man's unbreakable will, scratched his head. "My stubborn old man's made up his mind, so throwing a tantrum won't get me anywhere. Besides, I'm interested in what kind of country Souma's building, too."

He wouldn't have fully accepted suddenly being told he would be entrusted to a foreign country, but it was very like Kuu to already be thinking about it positively.

"I see," I said. "Welcome aboard, Kuu."

When I offered him my hand, he took it firmly.

"Ooh ha ha! But since I'm imposing myself as a vassal, that means you outrank me, doesn't it? Still, I'm from a foreign country, so calling you Your Majesty doesn't feel right. That's why I'm going to call you Bro from now on."

"Uh, 'Bro'?"

"Yeah. Think of me like your little brother. Well, there we have it." Kuu put a hand on his hip, grinned like always, and said, "I'm counting on you from here on, Bro!"

HOW A REALIST HERO REBUILT THE KINGDOM

EPILOGUE

An Unsettling Presence

With the tripartite agreement successfully concluded to found a medical alliance between the kingdom, Republic, and Empire, a feast was held to celebrate that night at the inn that had served as the site of the meeting.

Since coming to this country, there had been parties held whenever there was an excuse, but this time, there were numerous people in attendance, so it was the largest yet.

It was unfortunate that one of the three leaders, Maria, who had attended by Jewel Voice Broadcast, was unable to attend.

"Please, come to my country someday," she said before terminating the communication. *"When you do, let's drink together."*

"Yes. Someday."

Considering how far away the Empire was, though, I didn't know if that day would come or not. If the political situation in the world stabilized, we'd eventually be able to travel to each other's countries for meetings, but there was no indication that would happen any time soon.

"Bro! Are you having fun?!" Kuu, who was already drunk,

broke in. He suddenly put his arm around my neck, and the impact nearly made me drop my drink.

"Whoa! That's dangerous… I mean, get away from me. I'm not into getting touchy-feely with guys."

"It's 'cause you look so gloomy, Bro," he cackled. "You've gotta have fun when drinking."

Kuu moved away from me with a laugh.

"I'm enjoying myself," I said, relieved he had backed away. "At least as much as anyone else."

"Hm? Well, okay then."

Because so much time had passed since the start of the party, everyone was off doing their own thing now. Juna poured drinks for Sir Gouran, who was now our sworn friend, while Aisha and Hal had a drinking contest, and Kaede egged them on.

Leporina took care of Tomoe, who had been knocked out by the smell of alcohol, and Roroa talked to Taru, whom Kuu had invited. It was quite the chaotic scene.

"You seem to be in an awfully good mood yourself, Kuu," I said.

"Damn straight. I mean… You know." Kuu raised his thumb and indicated Taru, who Roroa was talking to.

I see. He's in a good mood because of that…

"That" had occurred a few hours before.

When the meeting finished, Kuu took us to visit Taru's workshop on the hill near Noblebeppu. He intended to tell his childhood friend Taru that he would be staying in the Kingdom of Friedonia for a while.

While we were there, we revealed our identities, too, but she wasn't especially surprised. For a craftsperson like Taru, maybe the position of her clients didn't matter so much.

"So...that being the case, it's been decided I'll go to the kingdom to study under Bro, and I'm only taking Leporina with me," Kuu finished, resting his foot on a bucket that was lying around, and adopting the pose of a sailor with his foot on one of the short posts used for mooring boats.

He might have thought it was a cool way of saying goodbye, or he might just have been trying to act tough, but either way, resting his foot on a bucket wasn't going to accomplish that.

While we all looked at him coolly, Kuu continued his speech. "But don't you worry, Miss Taru. Our parting will be a brief one. I'll stay with Bro, learn from how he rules, and I swear, someday, I'll come back to you as a real man. I look forward to the day when I return in glory to my old hometown."

Even though Taru said anything, Kuu kept on giving his parting speech.

Meanwhile, Taru paid no heed to his words, and continued pounding hot metal.

I don't know... It was the sort of scene that made me feel sorry for Kuu.

The lack of response from Taru upset Kuu. "Hey! Hey now, Miss Taru! Here I am, giving you my farewell speech, so give me a little response, would you? You'll be lonely without me, right?"

"Not particularly. I'm not interested in where you go, dumb master."

"Not interested...? Isn't that kind of harsh? Even if you aren't interested, your childhood friend is here to say goodbye, so be a little nicer to me."

"Having you yammer on at me when I'm smithing is nothing but a nuisance."

There was nothing he could say to that, so Kuu slumped his shoulders in disappointment.

Yeah, well, if the girl he liked was going to treat him that way, of course he'd get dejected.

I guess I'll listen to him vent at the party tonight... I thought with a sigh.

But then I heard the sound of Taru putting the metal she'd been striking into the water. She laid out a number of metal products on the table, including the one she had just been working on. That shape with a small blade on the end was nothing if not a scalpel.

"I tried making the thing you ordered with various metals," she told me. "Iron, copper, silver, and a number of alloys. Do you know which was the best suited for it?" She cocked her head to the side.

Ohhh, so a sample scalpel was what she'd been working on.

Even if she asked me which was best, I wasn't a doctor, so I didn't know. There were metal allergies and such to consider, too, so it couldn't be decided on strength and cutting edge alone.

"I'll have to go back to my country and ask someone who'd know."

"I see... Well, I'll go to the kingdom, too, then," Taru said offhandedly.

Everyone's eyes went wide. The most surprised of all, though, was Kuu, who had been giving his parting speech until a moment ago.

"Huh?! You're coming too, Taru?!"

"Not because I want to be with you, dumb master," Taru said willfully. "I'm going to the kingdom for my own reasons." Then she stared at me and said, "I heard the king requested a craftsperson of the Republic to come and offer guidance, in case it becomes necessary to make medical equipment for him. I volunteer to be that craftsperson."

"You're going to come teach?" Kuu gaped.

"I'm interested in Friedonia's techniques, too," she said with unswerving eyes. "I don't just want to teach; I want to learn."

"Fine. We welcome you, Madam Taru." I extended my hand to her. "Let me prepare a dedicated workshop for you in the castle town. I'd very much like to have you come to our country as a craftsperson."

"I'll be in your care." Taru firmly took my hand.

It looked like Kuu was dumbfounded by this sudden turn of events, but he quickly pulled himself together and cackled. "Oh, I see! In the end, you're coming, too! I don't care why. I'm glad we can be together!" He slapped her hard on the back.

"Ouch! Don't hit my back." Taru had a bothered look on her face.

Then again, since she was just sitting there and taking it, maybe she wasn't so unhappy about it? Maybe she was coming in order to be with Kuu?

"How should I say this…? She has a complicated personality," Juna said with a wry smile.

"Maybe it's actually for a really simple reason, y'know?" Roroa said with a happy smile, standing on the opposite side of me.

In conclusion, it seemed that a woman's heart was a thing of mystery: complicated, yet simple.

So, with Taru deciding to join us, Kuu was in high spirits. He'd been downing fermented milk since the start of the party.

Kuu went over to Taru, and Roroa came over to me.

"Hee hee," she grinned. "Ever since we came to this country, it's been nothin' but parties."

"You're right… Hey, wait!"

Roroa laid down and to use my lap as a pillow. Good grief.

I placed my hand on Roroa's head, and rolled her head around in my lap. "It's unseemly, suddenly lying down like this."

"I ain't drunk. You've gotta keep things free and easygoing when there's drink goin' 'round," Roroa said with a smug laugh as I rolled her head around. "So, Darlin', what's next? More travels?"

"What's next," huh?

"We have Kuu to consider now, so I think we'll go back to the kingdom for a while," I said. "I'm sure I have work piled up that needs my attention, and I'm concerned about Liscia, too. Besides…"

"Besides?"

"No, it's nothing."

"Hm?"

There were question marks floating over Roroa's head as I continued to pat her.

At last, Roroa smiled in satisfaction, and not long after that, she was snoring. When the usually boisterous Roroa was asleep, she looked like a sweet young maiden. While looking at her sleeping face, I thought about what I had nearly said before.

Besides... What Maria was saying bothers me.

After the meeting, when I was saying my goodbyes to Maria, her previously relaxed expression had suddenly become serious.

Just I was wondering what was up, she told me in a quiet voice, "Lately, the monsters in the north have been becoming more active."

HOW A REALIST HERO REBUILT THE KINGDOM

MIDWORD

THANK YOU for buying *How a Realist Hero Rebuilt the Kingdom* Volume Seven. This is Dojyomaru, who is worried that these midwords are appearing earlier and earlier in each volume.

This time we had the Republic Arc. With Kuu, Leporina, and Taru from the Republic of Turgis joining the cast, a new era is coming onto stage, with young people in the lead roles... And yet, Liscia is now off on maternity leave.

I don't think you'll find many series in which the main heroine is away from the story temporarily because of maternity leave.

The composition of this story is as odd as ever, but I do hope you'll stick with it.

Now then, in regard to what I wrote in Volume Four about the true value of web novels, there was some response to it, so I think I'll say just a little more.

When Volume Four came out, I boastfully wrote that the true value of web novels was that you could write as much as you wanted without worrying about the length, but they also had one other strength.: *You can choose the timing for when they're published as books for yourself.*

That was it.

Of course, unless you choose to self-publish the physical books, it is necessary to have a publisher approach you about print rights. What I'm talking about is the timing for releasing the physical books after you've been contacted by a publisher.

For instance, with a new author's award, the results are announced on the publisher's homepage with a bang.

"This novel won a grand prize. It will be published soon."

It's announced in a way that also acts as advertisement. New works need to attract the attention of readers, so this is the right way to do it. However, this also places a time limit on publishing the work. If there's too long a gap, people ask, "When is that work that won the grand prize going to be published?"

On that point, when it comes to web novels, even if the request to publish the novel in print comes, it's possible to delay your response. If you aren't confident, or are concerned about readers' responses to as-yet-unpublished sections of the work, or if you don't have enough material built up, you can defer your response to the request to publish.

Naturally, there may be some publishers who won't allow you to put things on hold. However, publishers like Overlap will wait if you ask them to.

Now, as for how I can say that with such certainty, that's because, with my own *Realist Hero,* I actually delayed my response for about half a year after I was approached. (By the way, I've checked with my editor if I can talk about this, and I received the okay, so have no worries there.)

The request to publish *Realist Hero* as a novel came just as I was writing the finale of Volume One of the web novel version. That was around the time when people had started to take notice of this story. However, I asked to defer my response.

My reason was, "I didn't know if the Subjugation Arc that will be Volume Two or the Post-war Arc that will make up parts of Volumes Three and Four will be accepted by the readers," and, "If I can't write through to the last scene of Volume Four, I'm not confident I can conclude the story."

Thanks to that, I was blessed with readers who stayed with me past the Subjugation Arc and Post-war Arc, and I found the confidence to continue writing this story, so I decided to accept the request around the time I wrote the last scene of Volume Four.

And that brings us to the present.

If I had immediately accepted the publication request back then... I'm sure I'd be in a different situation now. I'm a slow writer, and there were a few times I pulled down something I wrote, thinking, "This isn't it," and then reworked it.

If I'd started my career as a professional author with no confidence or stock of material... The thought scares me. Probably I wouldn't have had as much leeway, and would have had even less freedom to write the story the way I want. In my case, there was the risk that after messing up once, my will might have broken.

Writers are self-employed and responsible for themselves. If there are any aspiring authors out there reading this, I want you to remember that this sort of choice is an option.

It's okay. Overlap will wait. (This is important, so I said it twice.)

Now then, I'll wrap things up here for this time.

Now, I give my thanks to Fuyuyuki, with apologies for requesting four new character designs this time, to Satoshi Ueda, whose rough drafts for the manga I've been enjoying reading, and to my editor, the designers, the proofreaders, and everyone who now holds this book in their hands.

This has been Dojyomaru.

After this, we have stories that take place after the return from the Republic. Please, stay with us to the end.

SIDE STORY 1

After Returning to the Country Arc 1: The Weather Girl

"IN REGARDS TO THE MEDICAL ALLIANCE that was recently signed with the Republic..."

"Mom, it looks like that program's about to start," a child said.

"Yes, it is," his mother agreed. "It really is a lifesaver."

The mother and child had come to the fountain plaza to watch the Jewel Voice Broadcast. Recently, during the evening news program broadcast in the Kingdom of Friedonia, one segment had become especially popular.

The beautiful half-elf news broadcaster, Chris Tachyon, turned towards the viewers. "Now, we bring you tomorrow's weather. Nadeeen?"

A cheery melody and song started to play.

What will tomorrow's weather be?

Rain, my whiskers are telling me.

Later, the skies will clear at last.

Here's the Friedonia Weather Forecast!

A girl in a black dress which looked like it had scales embedded in it made her entrance, singing as she came in.

This girl with an adorable face had long, black hair and looked to be about fourteen. There was a black lizard tail growing out of her rump, and her head bore antlers more magnificent than those of the sea serpent race.

Her name was Naden Delal.

This dragon had recently come from the Star Dragon Mountain Range to the Kingdom of Friedonia in order to marry Souma.

Even though she was a dragon, she wasn't the usual Western-style dragon, but an Oriental-style ryuu. Her true form was large and serpentine, and when she had first descended on the castle in her ryuu form, the people of the castle town had panicked as if a monster was suddenly attacking. The panic died down once the castle announced her identity, though.

Naden bowed her head to the citizens who were watching the broadcast. "Good evening. I'm Naden, here with tomorrow's weather."

Then she raised her eyes, looked in Chris' direction, and tilted her head a bit.

"Hey, I think this every time, but is there any reason for me to sing as I come on?"

"Because every weather program needs a song...is what His Majesty Souma believes," Chris responded with a businesslike smile.

"I-I see..." Naden had no choice but to accept that answer.

The people watched with relaxed expressions on their faces as this exchange occurred.

When it was first announced that Souma was bringing back

a dragon fiancée from the Star Dragon Mountain Range, the people had been abuzz that he might be the second coming of the original King of Elfrieden.

The first king had been summoned as a hero like Souma, then built the precursor to the Kingdom of Friedonia, the multi-racial Elfrieden Kingdom, and taken a dragon as his wife despite not being from the Nothung Dragon Knight Kingdom. He was seen as a great hero by the people of this country.

However, Souma was very different from that hero, his reign being plain and steady.

The girl who became his fiancée, Naden, gave less of the impression of a god-beast and more of an innocent girl, so the people's passion had gradually faded.

Even so, it wasn't that she was unpopular with the people. She actually had a deep-rooted popularity with the elderly population. They looked on her not as a future queen, but as they might look on a daughter or granddaughter.

Naden was enjoying life in Parnam in her own way, too.

Her position made her the second secondary queen, so she wasn't confined to the castle, and often went down to the castle town to walk around and buy things to eat. Normally, the castle guard would have had to worry about her being abducted, but as a ryuu, there were no ropes that could bind her, so she was free to do as she pleased inside Parnam.

It was Souma's intention that Naden, who was unrestrained and similar to the independent women of Souma's old world, not be made to feel suffocated within the capital.

However, when she helped a lost child find his friends, played with them, and then came back to the castle covered in mud, she did get an earful from Princess Liscia.

For Naden and dragons like her, most of their accomplishments were made on the battlefield. That she could act as freely as she did was proof of just how peaceful the kingdom had become.

That was something to be welcomed, but it was boring to have nothing to do until a crisis came. That, and she wanted Souma to rely on her for something other than riding on her back, too.

"Hey, Souma. Is there something I can do?" Naden tried asking.

"Oh, good timing. There's actually something I wanted you to do."

The job Souma had prepared for her was this position as a "weather girl."

A ryuu's whiskers were sensitive to the air currents, and it was said that just a slight gust of wind was enough for them to know the weather in that area for the next week. Souma was apparently planning to put that to use and make a weather forecast.

The Jewel Voice Broadcast could only be seen with video in the large towns and cities where receiver equipment was set up, but even remote villages in the countryside could receive something like radio. Basically, broadcasting a weather forecast on the Jewel Voice Broadcast would communicate the weather to every person in the country.

"So, there you have it," he explained. "Can you do it, Naden?"

"Roger that. I'm on it."

Thus, Naden was now this world's first weathercaster.

And so, once again today, Naden reported tomorrow's weather to the entire kingdom.

"Umm...for tomorrow's weather, we expect there will be not a cloud in the sky, and it will be a generally feel-good kind of day. It should be a good day for doing laundry. In the Amidonia Region in the west of the country and around Altomura in the south, there may be scattered showers along the mountains in the evening, so be sure to take the wash in early. Also, in the northeast, the skies over Lagoon City will clear tomorrow, but there is the possububbly...of thundershowers, so be careful."

Ah, she flubbed her line!

Naden tried to carry on as if she hadn't misspoken, but the viewers smiled. They never tired of seeing this adorable queen-to-be.

Though she tripped over her words, Naden's forecasts had a reputation for accuracy.

Those in the farming and fishing industries were particularly grateful for her storm warnings. If a storm came, the produce they had worked so hard to grow might be blown down by the winds, or the seas might become so wild that going out in a boat would be a disaster that put their lives at risk. However, if the arrival of storms could be predicted in advance, it was possible to prepare for them.

For farmers, they could harvest their produce, or reinforce the plants so they wouldn't be knocked over.

For fishermen, they could dry-dock the boats and ensure they weren't swept away by the waves.

This had led to an increase in the country's food production.

There were even rumors that some fishing villages had already begun to worship Naden as a goddess who guaranteed good catches. Eventually this might be tied to Urup's sea god worship, and she would then become Ryuujin, the dragon god of the sea. For now, though, Naden was only a weather girl.

Now, how was Naden's weather forecast produced?

Let us take a glimpse at the production process.

◇ ◇ ◇

"Souma! Wake up!"

"Aah! Wh-what?!"

Suddenly, there was an impact on top of my stomach. I had been deep asleep until moments ago, so I was panicking, unable to process the situation when I saw Naden sitting on top of my belly. It seemed the impact had been Naden body-slamming me.

I glanced around with my head still fuzzy. This was... Right, the governmental affairs office.

Upon my return from the Republic of Turgis, Hakuya gave me a mountain of work that had piled up, so I'd been working through it until late at night. I went to sleep in the simple bed in the office.

Even while in the Republic of Turgis, I had kept using my magic, Living Poltergeists, to move Factory Arm #1 and do paperwork, but no matter how much I did, more work for the king kept pouring in. Honestly… Here I was, finally back in the country, but I couldn't even go visit Liscia, who was resting in the former king Sir Albert's domain.

That being the case, I was now very sleepy, and I didn't want to wake up yet, but Naden wasn't going to allow that. Turning sideways to form a cross with the bed in which I was sleeping, Naden stretched out and rolled back and forth on top of my stomach.

"Soumaaa, wake uuup."

"Sorry, Pa*rasche," I murmured. "I'm exhausted. I'm so very sleepy."

"Who is Pat**sche supposed to be? Get up already."

Like an elementary schooler trying to wake her father up on a Sunday, Naden shook her body back and forth. In this state, I couldn't get back to sleep, so I reluctantly decided to get up.

Once I had sat up, I shot Naden a somewhat resentful look. "I was up late working last night. Let me sleep a little longer."

"What are you talking about? If you don't get up, I can't do my job, you know?" Naden got off the bed and put a hand on her hip.

"Job?"

"I have to predict the weather, right?"

"Oh, jeez. Fine, I get it."

It was an important job, after all, so I gave in and got out of bed.

When we began producing broadcast programs for this world, I wondered if there was a way to make a weather forecast a reality.

In my old world, it was a given that there would be a weather forecast during news programs, so I had never felt all that grateful for them. However, coming to this world, where people lived without a weather forecast, brought me to the painful realization that it had been an incredible thing all along.

If they knew the future weather, people could be more productive.

When was it time to do laundry? When was it time to sow seeds? When was it time to go out fishing? When was it time to fix the house in preparation for a storm? By knowing future weather, it was possible to prepare in advance for these things. It made people's lives more efficient.

Now, the perfect person to make such a weather forecast had come to me.

In her ryuu form, Naden's two long whiskers were highly perceptive sensory organs, and just a slight breeze across them would tell her the weather in that place for the next week. That was why I had Naden fly around the kingdom every few days and investigate what the weather would be like in each area.

In addition to Naden, there were people who had lived in those regions for generations who could predict the larger changes in the weather. It was useful even if it was just something like, *"If there's clouds around that mountain, there will be a passing shower the next day."* We had them send that sort of information to us by messenger kui, and kept statistics in the capital.

By using Naden's weather forecast as the backbone, and the reports of the people who could tell the weather in all of those different places to flesh things out, we were able to put together a reasonably precise weather forecast.

It was popular with the people, who said she was pretty accurate.

"La, la, la!" Naden sang.

If I were to raise just one complaint, it was that every time she flew around the country, Naden dragged me along with her.

I was riding on Naden's back as she sang to herself and swam through the sky, my head nodding unconsciously as I was hit by waves of drowsiness.

Those who had a contract with a dragon were protected by their magic, so I wasn't affected by wind pressure or gravity, and I wouldn't fall off. That meant it was very comfortable, which only made me drowsier. It was like how sitting on the train as it swayed made you feel awfully sleepy.

Naden, for her part, felt good having me ride on her back when she flew. She'd explained before that having her partner on her back "feels like it scratches an itch, or like something is where it belongs."

It was a sense that was hard for a human to understand, but those were the sorts of creatures that dragons were.

That was why I was being dragged along for this. It was also why Naden was singing so cheerfully.

In her ryuu form, Naden didn't speak. She communicated using something like telepathy, so I could hear her singing right in my brain. Naden was surprisingly good at singing, and it was relaxing to listen to, which only made me sleepier.

"And we're here," Naden said. "Hey, Souma. We're over Lagoon City now."

"Huh...? Oh, yeah."

"Hold on, are you sleeping while we're having such a nice sky-walk?" Naden asked, sounding miffed.

Even with her ryuu face, I could tell she was puffing up her cheeks. "It feels so comfortable on your back, I can't help myself."

"Grrr...when you say it that way, it doesn't feel so bad..."

I pulled a stack of paper, an inkwell, and a feather pen out of the bag hanging from my shoulder. "Now, that aside, let's get to work."

Naden still had a somewhat dissatisfied look on her face, but she must have shifted into work mode, because she let her two whiskers drift in the wind. Then...

"Lagoon City will be sunny today. All day tomorrow, too. It will be clear the day after as well, but will cloud over in the evening. Three days from now, it looks like we'll see light showers starting in the morning. Those will last all day."

Naden put together a weather forecast for this area. I wrote it down word for word, being sure not to miss a thing.

"Four days from now, it will be cloudy, and five days from now, it will also be cloudy, but will clear up in the afternoon. Six days from now, it will be clear all day. Seven days from now, again, it will be clear all day."

We knew the weather for up to seven days from now, which was to say a total of eight days.

In this world, a week was eight days, so we had our weekly weather forecast for this region done.

Putting away what I had written, I let out a sigh of admiration. "Your whiskers sure are convenient, Naden."

"Hee hee! You can praise me more, you know?"

"Hey, you're number one! Now, if we just knew the temperature for the next week, it'd be perfect."

"That's expecting too much!"

I tried teasing her, and Naden got mad. Expecting too much, huh...? No doubt about that.

It was good fortune that Naden had come to be my fiancée. Not just for me, but for the whole country. If I forgot that, I was going to be punished for it.

I stroked Naden's back. "I'm grateful. Thank you for coming to be with me, Naden."

"Ohhh... When you're so straight with me, it makes me feel shy. Hee hee..."

"It's how I really feel. Now, on to the next place."

"Roger that! I'll carry you anywhere, Souma."

"Oh? Then the Republic of Turgis—"

"I hate the cold!"

While having those sorts of inconsequential conversations, we flew all around the country.

And, well, that was roughly how the weather forecast was produced. Today, Naden was relaying that weather forecast to the people watching or listening to the Jewel Voice Broadcast.

"This is Naden. I will now report on tomorrow's weather."

HOW A REALIST HERO REBUILT THE KINGDOM

SIDE STORY 2

After Returning to the Country Arc 2: Kuu's Stay in the Kingdom

THE MIDDLE of the 7th month, 1,547th year, Continental Calendar:

The roofs of the houses in the residential quarter of Parnam were uniformly orange.

If you looked down from Parnam Castle toward the center of the city, the castle walls that surrounded the city, and the small mountain nearby, it would look like a vast sea of orange.

A shadowy figure bounced along the top of those orange roofs.

The figure was running as it bounded from roof to roof, but then stopped on one roof to wipe its sweat. It was around the time that the sun was high in the sky.

Summer had begun in earnest at this point, and the kingdom was now seeing hot day after hot day.

"Man, it's hot," grumbled the figure. "It'd never get this hot in the republic."

The figure was the guest from the republic, Kuu Taisei.

It had been two months since King Souma of Friedonia formed a medical alliance with Gouran, the Turgish Head of State; and Empress Maria of the Gran Chaos Empire.

In order to see how Souma reigned and learn from it, Kuu had come to reside in Friedonia with his attendant Leporina and his childhood friend Taru.

He was staying for free at Souma's place, but because he wasn't a formal vassal, he didn't have any particular work to do, and he was spending most his time traveling around the kingdom to learn.

Kuu would submit a request to visit and learn about a place, and if Souma gave his permission, he would have relatively free rein to look around inside the Kingdom. He went to many places that way, and had registered as an adventurer along with Leporina, making a small amount of coin on the side by taking on quests.

Kuu crouched on the edge of the roof, looking out over the town of Parnam.

Still... I know I heard about it from Bro, but this country's even more amazing than I expected.

There were so many things he had learned simply by coming to live in this country.

The flashy things had caught his eye first. Initially, those were the broadcast programs of the Jewel Voice Broadcast. The idea of using the Jewel Voice Broadcast, which had only been used for official proclamations before, to provide entertainment for the citizens was amazing.

The singing program where many diverse loreleis sang, the news program where Chris Tachyon reported the events and incidents that happened in the country, the weather forecast run by one of Souma's fiancées, and more... They were all new to Kuu, and drew his interest.

Of them all, the tokusatsu program called *Overman Silvan* was his favorite.

It was good stuff. Watching a hero fight for good and punish evil got him fired up.

Kuu was so into *Silvan* that, when he watched them shooting the program in the castle, he had even gotten the autograph of Ivan Juniro, the actor who played the main character. It was incredible that in an era like this, the son of a nation's head of state would be begging an actor from another country for his autograph.

Now, as for the next flashy thing that caught his eye, it was religious functions.

Generally, nations that put a lot of fervor into their religious functions tended to be monotheistic, but the religious functions in this multi-racial, multi-religious state were surprisingly popular.

It seemed that ever since Souma had issued a proclamation saying that, "Any religion which registers with the government will be recognized as a state religion," this country had gained a variety of state religions, and they had come to hold large religious functions to attract believers.

Furthermore, by turning those religious functions into national events, it was even possible for members of other religions and sects to participate.

The result was that, with the exception of the most fervent believers, there was an increase in the number of citizens engaging with multiple faiths, and a cooperative relationship where different religions lent each other space for events was built.

If it was possible to hold multiple faiths, then there was no need to fight to steal each other's believers.

This sort of buffet-style approach to religion seemed like something the comparatively tolerant Mother Dragon worship might allow, but one that Lunarian Orthodoxy—with its focus on unity through the belief in one god—would hate.

However, the head of Lunarian Orthodoxy within the kingdom, Bishop Souji Lester, had said, "Multiple religions? Eh, sure, why not?"

And with that one utterance, they were gradually worked into the buffet of religions.

Souji was as impious as ever, but his loose management had the support of Orthodoxy's adherents in the kingdom. For the adherents who had lived in the kingdom a long time, they hadn't been happy about taking orders from the Orthodox Papal State about all sorts of things, even though it was the center of their religion.

On that point, Souji had said, "If you keep things in moderation, you can do as you like," and left them to their own devices, so it was easier on the believers.

There was now open religious dialogue in the kingdom between all faiths, and they were in an exquisite state of harmony.

If you went into town, one weekend there would be a Lunarian Orthodox festival, and the next weekend there would be a day of celebration for Mother Dragon worshipers, and then the following weekend the sea god worshipers would have a ceremony opening the seas... There was always some excuse to hold an event.

And so, people would gather where there were events, and things and money would gather where there were people. Holding religious events was tied directly into increasing economic activity.

Well, it's easy to look at the flashy things, but what's really amazing is the stuff you don't see.

Kuu stood up and began bouncing along the roofs again.

Beneath him, the people of this country went about their lives. He crossed a commercial street where wives were out shopping, and then down a craftsmen's street where the sound of hammers echoed unceasingly.

As he ran, Kuu had a thought.

The really unbelievable thing about this country is how easy it is to live in.

The kingdom as it was now still had those orange roofs, which gave it a sort of retro appearance, but beneath that, it had become incredibly livable.

The large cities had running water and sewer systems, and garbage collection had been nationalized, leading to an improvement in sanitation. Despite this being a large city, the air wasn't that bad, and the water used for daily consumption wasn't contaminated.

There was a transportation network, and many people came and went. The result was a distribution network for products, stabilized prices, and high public order because the military could be quickly dispatched anywhere.

If a person lived in the kingdom for even a few days, living in any other country would start to feel inconvenient.

The only country that could compete with this one for livability had to be the great power of the west, the Gran Chaos Empire. The Republic of Turgis wasn't anywhere close.

Dad, we can't just stay where we are.

The republic had formed an equal medical alliance with the other two countries, but at this rate, an incredible gap would form between them someday. In order to prevent that, Kuu would learn how Souma ruled here, and find a path of development for the republic.

"For that...I need to take a good look at Bro's country!" Voicing his resolve, Kuu let out a laugh.

Then a sort of weak voice came from behind him. "Y-young masterrr. Wait for meee."

When Kuu stopped and looked back, a girl with bunny ears came over to him, wheezing as she did. It was Kuu's attendant, Leporina.

"Sheesh, you're slow, Leporina. What happened to your usual healthy legs?"

"Hahh...hahh... I-It's because you're running on top of these roofs, young masterrrr. Unlike your snow monkey race, the white rabbit race aren't used to running in high places. Besides, there are proper roads, so let's walk on those."

"It's faster to cut across the roofs than to waste my time

dragging my feet on the ground, isn't it? I'm inviting Taru to lunch. If I don't hurry, lunchtime will be over."

Kuu was in a hurry because he was meeting with Taru.

Unlike Kuu, who was a freeloader staying in Parnam Castle, Taru rented a house with a workshop attached near the craftsmen's street. It would have been fine for her to live in the castle, but she felt it would be a hassle commuting from the castle to the town every day. Kuu frequently dropped in at Taru's house.

Kuu was about to take off running again, then stopped and asked Leporina, "So, where was Taru at again?"

"You were running without knowing that?!" Leporina looked at Kuu with disbelief.

"No, I know where her house is. But she's gone to train the blacksmiths today, right? I dunno where that training place is... What was it called again?"

"It's Ginger's Vocational School," Leporina answered.

Ginger's Vocational School was headed by Ginger Camus, the former slave trader. It taught children to read, write, and do arithmetic, while also being an academic institution where many fields of study and technologies in their dawning days were researched.

Of all the fields of study and technologies researched here, those deemed to have promise for the future were recognized, and if several researchers on a subject were able to be secured, an independent new specialized school would be created. For that reason, Ginger's Vocational School was called "a school for schools."

The field of medicine had just recently become independent, and the former capital of the Carmine Duchy, Randel, was now home to a school for doctors and nurses: the Randel Medical School.

Now that enough personnel had developed to the point that they could teach basic medical knowledge, Brad and Hilde were freed from their teaching duties. They had opened a medical practice in the new city of Venetinova, so there was no longer any reason for them to be tied down to the capital.

The reason the school had opened in Randel was because there was a practice ground for the National Land Defense Force nearby, which meant an endless supply of soldiers with fresh wounds who would make good guinea—er, test subjects.

Incidentally, though Brad and Hilde had made their return to the field like they wanted, they were still occasionally called to the Randel Medical School to hold lectures. Though they had quit their positions as teachers, they were now living legends in the world of medicine inside the kingdom.

It seemed that Hilde kept refusing because she was currently pregnant, but once she gave birth and had gotten used to raising her child, she was sure to receive multiple requests for lectures.

Pertinent to Kuu, however, was that Ginger's Vocational School was the place where Taru was teaching blacksmithing techniques.

Leporina sighed and ran ahead of him. "I guess there's no helping this. Follow me, young master."

Boing! Boing! Leporina jumped across the orange roofs. It looked like, in the end, they'd be going over the roofs after all.

"All right! Sorry for the trouble!" Kuu followed her with a laugh.

With Leporina leading the way, Kuu came to a place with wide grounds surrounded by a brick wall with a number of buildings inside. This was apparently Ginger's Vocational School.

When the two of them came to the gate, they saw a single maid inside the gate sweeping the ground with a bamboo broom. The maid was a beautiful girl whose triangular ears and fluffy tail were typical of the beastman races.

"Oh! I found me a cutie!" Kuu cried excitedly.

"Ohhh...not this again..." Leporina's shoulders slumped.

Kuu was into women who had fluffy beastman parts. If they had breasts, that was even better.

That was why he'd asked Tomoe, "Would you be my bride?" on their first meeting, and then set about trying to woo her. He'd have to hold out hope for the future in the breast department, though.

On that point, the beastman maid in front of Kuu was checking all his boxes. "Ooh ha ha! I wonder what kind of beastman she is. Maybe I'll go woo her right now."

"He said, despite having eyes for no one but Taru," Leporina said under her breath.

"Huh? Did you say something?"

"No, nothing... Or rather, I'll tell Taru about this later, you know?"

"Urgh... I-It's fine to look, isn't it?"

Kuu pouted. He was so easy to understand.

While the master and servant duo were arguing, the beast-man maid who had been cleaning noticed Kuu and Leporina were there. The maid narrowed her eyes warily. Readying her broom in front of her chest, she approached them with determination.

"What business do you have at our school?"

"Huh?" Kuu and Leporina, who had been in the middle of an argument, looked at her with dumbstruck faces as she suddenly interrupted them.

The maid gave the two a slight bow, never taking her eyes off them. "I am Sandria, a maid in service to Lord Ginger, the principal of Ginger's Vocational School. Pardon me, but...what business, may I ask, do you have at this school?"

There was a dangerous tone in her voice. Like she was wary of them, or she was angry. Kuu paid no mind to the atmosphere Sandria was exuding, and casually gave his name.

"Hm? I'm Kuu. This here's my servant Leporina."

Unlike Kuu, Leporina sensed the disquieting atmosphere and gave a more hesitant greeting. "I-It's a pleasure to meet you."

Sandria held her bamboo broom with a backhand grip and pointed the end of it at Kuu's forehead. "What have you come here for...is what I am asking you."

Sandria's brow was furrowed. That hostile stance got Kuu angry, too.

"What's this, out of nowhere? Is this how your school greets guests?"

"I don't think we call those who attempt to enter our school while armed 'guests.'"

"Armed? ...Oh, I guess we are." That was when Kuu finally figured it out.

Kuu had a cudgel slung over his back, and his attendant and bodyguard Leporina was carrying a bow and arrows on hers. Sandria must have been wary that they were brigands, here to attack the school.

Educational institutes were the places where the wisdom of a country was gathered, and it was entirely imaginable that they would be targeted by brigands, or agents of other countries after their researchers and results. The two of them had been careless.

When Kuu realized that, he offered his cudgel to the maid. "Sorry to come so suddenly and surprise you like that. We're just here to see someone."

"That's not how it looks, though?" Sandria said and indicated behind Kuu with her eyes.

When Kuu turned, Leporina had nocked an arrow and taken aim at Sandria.

"Wait, Leporina?! Why are you doing something so threatening?!"

"I-I thought my young master was in danger, so..."

She had immediately gone into crisis mode when thinking her master was in danger. That was the very model of what a servant should do, but in this case, it was only making the conversation harder.

"Calm down! It's just a broom!"

"Rest assured. This bamboo broom has something inside."

With a flash, a blade about the size of a knife slid out of the bamboo broom from the side she was holding. Sandria pressed the sharp edge to Kuu's throat.

"It's a cane-sword?! Why's a maid carrying something so dangerous?!"

"There are many individuals carrying out unusual research at this school, you see."

"Please, don't move!" Seeing the cane-sword, Leporina drew back her bowstring even further. "If you move a muscle...I'll fire."

"Very well," the maid said. "I will, at the very least, kill your master before that."

There were two beautiful women on either side of Kuu staring each other down. If it weren't for the weapons, this would be a situation any man would be jealous of, but even Kuu couldn't enjoy this one.

"Would both of you calm down already?! Ugh, someone do something about this!"

Perhaps Kuu's shout reached someone, because a young man came over. "Um...San? Just what kind of situation is this?"

There was a skinny, frail-looking young man standing behind Sandria, and his cheeks were twitching as he looked at this scene in bewilderment.

"You mustn't, Master!" Sandria shouted, looking panicked for the first time.

His name was Ginger Camus. Despite his youth, he was the principal of Ginger's Vocational School.

Ginger had just come over to invite Sandria to have lunch with him, but he panicked when he saw the situation near the gate.

Sandria had a broom with a knife on the end pointed at a young boy who looked like a monkey beastman, and a girl who looked like a rabbit beastman had her bow drawn and aimed at Sandria. Ginger had been taken aback by the dangerous scene, but...

"S-stop, please!" he yelled.

The next moment, his body was moving. Ginger interposed himself between Sandria and the archer so as to block the line of fire, and even in his terror, he managed to spread his arms and shout at Kuu and Leporina, "This is a school sanctioned by His Majesty King Souma! Please, stop with this violent affront to it!"

"Like. I. Keep. On. Saying. This is all a misunderstanding—"

"Master?!" Cutting Kuu off, Sandria threw aside her broom-sword, embraced Ginger, and spun them around to change their positions. She ended up exposing her back to Leporina, who was still taking aim with her bow.

"Wait, San! That's dangerous!" Ginger shouted.

"I will protect you even if it costs me my life, Master."

There was Ginger who was worried for Sandria, and Sandria who was risking her life to protect him. It was a scene that showed at a glance what their feelings for each other were like.

Having been shown that scene, Kuu awkwardly scratched his cheek as he said to them, "Uhhh...sorry to stop you when you're all fired up, but we aren't here to attack the place. Hey, Leporina. I'm free now, so how long are you going to keep holding that bow?"

"Huh...? Ah! Yes, sir!"

Leporina had been so focused on her task that only now did she realize Kuu had been released. She hurriedly lowered her bow and returned the arrow to her quiver.

With a laugh, Kuu turned to Ginger and Sandria and said, "Sorry to make a scene. I'm Kuu Taisei. I'm from the Republic of Turgis, but I'm currently freeloading at my bro Souma's place. Well, think of me as something like his little brother. Bunny ears here is my servant, Leporina."

"N-nice to meet you. Oh, and sorry for the trouble." Leporina bowed her head.

Ginger somehow managed to pry Sandria off of him, and stood in front of Kuu. "You're an acquaintance of His Majesty's, then. I am Ginger Camus, the one tasked with managing this school. This is my secretary, Sandria."

"I am Sandria." Sandria lifted the hem of her skirt a little and curtsied.

Her discomposure from earlier seemed like a lie, and she wore a look on her face like nothing had happened. However, she must have felt embarrassed inside, because her cheeks were just a little red.

Still, the only one there who would notice that was Ginger, who had been with her for a long time.

Kuu smiled and shook Ginger's hand. "Nice to meet you, Ginger. You've got a good subordinate there who cares for her master."

"Yes. She is a reliable partner."

"Guess I can't take her for myself, huh? Her looks are just my type, though."

"Huh?!"

This sudden talk of taking her away and how she was Kuu's type made Ginger panic.

Compared to that, Sandria didn't seem flustered in the least. "I regret to inform you that I have already devoted my body, my heart, and every last drop of my blood to my master."

"Whoa, San, what are you saying?!" Ginger cried.

"It goes without saying that if my master orders me to spend the night with him, I am prepared to bite back my tears and do it."

"Don't say things that make me sound bad! I'd never order any such thing!"

Ginger was panicking. That seemed to satisfy Sandria somehow.

Looking at Ginger get toyed with by his maid, Kuu found himself sympathizing despite himself. "I dunno how to say this, but...you've got it rough, too, huh?"

Now that Kuu thought about it, he felt like his bro Souma, who was also the king of this country, had times when he couldn't stand up to his fiancées, either. Were the women being stronger than the men a part of this country's national character?

She's too sadistic, so I can't bring myself to ask if she wants to be my wife, like I did with little Tomoe... Wait, huh? Is that what she's aiming for, maybe?

Had she been trying to keep Kuu from being interested in her by deliberately being sadistic to Ginger? So Kuu wouldn't try to take her away from him? Considering the loyalty she'd demonstrated by using herself as a shield to protect Ginger, it wasn't out of the question.

Kuu thought that while looking at the two of them, but...

"Master...will you keep me by your side for life?" Sandria asked.

"Of course. You're an important partner to me. I can't run this school myself, after all. So...please don't leave my side."

"Those are not quite the words I wanted to hear, but...of course I will stay at your side, serving you always, Master."

A correction, Kuu thought. *It seems a good half of it was just Sandria's personality.*

Ginger seemed a little airheaded, so he'd been able to dodge it without recognizing her intentions, but if the maid had said that to Kuu, he'd have picked up on it, and she'd have had him right there.

"That's one scary maid," Kuu said to Leporina in a quiet voice.

Leporina giggled in reply. "That just shows how important Ginger is to her. Did you see that show of devotion, young master? If it's for the man she loves, a woman can become as calculating as she need to be."

"Is that how it works...? I'm just a little afraid of girls now." Kuu sighed. "Thank goodness my servant's so simple."

"Oh, I wouldn't be so sure about thaaat," Leporina said with a mischievous smile. "Do you think any simple girl would be allowed to serve as your bodyguard? You might not think it when you look at me, but Master Gouran regards me quite highly, you know?"

Leporina puffed her chest out with pride. Though her chest was held down by the breastplate she wore, when she took that pose, it was clear she had more than Taru.

For an instant, Kuu almost stared, but the fact of her chest size rubbed him the wrong way, and he forced himself to look away.

"Hmph... Well, I'll recognize your skill with the bow, at least."

"It's not just Master Gouran, you know? I'm childhood friends with Taru, too, and we get along great. When that time comes, I'm confident the two of us can get along."

"When what time comes...?"

"That time is that time." Leporina dodged the question with her usual weak smile.

That smile made a shudder run down Kuu's back. While he'd always been under the impression that he was running Leporina around, she had become an important person to him at some point. If Leporina got fed up with him, that would hurt his relationship with Taru, whom she was also close to. At this point, she had become so reliable a presence for him that he'd never dream of replacing her with another servant.

While Kuu was still confused, Leporina started giggling. "Hee hee, I'm just joking. You always run me ragged, so I wanted to tease you a bit. Sorry."

"T-tease me?"

"Yes. You don't have to worry about what I said just now in the slightest."

O-oh, so that's how it is... Is it?

Kuu was almost satisfied, but there was a small part of him that couldn't accept it.

Leporina said she was just teasing him, but Leporina's position hadn't changed. Kuu didn't know anything about stories from Earth, but this must have been how Sun Wukong felt in the palm of the Buddha's hand.

In fact, Kuu didn't know what Leporina was really thinking at all, which was this:

Hmm...the young master seems like he's misunderstanding what I meant by "when that time comes." While the confused Kuu glanced furtively at her, Leporina smiled wryly. *Hee hee, I'd never do anything you wouldn't like, Master Kuu. I know very well how you and Taru feel. That's why, when the time comes, I'm confident I can get along with Taru. I won't get in the way of the two of you, so don't treat me badly, either. Okay, Master Kuu?*

Leporina gave Kuu a troubled smile.

Noticing that smile, Kuu thought, *Eek... Bro, I don't get girls after all...*

He felt like he could understand Souma's feelings just a little.

"What's wrong, dumb master?" Taru later asked Kuu, who had a slightly odd look on his face while they were eating.

When Kuu explained to Ginger and Sandria that he had come to invite Taru to lunch, they'd suggested they all go together, and the five went to the cafeteria inside Ginger's Vocational School.

Kuu laughed awkwardly and said to Taru, "Well, you know... a lot happened." He glanced at Leporina, who was standing next to him.

Kuu, Taru, and Ginger were seated at the table, while Leporina and Sandria were acting as servers. It had ended up with them in positions like it was a meeting, but Kuu and Ginger were able to have a rousing conversation about their respective circumstances.

"I see," Ginger said. "You're the son of the head of the Republic of Turgis. Even though she didn't know any better, San—our Sandria—was awfully rude to you."

When Ginger bowed his head, Kuu laughed. "Don't worry about it. It's partly my fault for showing up without an appointment."

"The dumb master was just being dumb. There's no need for you to bow your head to him, Sir Ginger," Taru said with a cool look on her face.

Taru was as merciless with Kuu as ever, but her behavior made Ginger's eyes go wide.

"You're a craftsperson, aren't you, Taru? Aren't you being a little too casual towards the son of your head of state?"

"Hm? The dumb master is just the dumb master. That's all."

"She's a childhood friend of mine, you see," said Kuu. "We don't stand on ceremony. I mean, she likes me enough to follow me to this country—ack!"

Kuu tried to put his arm around Taru's shoulders, but Taru elbowed him.

She looked away from him and said sharply, "The dumb master has nothing to do with it. I came here at King Souma's request."

"Ouch... Seriously, you sure can't be honest with yourself."

"You're just too honest with your desires."

Seeing the lively exchange between Kuu and Taru, Ginger more or less figured out their relationship and smiled wryly. "Ha ha...I think I get the idea."

Kuu munched on some bread as he asked Ginger, "So, is Taru getting along fine here?"

"Yes. The people in our blacksmithing department are happy to have a talented craftsperson here."

"The people here are passionate about their studies," Taru said with a serious look on her face as she drank her tea. "They have a long way to go, but I think they'll master it eventually."

It was moving for Kuu, who rarely ever saw Taru praise anyone, to see that face.

"You even have a blacksmithing department...?" Kuu said in amazement. "What other research do you do here?"

"All sorts, really," Ginger said. "Mostly sciences and technologies of all kinds. We study a wide range of topics, from things we know are important, like agriculture, to things that, at first glance, are not important at all. For example, we have a newly created Department of Dungeonology."

"Dungeonology?"

"Yes. The study of dungeons, which exist everywhere on this continent, and are a place where monsters exist outside of the Demon Lord's Domain. We record and categorize the layout of dungeons, and the monsters that reside within. It was established with the sponsorship of His Majesty, who wanted to know more about monsters."

"My bro Souma?"

If Souma was involved, there had to be some meaningful intent behind it. *Monsters, huh…?* Kuu developed a pensive look on his face, but Ginger continued without noticing it.

"We cooperate with the adventurers' guild and ask active adventurers to tell us about their experiences for our studies. Occasionally, we have novice adventurers use the gym here, and have veteran adventurers come to train them… Though, for some reason, San goes and joins them in training."

"As one who serves you, Lord Ginger, I want to have at least a bare minimum knowledge of self-defense," Sandria said unabashedly, causing Ginger to smile wryly.

"So that's why…" Kuu felt like it finally made sense. Her moves when she put that broom-sword to his throat were something an adventurer had taught her.

Kuu crossed his arms and leaned back in his chair. *Dungeonology, huh? Even that's a subject for academic study in this country…*

For Souma, whose policy particularly emphasized the importance of basic research, Ginger's Vocational School was a clear representation of scholarship. They were building a pile of plain and possibly useless research. However, even if that research was seen as useless, it was not meaningless. That pile of research would eventually become a driving force for the development of this country.

Through his interactions with Souma, Kuu had gotten to the point where he could think that way. *It's a country that's even more incredible than it looks. We can't let them outdo us.*

Then something occurred to Kuu. "Hey, Ginger. This school... Could me and Leporina attend it, too?"

"Dumb master?" Taru asked.

"Young master? What are you saying all of a sudden?"

Taru and Leporina cocked their heads to the side, but Kuu ignored them and made his request of Ginger.

"Please. I want to learn all sorts of stuff in this country, too."

Having received such an earnest request, Ginger scratched his cheek.

"Erm...we don't turn away anyone who wants to learn, but you're from another country, right? I'm sorry, but I think you'll need permission from His Majesty."

Kuu stood up with a look of glee on his face. "Got it! I'm gonna go get permission from my Bro right now!"

"Huh?! Right now?!"

"Strike while the iron's hot, they say! C'mon, Leporina, let's get going!"

"H-hold on! Wait, young master!"

Kuu took off, and Leporina rushed after him. The two had run off like a storm, and Ginger was left dumbfounded.

"What can I say? He's a very decisive individual, isn't he?" Ginger said at last.

"It's always like this," Taru said while quietly drinking the tea Sandria had poured for her. "Oh, Master Kuu... You really are dumb."

However, when she whispered those words, she was smiling just a little.

Some days later...

"All right, Leporina, let's go study in the Department of Dungeonology today. I hear we can see a dungeon relic provided by the House of Maxwell."

"I-I get it, so please stop pulling. Jeez."

At Ginger's Vocational School were Kuu, who had been attending with enthusiasm since receiving clearance from Souma; and Leporina, who he was dragging around with him, but who didn't seem to mind it, and...

"Oh, dumb master, you're so dumb."

There was Taru, watching the two of them from a distance, with the corners of her mouth turned ever so slightly upwards.

What would they study in this country, and what would that bring about in the Republic of Turgis?

That, we will not learn for a while yet.

SIDE STORY 3

After Returning to the Country Arc 3: The Flower that Blooms in the Field and the Bird in the Cage

THE SUMMER SUN had begun to set, and it was getting a little cooler.

I was in the governmental affairs office, fighting with the documents that had piled up while I was away in the republic. Why, when I was working so hard, did the amount of work left not seem to be decreasing?

There was always work I needed to do. I couldn't fight twenty-four hours a day...I wanted to go home. This *was* home, though...

Augh...I can't concentrate anymore!

I had been working in the office all day, so my mind was exhausted. Physical labor brought about lethargy of the body, but mental labor brought about impairment of mental function.

I leaned back in my chair. The sense of exhaustion felt stronger than usual.

It's because Liscia's not around.

Ever since Liscia, who had always helped me in a secretarial role, became pregnant, she had been resting in Sir Albert's former domain. I still hadn't found time to go see her.

After all these days without her, I now understood that I found Liscia's mere presence soothing. Even when I was tired, when I looked at her well-balanced proportions wrapped in a red military uniform, I felt like I could try a little harder.

If I told her I'd been ogling her during work, would I be in for another lecture...?

I wanted to talk to Liscia... No, for now, it didn't even have to be Liscia. I just wanted someone to talk to.

Sigh... Time to call it a day, I guess.

If I forced myself to work and entered the wrong information somewhere, it was bound to create more work down the line. I was losing my concentration, so it would be better to leave the rest until tomorrow and get some rest.

There was a sudden voice from the terrace, which should have been vacant.

"Your Majesty, may I have a moment?"

Considering the time, it was probably one of the Black Cats. It used to make me jump every time I suddenly heard my name, but it had happened often enough that I was used to it now.

As expected, the unit's second-in-command, Inugami, was the one to open the terrace door and come in.

"Did something happen?" I asked.

"Yes, Sire. I have something I would like to report."

After I heard Inugami's report, I was left agape.

"Huh? Why is she here?"

"It will do you no good to ask me. I suggest you address the matter with the person in question."

"I guess you're right... But I'm impressed they knew."

"The one who found her was a member who went to the Republic of Turgis," the man said. "If any of the other members had found her first, it would have been dangerous. For her, of course."

"I know. How could she do something so dangerous...?"

I pressed my palm to my forehead and sighed. Seriously, what was she thinking?

"So, what will you do?" Inugami asked, looking to see how I would respond.

"Can you lead her here...?" I asked wearily.

"You wish to meet with her?"

"We could run her off, but she's not the type to give up."

"Understood. Please wait a moment."

Inugami went out to the terrace. He had to be going to get her.

I leaned back in my chair, thought about what was to come, and became a little gloomy.

◇ ◇ ◇

Earlier, just before sunset...

Parnam was bustling with people who had finished their daily toil. Among them was a green-haired girl walking down a shopping street, muttering to herself.

"Yeesh, everyone just goes off whenever they want..."

It was Juno, the adventurer. The party she was a member of had returned from the Republic of Turgis to their usual base of operations in Parnam, the royal capital.

Juno stuck her hand in the pouch at her waist. There was more money in there than usual.

Here I am with hazard pay, but I don't really want to drink alone...

The emergency quest they took in the republic had resulted in a hefty reward. Even divided between the five of them, the money was enough to pay for all of their new equipment, and they had decided they would each spend the day doing whatever they wanted.

The swordsman Dece had invited the mage Julia, who he had a thing for, out to dinner, while the brawler Augus had said he was off to party hard at a place with pretty girls. The priest Febral was childhood friends with the innkeeper's daughter, so he had gone to see her.

All of that being the case, Juno was now left out.

Isn't there something interesting around here...?

"Hm?"

Suddenly, down the road, Juno spotted something: a roly-poly silhouette that walked with slow, easy steps.

"I think I've found it," she said with a grin. "Something interesting."

The object walking down the street was the kigurumi adventurer, Little Musashibo.

He had once been treated as an urban legend and viewed as an oddity by the townsfolk, but because he was now a major character on the Prima Lorelei Juna Doma's broadcast program *Together with Big Sister,* he was popular with the children.

"Hey, it's Little Musashibo!" a child cried.

"He's so round. And so big."

As proof of that, there were children waving to him now. That was an impressive show of popularity.

Little Musashibo gave the kids a thumbs-up.

Juno tilted her head to the side as she looked at the kigurumi adventurer.

Come to think of it, I saw a program with Little Musashibo in it, didn't I? Dece and the others were saying he probably just lent them his kigurumi suit, but those moves... He looks like the real deal.

Juno had learned to sense Little Musashibo's feelings from the way he moved, and she could see that it was the same person inside this Little Musashibo. Not only that, she had previously encountered him running errands for the castle.

Is it like I think...and he's got some connection to the castle?

Her suspicions were turning to certainty.

Juno tailed Little Musashibo. She kept a constant distance from him, her eyes on his back as she pursued. As expected, Little Musashibo headed for the main gate of Parnam Castle.

Little Musashibo showed something to the guards there. They saluted, and he was allowed to enter.

Did he show them something like a pass? But, even with a pass, would they really let such a blatantly suspicious person through?

Even if that kigurumi was appearing in a broadcast program produced at the castle, there was no knowing who was inside it, so shouldn't they be more cautious? Or did he have something that would make the guards let him pass just by showing it to them?

Was he a person with a strong enough connection to the castle that he would have a thing like that?

Juno understood Little Musashibo less than ever.

Even after waiting for some time after that, there was no sign of Little Musashibo leaving the castle. That he had only come to run a little errand seemed unlikely to be the case.

By the time she noticed the sun was setting, the area had gotten dark.

Maybe I'm right. Maybe he really is connected to the castle. Ohhh, I wonder how. But it's a castle... It's probably a bad idea to try sneaking in.

If she crossed the walls of Parnam Castle without permission, she would likely be arrested for trespassing. If that happened, it wouldn't just be her problem; she'd be inconveniencing Dece and the rest of her party, too.

Hmm, what to do?

Juno was trapped, paralyzed at the border of curiosity and reason. She did not realize that, at that moment, she had become a "suspicious person staring at the castle." Or that there was a group that existed to guard against such people and expose them if found.

Juno had long since gone from being the watcher to being the watched.

Ah!

By the time she noticed, it was too late. There were countless presences surrounding Juno.

No! How could a scout like me fail to notice until I was surrounded?!

Juno, who excelled at sensing the presence of enemies in a dungeon, had allowed them to close in on her. There was no doubt her opponents were skilled.

Wh-what do I do...? What now...?

Juno tried to get a feel for the presences. Polishing every nerve in her body, she searched for their locations.

When she did, she realized there was only one direction with no people in it. Despite being otherwise perfectly encircled, there were no people in the direction of the castle.

I smell a trap, she thought. *It's too blatant, but...it's not like I have any other choice.*

Juno resolved herself, and took off in that direction. The presences around her moved, too.

They aren't attacking? But I'm still surrounded.

While searching for the presences, she looked for a place from where she could escape. She was running in the direction where there were no presences, but she sensed she was being led somewhere.

Wait...I'm super close to the castle?!

Having focused on nothing but running away, at some point she had crossed the castle wall and gotten close to the castle itself. If she got caught now, she would be dealt with as an intruder.

Juno clambered up a wall, jumped around on the roofs, and ran desperately.

Eventually, she landed on a terrace. There was an open glass door.

C-can I go in here, hide, and wait them out?! she thought, and tried to enter the room.

"And stop."

"Wha—?!"

The young man who came out of the room blocked her way.

"There are important documents in here, after all," the young man said in a relaxed tone that you wouldn't anticipate from someone unexpectedly encountering a suspicious person on the terrace. "There are rules against anyone entering who doesn't have to."

However, as she was on the run, Juno was desperate.

"S-sorry! I might look suspicious, but I'm not! I was just being chased and they cornered me in here, so...um...hide me for just a little while?"

Juno ran her mouth as fast as she could, but the young man sighed.

"Calm down a little, Juno. I more or less know the situation."

"Huh...? Why do you know my name?"

"How many times have you asked that question now, I wonder...?"

With that, the young man took another step forward. When she saw his face, which had up until now been covered by a shadow, Juno's eyes went wide with surprise.

"I-It's you! You're the guy we just met in the republic, aren't you?!"

"Yes. We met in the refugee camp, too, I believe," the young man said with a wry smile and a shrug. "I might add, we've gone adventuring and drank together, too."

"Huh? What're you... Huh?!"

Then the young man pointed towards the room. Inside was Little Musashibo, approaching with slow, easy steps. Little Musashibo's "head" was wide open for the flabbergasted Juno to see. Inside, he was...empty.

The young man spoke. "I move it using my own unique magic. I am the person in the costume, despite being outside the costume, you could say."

"Then you're Mr. Little Musashibo's real identity?!"

"Well, yeah, that's more or less what I mean." The young man extended his hand to Juno. "It's a pleasure to meet you...though I suppose it's not the first time. Still, I haven't given you my name properly, so let me introduce myself. I am Souma Kazuya, the one who was controlling Little Musashibo."

"Souma Kazuya... Wait, that's the name of..."

While they were shaking hands, Juno's brow furrowed at the familiar name.

The young man smiled wryly. "Do I really make that little of an impression in my normal outfit? Yeah. I'm the provisional King of Friedonia."

At that point, Juno's mind went completely blank.

◇ ◇ ◇

It took some time for Juno to recover from her confusion.

"Th-then what? You're Little Musashibo, and you're the king, so that means Little Musashibo is the king? ...Ah! Sorry, I need to mind my manners."

"No, the way you normally talk is fine," I told Juno with a wry smile. She was babbling incoherently now. "I told you we were comrades before, didn't I?"

Juno puffed up her cheeks and looked away. "I don't want someone who was keeping something so important a secret as a comrade."

"I couldn't tell you *because* it was so important. Besides, even if I had, I doubt you'd have believed me, would you?"

"That's... Well, maybe not. Fine, I'll act like normal."

With that said, Juno sat herself down on the railing at the edge of the terrace.

I stood with my back leaned against the same railing, and we were finally in a position to have a relaxed talk.

Juno's eyes started darting around the area.

"What is it, Juno?" I asked.

"Nah, I was just wondering where the presences that were chasing me up until a moment ago went."

"Oh. Those are my people. I asked them to guide you here."

"Those were your underlings?! I was super scared, you know?!"

"It was your fault for spying on the castle. If you were unlucky, you might have been killed out of hand for being a potential troublemaker. Who knows what would have happened if they hadn't contacted me?"

At that reasonable argument, Juno groaned, unable to come up with a response. "Um... Sorry," she said. "I just really wanted to know who you were..."

Juno was acting meek. It wasn't like her, so I laughed. "Well, it's fine. And? How do you feel, knowing my true identity?"

"I'm relieved to have my doubts cleared up," she admitted. "But why's the king playing with dolls?"

"It was just an experiment at first."

From there I gave Juno a simple summary of how Little Musashibo had come to be.

Wanting to test the range of my ability, I'd registered him as an adventurer and had him go all sort of places. He had met Juno and her group because of that, we'd ended up adventuring together, and so on.

I also explained that I was able to see whatever Little Musashibo saw.

"Wha...?! Then you saw when my breastplate melted, too?!"

"Uh...yeah. It's a good thing you didn't end up showing your ribs as well as your breasts—ow!"

"Don't talk about my breasts!" Juno planted a hard kick in my flank.

I was just paraphrasing Dece, though!

"Ow...hey, I'm kind of the king, you know?" I complained.

"You said we're comrades, and to act like normal, didn't you?" My agony must have made her anger settle, because Juno was cackling. "Come to think of it, what happened to that awful salamander?"

"I sent in the military to put it down," I said. "We couldn't leave it be forever. We stripped the body down to its bones and sent it to a research institute. There's a replica on display in front of the museum."

"Those massive bones were that salamander?!"

"Looks like it was the one that ended up showing off its ribs, huh?" I said jokingly.

"It sure did!" she replied, with a big laugh. "I see. Then the hand I saw when we were eating at the cafeteria was your hand?"

"Yeah. Because of the heat of the kigurumi suit and the alcohol I'd been drinking, I was a bit out of it, though."

"Ah! That's why the princess conveniently came along, huh?" Juno clapped her hands, seemingly satisfied with the explanation.

Was she talking about the time I'd collapsed at the banquet and Liscia had shown up to collect me? Now that I thought about it, Juno knew Liscia, didn't she? If you included the time in the refugee camp and our encounter in the republic, she'd also had contact with Aisha, Juna, and Tomoe.

When I told her that, Juno was taken aback.

"Without knowing it...we met some really important people."

"It sure is a small world," I agreed.

"Normally it's a little bigger!" Juno said angrily.

Her reactions were fun, so I was enjoying this.

Then, wiping her smile away, she spoke with a little concern. "But still, how is it being a king?"

"What's this, out of nowhere?"

"Nah, I was just thinking it must be a hassle."

"Well, yeah," I agreed. "But so is every job, right? Being an adventurer means you're always putting your life on the line, doesn't it?" I looked idly into the dark sky. *Oh, hey, the stars are out.* "King, adventurer, or baker, it's all the same. If you face your work head-on, you're putting your life on the line. If you keep trying hard like that, someone will help you. For me, it was my family and retainers, while for you, it's Dece and your party, right?"

"Sure is," she agreed. "'The longer you walk, the more hands there will be to support you.'"

"I've heard that before."

"It's a line from a children's song. The one we sing to children when they start to walk."

Ohhh, the one Juna had sung for me that one time. When I felt like I might be crushed by my responsibilities as king, and I couldn't sleep, Juna sang me a lullaby...

It had been a long time since then, and the number of hands supporting me had gone up, but how far had I been able to walk?

"I'd actually like to ask you something," I said. "What do you think of this country, Juno?"

"What do I think?"

"I mean, do you think it's a good country? I want your frank opinion."

"Hmm...it's an easy country to live in." Juno placed her hand under her chin and thought as she spoke. "There's a wide variety of foods, and, as an adventurer, being able to get around by rhinoceros train is nice and easy. Having proper roads makes quests to protect traveling merchants easy, too. Oh, also, this country terminated its contract with the guild to conscript all adventurers in the country in times of war, right? Being able to stay here and know we won't be drafted if a war comes is good."

"I see, I see..."

Like I thought, it was different from what an ordinary citizen thought of as a "good country." I didn't often get the chance to hear opinions from adventurers, so it was interesting.

"Turning that around, it makes it easy for adventurers to gather here, though," Juno said. "If too many adventurers gather, the competition for dungeons gets higher, so you could say that's a problem."

"Well, for the country's part, we're happy to have dungeons cleared earlier."

"For us adventurers, they fill our bellies, and feed our spirit of adventure. You went on an adventure using that doll, so you understand, don't you? That exhilaration."

"Well, yeah... I know the stories of your feats of martial prowess are a source of entertainment for the people, too."

Besides, dungeons played a role in the local economy. That was why the state shouldn't get involved more than necessary. I wanted dungeon cores for the Jewel Voice Broadcast, but I also wanted to avoid causing any unexpected problems.

"So, well...do your best, adventurer!" I said.

"Don't talk like it has nothing to do with you! If you can use that doll, you can be an adventurer too, can't you?"

"But now you know I'm the one controlling it. I was thinking of stopping the adventuring."

"That'd be a waste, you know," she said. "Now I know the doll's empty, so I can use it to slow down the enemy, sacrifice it, or use it as bait without hesitating."

"You're totally planning to get it wrecked. It wasn't cheap, you know."

"Hey, let's adventure together again. I swear I won't say a word about who you are."

Juno put her hands together and pleaded, so I shrugged.

"Well, if your tongue slips, I can just have him retire then, I guess."

"I'm telling you, it won't!"

From there we argued over some silly things, and by the time I realized it, a fair amount of time had passed. It felt like having a good conversation with a friend I hadn't seen in a long time. Talking with a like-minded companion really was fun.

That was why...

"I hope we can talk like this again sometime." Those words came out of my mouth naturally. "I want to hear more about the castle town, and about all sort of other inconsequential things."

"You want to make me your spy?" Juno asked.

"That's not it. I have better spies available, after all."

"Well, of course you do. I learned that firsthand." Juno clutched her chest and trembled a little. She must have been truly terrified to be chased by the Black Cats.

"If I'm in the castle all the time, I feel like I'll be disconnected from the people," I said. "That's why I want to hear about the little things that are going on in town. Like how one lady was saying, 'These vegetables are too expensive! Make them cheaper!' or how Gonbe's baby caught a cold."

"Who's Gonbe supposed to be?" Juno chuckled and nodded. "Sure. When I've got free time, I'll chat with you. Is this a good time of day?"

"Let's see. I'll tell the spies to show you in."

"I'm getting an escort from those guys...? Well, it's fine." With that said, Juno stood up on top of the railing. "We really got talking, didn't we? I should be off."

"Yeah. Be careful on your way back. I'm looking forward to the day we can talk again."

"Sure thing. I'll try to have an interesting story ready for when that time comes."

"All right, I'll have something to eat prepared next time."

"Sounds good. The food in that cafeteria was delicious, after all." Juno turned to go, but then she suddenly looked my way. "If you get sick of living in the castle, just tell me. I'll take you on an adventure any time," she said with a smile.

"Well, if you get tired of living like a tumbleweed and want to settle down somewhere, tell me," I replied with a laugh. "I can introduce you to any number of places where you can live where you work."

"Ha ha, nice comeback. Well, later then."

"Yeah. See you next time, Juno."

Juno jumped down from the railing, bouncing along the rooftops as she vanished into the darkness of night. As would be expected from the party's scout, she was nimble.

Watching Juno's back as she left, I whispered to myself, "If I get sick of living in the castle...huh."

That day would surely never come. There were people precious to me here.

There is a debate over which is happier, the flower that blooms in the field, or the caged bird.

It is meaningless.

The flower and bird each have their own happiness.

SIDE STORY 4

After Returning to the Country Arc 4: The God-Protected Forest's Longest Day

THE MIDDLE of the 8th month, 1,547th year, Continental Calendar:

On this clear day, I was flying through the sky on Naden's back while she was in her ryuu form.

This height had scared me at first, but after being sent out to do weather reporting enough times, I was now completely used to it. Now, I could even sleep at an altitude of 1,000 meters.

Though Naden gets mad if I sleep...

"Is something the matter, Sire?" Aisha asked.

"It's nothing," I told her.

It was just that today, Aisha was seated behind me with her hands wrapped tightly around my waist. That was because we were heading to Aisha's homeland, the God-Protected Forest.

"Still, why are we going to the God-Protected Forest so suddenly?" Aisha asked.

"Because we got engaged, but I haven't gone to give my regards to Sir Wodan. We've been communicating with letters, but I've been meaning to find the time to go see him."

"It's to see him about the betrothal?!"

"Yeah. I've already talked to Liscia's parents, and Juna's guardian is Excel, so I've spoken with her. For Naden, Tiamat is like her mother, so the formalities are taken care of there, too. As for Roroa's parents...I intend to visit their grave soon."

There was a grave for the Amidonian royal family near Van, the former capital of the Principality. Roroa's parents lay at rest there. I couldn't imagine Gaius would have blessed our marriage, but I had to believe that Roroa's mother, a cheerful woman according to Sir Gouran, would have pacified him.

"So, that being the case, we're visiting Aisha's family home, huh?" Naden asked.

"Urgh... If that's what this was about, you could have told me. I'm not mentally prepared..." Aisha ground her forehead against my back.

Leaving the confused Aisha alone for a bit, I talked to my other fiancée, who was kindly giving us a ride. "Sorry, Naden. For making you give Aisha a ride again, too."

I gave her a pat on the back. She turned her ryuu head around to look our way and replied, "I don't really mind if it's Aisha," using her telepathy. "She's ridden me before. Besides, 'the partner of my partner is like my partner.'"

"Yeah, you were saying something like that before."

Aisha, who seemed to have recovered from writhing in embarrassment, tilted her head to the side. "Hmm...if Naden and I are partners, which of us is the husband?"

What is this stupidity Aisha is suddenly spouting? I thought, but Naden pondered the question with a surprising amount of seriousness.

"Hmm, wouldn't it be you, Aisha? You're strong, after all."

"In your ryuu form, you're strong, too."

"But compared to Juna, you're more of a husband type, wouldn't you say?"

"Comparing me to Juna isn't fair! She's more of a woman than anyone."

"In this form, my breasts are bigger than hers... Wait, saying that just makes me sad. But when you think of it that way, isn't Liscia the most like a husband?"

"Lady Liscia is gutsy," Aisha agreed. "In a way, she's better husband material than His Majesty."

"You're just saying whatever you want..." Hearing the two of them talk, my shoulders slumped. It was true enough; I was nowhere near as gutsy as Liscia. "Still, in the end, you'd both prefer to be the wife, right?"

"Well, of course."

"For my part, I need both of you to be my brides."

"Sire!" Aisha cried.

"Souma!"

The two both smiled bashfully. I was embarrassed having said it, too.

"It's awkward having my superior flirting right beside me, you realize?" Hal complained.

He was flying beside us on the back of Ruby, who was in red dragon form. He looked at us with a face like he'd been forced to drink boiled sugar.

His mount was looking at Naden with her golden eyes, too.

"You, too, Naden," Ruby rebuked and then looked away sulkily. "If you're a dragon of the Star Dragon Mountain Range, keep yourself together when your knight is riding you. That is the dignity expected of a knight's partner."

"Souma's not a knight, he's a king, so there."

"Don't quibble! That makes him higher than a knight!"

"Oh, jeez, shut up!"

The two of them started arguing high up in the sky.

While they weren't as hostile as they had been when I'd first met the two of them, neither of them had changed their stubborn personalities, so fights like this were a daily occurrence.

That said, they did it as friends.

As my fiancée, Naden's position was far higher than Ruby's, but the fact they could fight on equal terms showed that Naden and Ruby didn't let that come between them. They were each the only person the other knew from their homeland in the kingdom, after all.

Then Naden said, "Nyahh!" and bared her teeth. "You can stop worrying about me and get along with your own knight, can't you?! That fox-eared mage isn't here today, so you can get as lovey-dovey as you want."

"Wh-what are you saying?! I wouldn't—"

"Oh, my, what's this? Your face is all red, Ruby!" Naden teased.

"It's naturally that color!"

After that, Naden and Ruby kept shouting and having a good time. Where did the dignity expected of a knight's partner go...? Well, if they were getting along and fighting with each other, I could let that go.

"But there wasn't any need for me to come, was there?" Hal asked. "If Young Miss Aisha and Young Miss Naden are with you, isn't that enough to protect you?"

It was true. When I had Aisha, the greatest warrior in the kingdom, and Naden, who in her ryuu form could probably take on over ten wyvern riders at once, with me, there was no point in bringing Hal for protection.

However, there was a good reason for bringing him along.

"When I sent Sir Wodan a letter saying, 'I will come to visit soon,' I was asked to bring you with me, too," I explained. "It seems Sir Sur has been wanting to see you."

"By Sir Sur, you mean... Ohhh, that dark elf who came to reinforce us before, huh?" Hal said, clapping his hands.

Back when the Forbidden Army and the Army stared each other down near Randel, a unit of dark elf archers had rushed to their aid as thanks for the relief they'd received after the landslide disaster. The one leading those reinforcements had been Sir Sur. Our troops were stretched thin at the time, so I was still really grateful for that assistance.

"But why does he want to meet me?" Hal asked. "He's already repaid his debts, hasn't he?"

"Oh, well, it seems the one who really wants to meet with you is Sur's daughter. She was apparently one of the people you saved while searching for survivors with me."

"Yeah, I don't remember her. We saved a lot of people that time, after all."

"Even if you've forgotten her, she hasn't forgotten you. You're the man who saved her life, after all."

"Only because that was the mission!" Hal scratched at his head. He wasn't good at accepting excessive praise. He might run wild at times, but that straightforward nature of his was very like Hal, and it left a good impression on me.

"Let her thank you, at least," I said. "Now then... Come on, Naden, Ruby, don't just keep fighting forever. Let's hurry on to the God-Protected Forest. Sir Wodan is waiting for us."

"Oh! Yeah. Roger that."

"R-roger."

With the two dragon girls having come to their senses and picked up the pace, we headed for the God-Protected Forest.

The green leaves of the God-Protected Forest shone in the summer sun.

When we'd come to provide aid before, we stopped the rhinoceros train outside and headed for the village on foot, but this time we were coming from the air, so we could land directly in the dark elf village.

"H-he really came on a dragon!" an elf exclaimed.

"That's a big'un..."

They weren't wary because we had notified them in advance,

but the dark elves curiously watched the ryuu and the dragon descend from a distance.

When we touched down and Naden and Ruby took human form, the people who were watching rushed in like a dam had just burst. Surrounded by dark elves of all ages, from children to adults, we ended up getting manhandled.

"What?! You girls are dragons?!"

"Wowwwie! Hey, transform again!"

"Why, King Souma, how good of you to come visit."

"You were a great help last time."

"Hey, Lady Aisha, good of you to come back."

"Lady Aisha, congratulations on your betrothal to His Majesty."

"Is this red-headed girl Sir Hal's partner? She's a beauty."

"Who is this black-haired kid? ...Huh? She's not a kid?"

That was about how it went, with the questions flying fast and it not being clear who was saying what to whom until somebody clapped their hands.

I looked in that direction to see Aisha's father, Sir Wodan, looking on with a wry smile.

"Everyone, His Majesty and his entourage have only just arrived. It is rude to surround and interrogate them like that."

When Wodan lightly told them off, the dark elves stepped back, seeming a little embarrassed.

Now that we were free from the crowd, we could finally catch our breaths. "You're a lifesaver, Sir Wodan," I said gratefully.

"No, no, the villagers were being rude. However, this is because when they learned that you, who came to the aid of our village, were coming to visit, they all became excited to welcome you. Please, forgive them."

"Don't worry about it. I'm grateful for the warm welcome."

Sir Wodan and I exchanged a firm handshake. In that moment, the dark elves started clapping.

I dunno, being this welcome was kind of embarrassing.

"Now, it won't do for us to stand here talking forever," Sir Wodan said, indicating which direction he wanted us to go. "Please, come to my house."

"Chief." A hand went up from inside the crowd of dark elves. It belonged to Sir Sur, who had led the reinforcements that came during our battle against the Army. "I wanted to invite Sir Halbert to my own house. Would that be all right?"

"Hmm...what do you say, King Souma?" Sir Wodan asked.

I smiled and nodded. "I don't mind. That was why I brought him along in the first place."

"Thank you," Sur said. "Now, Sir Halbert, please come to my house."

"O-okay?"

Hal was dragged off with Sur pulling him by the arm. Ruby hurried after them. Afterwards, Aisha, Naden, and I went to Sir Wodan's house.

Looking at the village along the way, I could see almost no signs of the disaster that had happened here before. Their houses were in a forest to begin with, and many were simple, so it must not have taken long to rebuild them.

"You've come a long way towards recovering," I commented.

"That is thanks to your generous provision of materials," Sir Wodan said. "Thank you, sincerely."

"I ought to thank you for sending those reinforcements during the recent war."

"It was nothing. Those are the times when we most need to help one another."

As we walked, we entered Wodan's house. We were shown through to the living room, where Wodan offered me the head seat at the table, but I firmly declined.

"I'm not here as a king today, but as a single man, here to take Aisha to wife. Please, sit at the head of the table, Sir Wodan."

"I see."

Sir Wodan sat in the head seat, while I sat across from him. I had Aisha sit next to me, and Naden sat a little behind us, waiting.

Then I bowed my head. "Even though my betrothal to Aisha was agreed upon, I must apologize for having been so busy that it delayed my coming to give you, her father, my regards. Please, give me your daughter. Give me Aisha as my wife."

"P-please, Father." Aisha hurriedly bowed her head.

When I glanced over, Naden was bowing her head along with us.

Sir Wodan sighed a little. "Raise your heads," he said.

When I raised my face, Sir Wodan tried to force a smile, but failed. It was an awkward expression.

"I am sure Aisha requested this marriage, didn't she? There is no need for you to bow your head, Sir Souma. This is complicated for me as a father, but if it is my daughter's wish...it seems I must give you my blessing."

"Fatherrr..." Aisha said tearfully, her voice full of emotion.

Sir Wodan gave her a smile. Then, returning his face to normal, he looked me in the eye. "We dark elves are a long-lived race. Aisha is younger than you, and will live longer, I am sure. Even if you reach the end of your natural life, you will be leaving Aisha behind. Do you understand that?"

"Yes." The life of an ordinary human like myself, when looked at by a member of a long-lived race like Naden or Aisha, had to look like a short thing. Even so, Aisha and Naden both wanted to be with me.

In order to ensure they did not regret the time spent with me, I vowed from the bottom of my heart that I would endeavor to be a good king, and a good partner. Even if a time would come when we would be forced to part...

However, it seemed what Sir Wodan wanted to say was a little different than what I was reflecting on. He began to speak, sounding like he had found some sort of enlightenment.

"However, long-lived as our races are, if we cannot live to the end of our natural lives, it is possible for us to live a shorter time than humans. We can die in war or accidents. If we catch epidemic diseases, we die quite easily. My own wife, Aisha's mother, lost her life to such a disease. If you let your guard down because she is long-lived, Aisha may pass on before you do."

I was silent.

"So please, take care of Aisha. Give her a new family and fond memories for the time when, someday, you go on ahead of her." Sir Wodan quietly bowed his head.

A father's wish was always for his daughter's happiness.

I would soon be a father myself. I didn't know if my child would be a boy or a girl yet, but there might come a day when, like Sir Wodan, I would entrust them to someone.

I chose my words carefully and answered him in a calm tone. "Aisha is a far stronger person than I. From here on…I am sure she will defend me on the battlefield."

He was silent.

"That being the case, I will try to protect Aisha's smile from everything else. So that, someday, she can see me off with a smile. So that she will not regret our time together."

"Sire…" Aisha cried and drew closer to me.

I could hear sniffling from behind me. Aisha's tears had likely made Naden start crying, too.

Sir Wodan stood up and walked towards me. Then, placing his hands over mine and Aisha's, he smiled and said, "Sir Souma, I'm counting on you to take care of Aisha."

"Yes, Father, I will."

"Aisha. Be happy."

"I will…Father."

"Madam Naden, I am sure you will be Sir Souma's wife, too. Please, treat Aisha well as a member of the same family."

"Of course I will! Roger that!"

Having heard our responses, Sir Wodan smiled broadly and nodded in satisfaction.

◇ ◇ ◇

Meanwhile, around that time...

Having broken off from Souma and the others, Halbert ended up being practically dragged into Sur's house.

He walked where his hand was being pulled. With Halbert's strength, which was among the top in the kingdom, it would be easy to shake free of this hand, but he felt nothing but goodwill from Sur, and so he couldn't treat the man poorly.

Ruby hurried after the two of them.

Halbert turned his head back in her direction and asked in a whisper, "H-hey, Ruby, what's going on here?!"

"D-don't ask me," she whispered back. "Can't you get away?"

"If he were hostile, that'd be one thing, but I'd feel bad brushing off an invitation made with goodwill..."

"Then all we can do is wait and see how it goes, right?"

While the two of them were having that exchange, Sur turned back with a smile. "Okay, we're here. Welcome to my home."

"Huh?"

By the time they realized it, the two had been led to a small house with a thatched roof. It was clearly the abode of a farmer, but the roof was bizarrely steep.

"That's an awfully pointy house you've got, huh..."

Halbert's opinion was more or less exactly how it looked, so Sur laughed. "Here in this forest, when winter comes, we get a fair amount of snow accumulation. If we don't use roofs like this so the snow falls off, they'll collapse."

"You get that much accumulation?" Hal asked.

"Yes. Because of it, we cannot hunt in winter, and everyone spends their time indoors, mending things or doing maintenance on their weapons. Though last year's winter was different."

"How so?"

Sur indicated the pile of lumber next to the stairs. "Because we had lumber from the trees knocked down by the landslide, as well as from the periodic thinning His Majesty advised us to do. We were making pieces of traditional art before, like statues, but they seem to have become popular in the outside world, and are creating significant wealth for us. There are occasionally merchants who receive permission from both the kingdom and the God-Protected Forest to come buy them."

"Wow..."

"The most popular of them was... Let's see, I think I had one around here..." Sur said and began digging through the wood pile.

Not long passed before he pulled a long, thin object from the pile.

"Ahh, here it is." He held it up for Halbert and Ruby to see. "This is it. This is the most popular item."

"By this, you mean...a wooden sword?"

What Sur was holding up was a sword made of wood. What was more, it wasn't the sort of orthodox double-bladed sword used in the kingdom, but one modeled on the katana, which was the main style in use in the Nine-Headed Dragon Archipelago Union. On top of that, there was some sort of writing or symbols carved into the handle.

"His Majesty called this a souvenir bokuto," Sur said.

"Oh...of course Souma would be involved." Halbert said, shaking his head in exasperation.

Hal had gotten that feeling when Sur started talking about traditional art, but then said the most popular item was a bokuto. If it was the sort of thing where Hal couldn't tell at first glance what the point was, it had to be Souma's doing.

"Then what's engraved on the handle was him, too?"

"Yes. He says they're the characters that would represent the name of this forest in his world's language," Sur showed them the hilt and explained.

Halbert and Ruby couldn't read them, of course, but there were four kanji—神護之森—carved into it.

Incidentally, Souma had considered carving in the name of that one lake in Hokkaido, since no one could read what it said anyway, but when he imagined soldiers training diligently with one of those wooden swords in hand...he'd turned that idea down himself.

Sur offered the bokuto to Halbert. "Sir Hal, would you like one for yourself?"

Halbert stared at the proffered bokuto.

Ruby thought, *What are you staring so seriously for?* But eventually, Halbert quietly took it.

"Huh?! You're taking it?! It's just a wooden stick, isn't it?!" Ruby reacted to Halbert's actions with wide-eyed shock.

"I don't know why! I don't get it, but I really wanted it!"

Sur nodded as Halbert tried to explain himself. "I understand. There's something you find strangely exciting about it, as a man."

"That's right! If you see something like this, you can't *not* take it! Is there some sort of magic placed on these characters?"

"I don't really feel any magical power," Ruby said dubiously. Red dragons were sensitive to magical power.

Most likely, what Halbert and Sur felt was the same thing that all those boys who bought a souvenir bokuto on a field trip did. However, Halbert didn't know that was a thing, so he felt like he had been charmed somehow. That was the terror of the souvenir bokuto.

While they were having that inconsequential discussion, something burst out of Sur's house.

Halbert, being a warrior by nature, readied himself to fight the instant it happened, but when he realized it was a small child, his tension eased.

However, that was a mistake.

"Lord Hal!" the child cried, landing an energetic tackle on Hal's stomach.

"Guhhh!" Halbert let out a groan.

"Hal?!" Ruby cried.

He used his hands to give the worried Ruby a sign he was okay.

The one now hugging Halbert was a little dark elf girl. She was maybe twelve. Her hair was cut short, and she had a cute face.

With no regard for Halbert's reaction, the girl rubbed her face against his abdomen.

"Lord Hal! I've been wanting to see you!"

"Erm...are you Sir Sur's daughter?" Hal said, remembering Sur had mentioned she wanted to see him. This girl who'd performed a flying tackle-hug had to be her.

The girl let go, and politely bowed her head. "Excuse me for that. I am Sur's daughter, Velza." She raised her face and grinned. "I do not know if you remember me, Lord Hal, but I am one of those you saved from beneath the sand and dirt. Thank you so much for that." She bowed her head once more.

Halbert was flustered. "No, it's nothing you need to thank me for. I only followed Souma's orders..."

"It still made me happy. I will never forget the day you saved me. Nor will I forget you, Lord Hal, or my debt of gratitude."

"I dunno what to say..." Halbert was overwhelmed by the girl's persistent thanks.

"He he. She's a real polite girl, isn't she?" Ruby, who'd been left completely out of it, said to Sur. "She's so small, but she really has it together."

"Tell me about it. When did that tomboy daughter of mine get to be so pol—*ow*!"

"Sir Sur?!"

Mid-word, Sur began writhing in pain. Velza had kicked a piece of wood lying by her feet, and it landed a direct hit on Sur's shin.

Through all of that, Velza never once dropped her smile.

When Halbert and Ruby saw Velza smiling like that, it reminded them of an angry Kaede, and a chill ran down their spines.

Because Halbert and Ruby were both straightforward in their personalities, they often had fights without it getting ugly, but if they ever stepped over the line, they knew they were in for a lecture from a smiling Kaede. This girl's smile was just like Kaede's was at those times.

Velza ran over in front of Ruby. "Um...would you happen to be Lord Hal's wife, perhaps?"

Ruby was dumbfounded for a moment, but then she nodded. "Yes. I am Ruby, the dragon. I've formed a dragon knight's contract with Hal. Because the contract between a dragon and a knight makes them life partners, you could say we're engaged."

When Velza heard Ruby's response, she clapped her hands. "Oh, my! You're *that* dragon, Miss Ruby? To think he has become a dragon knight! That is Lord Hal for you."

Having said that with an innocent look in her eyes, Velza took Ruby's hands.

"I want to join the National Defense Force like Lord Hal in the future. If possible, I want to be assigned to Lord Hal's unit. It is a pleasure to make your acquaintance, ma'am."

"R-right..." It seemed Ruby was not entirely displeased to be referred to that way.

Seeing Velza worm her way into Ruby's good graces in no time, Halbert sensed the situation moving forward somewhere where he had no control.

Wh-what is this...? This feeling like the moat around my walls was filled in without me noticing...?

Meanwhile, Sur, who had recovered from his pain, plopped a hand down on Velza's shoulder with a sigh.

"It's rude making our guests stand outside forever. How about we take this indoors?"

"Oh, my! You're right! How careless of me. I was so delighted that Lord Hal was here, I got worked up despite myself. Now, let's go, Lord Hal, Lady Ruby."

Velza took Halbert and Ruby's hands and showed them inside the house.

To anyone else, it would look like a little sister having her big brother and sister indulge her. Halbert and Ruby didn't feel bad about having a little girl adore them, either.

However, behind the two who were being led by the nose by Velza, Sur wore a wry smile.

Goodness me, he thought. *She must take after her passionate mother... If you don't take her by the reins, you're going to be in for a rough ride, Sir Hal.*

While thinking that, Sur followed the three of them inside the house.

◇ ◇ ◇

That evening, after the pleasantries with Sir Wodan were out of the way, Aisha, Naden, and I went to visit Aisha's mother's grave.

In the God-Protected Forest, people were buried at the base of trees. The custom was to return their bodies, which were raised on the forest's blessings, to the forest.

We heard the rustling of branches and the buzzing of insects.

I knelt in front of the tree where Aisha's mother lay at rest, my hands together, praying in the Japanese style. Like I had sworn to Sir Wodan, I would protect Aisha from sadness to the best of my ability.

So, please, give me your daughter, I prayed.

After staying like that for a short while, I stood up and looked at Aisha and Naden. "I have something to say to the two of you."

"What might that be, Sire?" Aisha asked.

"What? Why so formal?"

They both gave me blank looks. I chose my words carefully. "It's about...after we're gone."

They both opened their eyes wide in silent shock.

This was something the two of them were going to have to face eventually, after all.

"If you let your guard down, even a member of a long-lived race can live a short life," I said. "What Sir Wodan was saying makes perfect sense. However, the more likely outcome is that Liscia, Juna, Roroa, and I will end up leaving you two behind. I make this request having thought about what that means myself."

I looked into their dumbfounded eyes and continued.

"Please...don't be lonely. I'm happy to have met you two. I don't want to make this moment one that you reminisce on sadly while thinking, '*Things were better back then.*'"

The two of them said nothing, just continuing to let me speak.

"I want you two to be happy when you remember. Ideally, you'll be able to smile and think, '*I'm happy now, but I was happy back then, too.*' Once we're gone, stay connected to our children, and to the long-lived people you know like Carla and Excel... And if you find a good partner, I don't mind if you get remarried."

The two of them looked down and said nothing.

"Make sure you're always connected with someone, and don't be lonely," I said. "Not ever..."

Aisha and Naden hugged me without a word.

They neither accepted nor rejected what I was saying. Because we each understood all too well how the others felt.

If they were in my position, they might have thought the same thing I did. If I were in their position, I'm sure I'd have felt the same as them. So there was no need for a response.

If the two of them remembered me saying this later, it might give them the push they needed if they ended up feeling lost when the inevitable happened. This was the best I could do for them. Their lack of response must have been their own way of being considerate.

I patted them both on the back and, with a laugh, I said, "I'm never letting go of you for as long as I live, though. I'm gonna be with you until you're sick of me."

"Okay," Aisha said. "Let's be together as long as we can."

"We aren't going to let go of you easily, either," Naden agreed.

They both had tears in the corners of their eyes, but they were smiling.

"Let's be sure we make children, too," Aisha added. "I'll do my best."

"Yeah," I said. "Definitely."

"One won't be enough, either," Aisha went on. "You'll have to work hard, Sire."

"S-sure... I'll do my best."

Seeing Aisha get so enthusiastic, I felt a bit overwhelmed.

Naden joined in, too. "If we have a ryuu, we'll have to leave it in the Star Dragon Mountain Range, so I'd prefer a dragonewt, if possible. I'd like to give birth to at least one ryuu to show my gratitude to Lady Tiamat, so... Oh! But if it's a dragonewt, that would be a member of the sea serpent race, right? What do we do if it grows up to be like Duchess Walter?"

A child like Excel, huh...

"Let's all work together to educate our child so that doesn't happen," I said fervently.

"Indeed," Aisha agreed.

"Roger that."

With that, we laughed while continuing to hug each other.

HOW A REALIST HERO REBUILT THE KINGDOM

SIDE STORY 5

After Returning to the Country Arc 5: Memorial Festival

END OF THE 8TH MONTH, 1,547th year, Continental Calendar:

It happened in the Royal Capital of Parnam, on a day when the summer heat was still far from fading, in the large room in Parnam Castle where the bureaucrats who handled finances worked (a.k.a. the Finance Room).

In one corner of that room was a set of sofas in a reception area. One of these was currently occupied by Roroa Amidonia, the former Princess of Amidonia, who was now a candidate to become Souma's third primary queen. In the other sat the Minister of Finance, Gatsby Colbert. Both of them wore dour looks on their faces.

There were a number of documents sitting on the table between them. These documents were the source of their current headaches.

"What will we do, Princess?" Colbert asked.

"Ain't nothin' we *can* do," Roroa said, leaning back in the sofa and looking up at the ceiling. Unusually for the ever-cheery

Roroa, she looked depressed. "Sure, I said, 'If any of you out there've got some interestin' festival to share, just you let us know.' I told the bureaucrats to come up with event ideas that could get the money movin', too. But still...ain't this one kinda bad?"

Roroa looked at the words on the document she had picked up with a face that looked like she had bitten into something unpleasant.

Colbert felt exactly the same way. "You're right. If done wrong, it could cause a major problem that would shake the foundations of this country."

"I know, right? Honestly! Festivals are supposed to be for gettin' the economy goin', so I want ideas that're more fun."

As Roroa slumped her shoulders and sighed, Colbert sympathized. He had been her associate ever since they were in the Principality of Amidonia, and was likewise an expert on economic matters, so he knew exactly how she felt.

"Then...do we ignore this one?" he asked.

Colbert's considerate words made Roroa hesitate for a moment, but eventually she resigned herself and shook her head quietly.

"No can do, I'm afraid. It's gathered a good number of signatures, hasn't it? I'd be scared to ignore it."

"That's true..."

"Besides, if we let either one of us be the final word of whether we end up doin' an event or not, that may end up leadin' to unneeded trouble. Our positions bein' what they are," Roroa added in a self-mocking manner.

Unable to watch her any longer, Colbert worked up his spirits and said, "I think it's best to consult with His Majesty here."

"We're gonna get Darlin' caught up in this problem? ...I don't wanna."

"Well, if we're going to carry out this project, we will need to receive permission from His Majesty, regardless. It's only a difference of whether it happens sooner rather than later."

"Well, yeah, you're right, but...havin' it be me goin' to ask him about it, and makin' Darlin' feel that way... Won't he end up thinkin' I'm a troublesome woman?"

Roroa's worries had, at some point, transitioned to those of a teenage girl.

Even with her unique financial sense, and even though she could make decisions that decided the fate of the principality, Roroa was still a seventeen-year-old girl. It was only natural she'd be concerned how the man she liked saw her.

For Colbert, who saw Roroa like a little sister, her attitude brought a smile to his face. "From what I know of His Majesty, he won't treat you badly over something as small as this, Princess."

"Ya mean it?"

"If you'd like, I could bring it up with him myself."

"Nngh...I'm thinkin' I gotta do this myself."

Roroa made her decision, stood up, resolved herself, and went to see Souma.

As he watched her go, Colbert cheered her on in his heart.

◇ ◇ ◇

"The 'Gaius Memorial Festival'?" I repeated.

Roroa was silent.

I was doing my paperwork in the governmental affairs office again today, as per usual, when Roroa had come in and presented me with a document that was a few pages long.

While thinking the usually energetic Roroa seemed awfully reserved today, my gaze had fallen to the papers, and…there was the title, "'Gaius Memorial Festival's Draft Proposal."

Gaius…huh.

By "Gaius"…it means Gaius VIII, right? The man who was Roroa's father, as well as the Prince of Amidonia.

The Principality of Amidonia had lost more than half its territory in a war with the king before Sir Albert. In order to avenge that humiliation, Gaius started instigating trouble inside the kingdom, aiming for an opportunity to take revenge.

Then, when I was having a disagreement with the former General of the Army, Georg Carmine, Gaius saw his chance and led the forces of the principality to invade the kingdom.

The forces of the principality passed through the Ursula Mountains, our southwest border with them, and laid siege to the central city of the southern grain-producing region, Altomura. Gaius intended to take Altomura while Georg and I were fighting, and annex the surrounding grain-producing region to his country. I was sure of that.

However, this was a trap Hakuya had set up using a fake insurrection by Georg to lure Gaius out. In order to root out troublemakers from inside the kingdom, we had needed to reduce the influence of their supporters in the princely family of Amidonia.

After ending Georg's fake insurrection and bringing the three dukes into line, we immediately declared war on the principality.

Then, making it look like I would launch a blitz invasion of Van, the capital, I waited for the forces of the principality that had retreated to defend their capital at a plain near Van.

Then, finally, the forces of the kingdom and principality had clashed outside Van.

In the end, the more numerous forces of the kingdom handily defeated the forces of the principality, who were already exhausted from their retreat. Even so, Gaius' forces showed serious grit in the battle.

Despite the total collapse of the forces of the principality, Gaius and his closest retainers launched a suicide attack to allow Crown Prince Julius to escape, and closed in on the kingdom's main camp, with me in it.

Because of my extreme situation, I had forced myself into the role of "king" so thoroughly that I hadn't felt anything at the time...but looking back now, it made me shiver.

In the end, due to the assistance of Carla and a number of other factors, the blade of Gaius' revenge never reached me.

Gaius fell on the battlefield, and I survived without further incident, but one misstep and I would have been the one to die there.

Gaius had become enough like a fierce god of the battlefield at that point to make me believe he really was one.

Hold a Memorial Festival for that Gaius...huh.

While I was still looking pensive, Roroa opened her mouth,

seemingly having found her resolve. "It's gathered a fair number of signatures in the Amidonia Region. It'll have been a year since the battle near Van in another month or so, won't it? They're sayin' they'd like to have a memorial for all the soldiers of the principality who died there."

"If it's been a year since that battle...then it's the first anniversary of their deaths," I said slowly.

Roroa was silent.

That meant it was going to be the first anniversary of Roroa's father's death.

I had been forced to kill Roroa's father for the sake of the kingdom. It happened on the battlefield, and she had never liked him to begin with, so Roroa often said to not let it bother me, but...even so, it left an unpleasant feeling inside me.

I already thought of Roroa as family. No matter what happened, I had to protect my family. I felt I had come this far with that as my core belief.

However...I had killed a member of my family's family. That was a fact that would never go away.

Maybe she got worried by my silence, because Roroa started talking with forced cheerfulness.

"This one's really got me beat. Even I dunno what to do. Runnin' an event like this has got the risk of inflamin' their patriotic spirits. But now that we've asked for event proposals, we've gotta carry through with it. Then there's my position as the former Princess of Amidonia to think of. If I ignore it, it could cause even more backlash."

Roroa was talking fast, one thing coming out after another. Her loquacity must have been a manifestation of her unease.

She was likely afraid that by suggesting this as the former Princess of Amidonia, she would cause discord in her relationship with Liscia and me. Her eyes quivered.

I couldn't blame her. She was trapped between her family, who was on the side of the Kingdom of Elfrieden, and the people of the Principality of Amidonia, who still looked to her as their princess.

I can't let Roroa keep looking like this forever...

I wanted Roroa to get back to laughing like her annoyingly cheery self.

"Sure, I don't see why not. Let's do this Gaius Memorial Festival." I set the paperwork down, acted like it was no big deal, and smiled for Roroa.

Roroa's face, which had been a bit downcast, popped right up and her eyes went wide. "Huh?! Ya really mean it?!"

"The name is probably fine as it is," I said. "But hold it not just as a memorial for the people of the principality, but for all the people who died in the war. There were more than a few casualties on the Elfrieden side when the forces of the principality invaded, after all. Rework it into an event that honors all of the war dead, please."

"That's fine, but... Really? It's really okay?" Roroa still looked worried. "My old man... Gaius VIII was an enemy of the kingdom, wasn't he?"

I rose from my chair and stood in front of Roroa. I placed a hand on her head as she looked up at me with uncertainty, and mussed her hair a little roughly.

"Whoa, Darlin'," not so rough," she protested.

"When you're acting reserved, it throws me off balance. I'll bet you've been thinking, 'I don't want him to hate me because of the bothersome situation in the principality,' or something like that, right?"

"Ah!"

It looked like I'd hit the bullseye. Roroa blinked repeatedly.

I sighed. "There's no need to worry like that. Liscia and the others will get mad that I've put you in a spot, you know?"

"Well, I'm your fiancée, Darlin'! It's only natural I'd be worryin'!"

"But if your positions were reversed, you'd get mad, too, wouldn't you?" I asked.

Roroa got very quiet, so I patted her head again, more gently this time.

"You don't have to worry. It wasn't that uncommon in my country to worship those we vanquished in war as gods once they were dead."

"It wasn't?" she asked worriedly.

"Yeah. Because the defeated bear holds grudges and regrets when it dies. In order to avoid being cursed by such things, we soothed their wrathful spirits, enshrining them as the protector deities of that land."

Kunitsukami, who was defeated by Amatsukami; Sugawara no Michizane, who was driven from the capital; Taira no Masakado, who had dreams for the Kanto region and was subjugated... It may have been my country's love for a good underdog story, but those who tried their hardest and failed were worshiped as gods and protector deities.

Of course, it was a calculating move, too. They did it to comfort their tragic souls and avoid being cursed by their grudges.

When I explained that, Roroa blinked in surprise. "I was thinkin' this when we had trouble with Lunarian Orthodoxy, but Darlin', your country had a real loosey-goosey view on religion. It's awfully secular, you could say..."

"Aren't beliefs and festivals that way by nature?" I asked. "I think memorial festivals are more for the people who are living than the dead, in order to compensate for the sadness of losing someone precious to us, or to let us come to terms with their loss and move on."

"Yeah... Ya might be right about that."

Roroa finally showed me a smile. Then, maybe having managed to get into a new frame of mind, she took on a face that combined her usual charm with a merchant's cunning.

"In that case, Darlin', since you're fine with givin' approval for the Memorial Festival, if we're gonna do it, let's make it a big showy event. That's what we were collectin' proposals for to begin with. I'd like a whole lotta people to be gatherin' for it and droppin' money."

Roroa grinned as if she were a child badgering me for something.

It was very much like Roroa to start a business negotiation the moment she got into a new frame of mind. It irritated me a little, but...it was better than her feeling down.

"A memorial festival that's got a showy event, huh..." Hearing that, I remembered one from my other world. "How about we do 'Tourou Nagashi'?"

"Toronagashi?" Roroa tilted her head to the side.

I'll keep it a secret that I kind of thought it was cute when she did that.

"It's a way of sending off the dead with fire. In my world, the waterside of seas and rivers had an association with death. Like the Sanzu River that separated this world from the next, for example."

"Ohhh. We've got that sorta idea in this world, too. There's a great river between this world and the next, and you need a ferryman to take you across it."

Ohhh, it was that way in this world, too, huh? If I recalled, the "water = death" and "waterside = the border between life and death" associations existed in both the East and West in my other world. It looked like it was the same here.

Surprisingly, that might be a fundamental understanding all living beings had.

"The Tourou Nagashi involves letting boats with offerings drift down the river, which is associated with death, to comfort the spirits," I said. "It absolutely feels like something out of a fantasy, seeing all those lights slowly drift down the river."

"Wow. It sounds pretty, even just from listenin' to you talk about it!"

Then Roroa grasped the hand I had resting on her head with both of hers.

"I'm takin' that idea! Let's do that Toh-roh Nagashi thing at the Memorial Festival! Now that it's decided, I can't waste time here! I'm gonna go have Mr. Colbert run the numbers!"

With that said, Roroa took off to leave the room...and stopped at the door. Then, turning her whole body around, she gave me a soft smile.

"Thanks, Darlin'," she said in a singsong voice, then took off from the room with vigor.

Unlike her arrival, I could hear her loud footsteps echoing off into the distance.

"That's how I like my Roroa..." I murmured.

Her echoing footsteps felt like a representation of her energy, and I loved them.

Having made up her mind, Roroa acted fast.

She immediately put together a budget with Colbert, and started moving on the Memorial Festival.

I was busy with my political duties in the meantime, so the only thing I did for the Memorial Festival was persuade Hakuya it was all right to honor Gaius, our former enemy.

Because of that, I left most of the preparations to Roroa and her people.

Now that I think about it, that may have been a mistake.

◇ ◇ ◇

The middle of the 9th month, 1,547th year, Continental Calendar:

I blinked and stared. "What is this...?" I whispered despite myself.

We were on the shore of a major river near Van, the capital of the former Principality of Amidonia. On that great river was, no exaggeration, a fleet. There were dozens of small, fast boats decorated in gorgeous colors, and they shone brilliantly on the evening river.

"What? It's the Toh-roh Nagashi, ain't it?" Roroa asked me with a blank look on her face. "The boats with lanterns on 'em are floatin' in the river, just like you were sayin', Darlin'."

"No, no, these are way too big... Oops. I never said anything about the size, did I?"

I'd only told her to send boats with lanterns down the river. I'd meant boats of a size you could carry in your hands, but from the way I'd explained it, I couldn't blame her for thinking I meant regular-sized boats.

However, when they got to this size, it was no longer Tourou Nagashi, and it was closer to another event called Shourou Nagashi, or the Spirit Boat Procession—the one from that famous song by Masashi Sada that my grandpa liked. The spirit boat in Nagasaki is paraded around on land, but I hear there are places where it's actually sent down a river.

Yeah... I'd heard funny stories of people who heard the song Shourou Nagashi and thought it was about Tourou Nagashi, but I never thought I'd see the opposite.

"On top of that, you've put a lot of work into the designs of all the boats, too," I added.

The small, fast boats on the river were all painted in super gaudy colors. Most had some sort of motif. Some were like Viking longboats, while others were designed like pegasi, or like Naden in her ryuu form, and still others were shaped like melons, daikon radishes, and other fruits and vegetables. There were even boats with music bands on board, and they were all playing cheery tunes.

The procession of lights and cheery music reminded me of the electrical parade in a certain kingdom-themed amusement park.

"It looks really fun, but this doesn't feel like a Memorial Festival."

"What're you sayin'?" Roroa asked with a look of exasperation. "It's partly your fault it turned out like this, now isn't it, Darlin'?"

"My fault?"

"That's right. When you were occupyin' Van, you taught the people here how much fun freedom of expression could be, didn't ya? Ever since, Van's been a city of the arts."

"So I hear. I thought it was better than them resisting, though, so I never thought much of it..."

"Because of that, a whole lotta young artists have been gatherin' here from around the kingdom. That bizarre fleet is a product of those artists' overflowin' passion."

"Seriously?"

To think my policy would result in this.

No matter what we did, there was always a result, good or bad, but that result wasn't the end of it. The influence of what we did carried on after the result. That would continue for as long as there were people to do things. When I considered that, the bizarre scene before me felt moving.

"If Gaius could see this, he'd go mad from rage," I commented.

"My old man? Yeah, I'll bet he would..."

Remembering Gaius's stern face, Roroa and I smiled wryly.

He'd made me fear for my life during our fighting, but now he only remained in my memories. The mood had gotten a bit grim, so I decided to change the topic.

"So that's why you prepared *this thing,* too?"

"The others are all super gaudy," Roroa said. "You want the boat we're ridin' to leave an impact, too, don'tcha?"

"Still...did you have to pull out the *Roroa Maru?*"

Indeed. We were currently on the deck of the amphibious transport ship, *Roroa Maru.*

If we kept using the Little Susumu Mark V to float over the water the whole time, the waves it caused would wreak havoc on the small boats around us, so we currently had it set to the minimum needed to make the rubbery part that held the air stretch taut, and were up on the shore.

There were a number of tables with delicious-looking food laid out on the deck, as well as a Jewel Voice Broadcast jewel set up to broadcast my opening remarks.

"Ha ha ha, that's just about right!" Roroa said with a jolly laugh. "If we've gotta have the soldiers runnin' security haul a jewel aboard anyway, it's better to have a big ship. It'll be a good demonstration of the amphibious transport ship, too."

Roroa was laughing, but Colbert, who was in charge of the finances, must have been holding his head. The gaudier she made the event, the more preparations were needed to guard it, after all.

Shrugging, I looked around the area. Juna and Tomoe were by the side of the ship, having fun pointing at the fleet and laughing.

"This scene is like something out of a fantasy," Juna murmured.

"It's really pretty, huh, Juna?" Tomoe agreed.

The duo of beautiful woman and pretty little girl made for quite a nice picture, standing there on a night when the lingering heat of summer had faded, with the dark river and gorgeous ships in the background.

Meanwhile, at the tables on deck, Aisha and Naden were devouring the food on the tables.

This was business as usual for Aisha, but Naden was the type who couldn't resist good food, either. They were technically supposed to be my bodyguards, but... Oh, well, they'd manage just fine.

With a wry smile at the two of them, Roroa said, "Would've been nice if Big Sister Cia could've made it, too, though."

"I considered calling her, but we can't make her push herself," I said.

The baby in Liscia's belly was apparently growing steadily. However, this was a crucial period, so I didn't want to make her travel a long way and cause her unnecessary stress.

"Besides, Liscia was insistent that, 'Roroa's the star for today, so make sure you be a proper escort for her,' in her letter. So I'll make sure I stay with you the whole time today."

"Ha ha ha, that's just like Big Sister Cia, all right." Roroa wore a wry smile with some happiness mixed into it. "Now then... My King, how's about we get this show on the road?"

"You've got it, my Princess Roroa," I said.

And I took the hand she offered me.

◇ ◇ ◇

"Soon it will have been one year since that battle."

Souma's voice echoed across the river chosen for the event. On the stage set up aboard the *Roroa Maru,* Souma was giving the opening address of the Gaius Memorial Festival in his role as king.

Roroa was standing next to him, staying close by his side.

By having the two of them stand there in harmony, they represented the solidarity between the Elfrieden Kingdom and the Principality of Amidonia, which had united to become a single country.

This scene was being broadcast throughout Friedonia over the Jewel Voice Broadcast. Souma continued with his remarks.

"Much blood was shed by both countries in that conflict, and lives were lost. The peace we have now rests upon those sacrifices. To ensure we do not forget that, we have decided to hold this Gaius Memorial Festival to reflect on the dignity of the late Sir Gaius."

Souma paused there for a moment, steadying his breath before he continued.

"Even now, I remember it. In the final stage of that battle, as he charged boldly toward me with his closest retainers, Sir Gaius cut a heroic figure. Unaffected and sincere. These are words that were made to describe a personage such as he. Though he was defeated, he was a true manifestation of the Amidonian people's spirit. Let me say this definitively. I feared Gaius VIII!"

The noisy river became quiet. Everyone listened to hear what Souma would say.

"The way he struggled onward, pursuing his revenge against the Elfrieden Kingdom, almost made him seem like a fierce deity. For someone from the Elfrieden Kingdom, he was an unusually difficult person to deal with. However, I cannot reject that tenacity of his outright. That is because there is no doubt that tenacity was for the sake of his people. It was to make the Principality of Amidonia rise. For a warrior like Sir Gaius, I am sure that was the only way available to him."

"Ohh, Prince Gaius," a person in the crowd moaned.

"Your gallant figure is burned into my eyes!" cried another.

"You maintained your pride as a warrior! Can there be any greater happiness?"

The lamentations of former officers of the principality could be heard from the boats.

Gaius' policies had prioritized strengthening the military, and they had placed no shortage of burdens on the people of the principality, but there were certainly still those who respected his dignity.

Every person had their good and bad sides. He was no longer among us, so why not let them turn a blind eye to his faults and fondly discuss their good memories? There was no need to continuing whipping him when he was already dead.

Knowing this was the most challenging part, Souma raised his voice.

"So, let me declare it here! Let the grudge long held by the princely family sink deep, together with Sir Gaius! I will inherit his love for his people! I will protect Princess Roroa here for all my life, and I will protect the lives and property of this country's people, irrespective of whether they come from the Elfrieden or Amidonia Region! If I should stray from this path and do anything to make Princess Roroa or her people cry, Sir Gaius would no doubt rise from Hades, stand at my pillow, and curse me to death! In order to avoid that, I intend to fulfill my duties as king to the best of my ability!"

When Souma declared that, loud applause rose up from the boats.

It looked like he had satisfied the hearts of the Amidonian people.

The king of the victors was giving a speech to the defeated people. If he was high-handed, they would push back against it, and if he was too weak, they would look down on him.

Souma had to be careful with these opening remarks, but he'd managed to do it by focusing on Gaius's dignity.

While internally feeling relieved, he wrapped up his statement.

"Okay, that does it for these stiff opening remarks! There is no kingdom or principality now! Let the grudges and sadness sink to Hades with the dead! Tonight, let us mourn the departed and celebrate the joys of living together! Now drink, eat, and sing, while remembering Gaius and all those who have left us! I hereby announce the opening of the Gaius Memorial Festival!"

With Souma's words, the greatest cheer yet went up.

◇ ◇ ◇

"Don't ya think you're praisin' my old man just a li'l bit too highly?" Roroa asked me with a smirk when my opening remarks were finished.

The people were already having a raucous good time out on the river. On the shining boats were people drinking, telling stories, listening to musicians play, and Juna and her loreleis were singing. There was no Elfrieden or Amidonia now, and the initial goal of remembering the dead was forgotten. But that was fine, because we should be celebrating. The living needed to celebrate the joy of life with everything they had.

"Whoa, whoa, Aisha," Naden burst out. "Isn't that a bit much at one time?"

"Urgh..." Aisha pounded on her chest like she was choking on something.

"See, I told you so. Tomoe, fetch some water," Naden said as she tended to Aisha.

"O-okay, Naden!"

Oh...that might be celebrating a little too much.

I shrugged my shoulders in exasperation and rested my hand on Roroa's head. "There may have been some exaggeration, but there was no lie in what I said. Sir Gaius acted in the way he thought was best for this country."

Our paths may not have converged, but I was sure he had lived his life to the best of his ability. As a fellow ruler, there were places where I could sympathize with him.

At the very least, I would protect Roroa and this country, the proof that he existed. I would tie the things I had inherited from him to the next era.

As I was renewing my will to do so, Roroa grinned at me. "And when you said you'll protect me for life...?"

"Of course I meant it."

"Hee hee hee. I really do love ya, Darlin'." Roroa wrapped her arms around my neck and jumped up, planting a kiss on my lips.

Ow! She had too much momentum and our teeth hit. I wrapped my arms around Roroa's waist, and Roroa was suspended in the air. It was an odd position to be kissing in.

When Roroa moved her face away from mine after a while, she gave me the best smile she had yet.

"Ya declared you'd do it, so I ain't gonna let it go if you don't take good care of me for life, Darlin'."

HOW A REALIST HERO REBUILT THE KINGDOM

BONUS SHORT STORY 1

The Master and Servant Aren't on the Same Page

THE REPUBLIC of Turgis, on the south of the continent:

Near the town of Noblebeppu in the east, a young snow monkey boy named Kuu Taisei, the son of the current head of the republic, was riding on a numoth as it broke through snow and ice. He was heading to visit his childhood friend, Taru the blacksmith, with his servant Leporina in tow.

Lying down on the numoth's back, Kuu stared idly into the sky.

There was a blue sky and white clouds. Partly because summer was approaching, today was a clear day. However, in this country, when the winter came, thick clouds would block out the sky, and frequent blizzards would impede the coming and going of the people. That meant they tended to stay cooped up inside their homes, making them even more introverted.

If only this weather would last a little longer...

Kuu was always saying being the son of the head of the republic didn't suit him, but he wanted to change the situation in this country. The winters here were too dark. He preferred things to be bright. He wanted the men and women in town to smile with good cheer. That was why he made the effort to at least smile himself, but it wasn't an issue he could fix without help.

If I just knew what to do, I could work hard to do it... he reflected.

"Thinking about something, Master Kuu?"

Leporina's face entered Kuu's field of vision. Because he was resting his head in Leporina's lap, her face appeared upside down when she looked down at him.

Kuu and Leporina were master and servant, but they had also known each other from a young age, so they were close. They had often played together with Taru in their youth, and at those times Leporina had been like a big sister to the two of them because she was a little older. That was why it didn't feel unnatural to be resting his head in her lap.

"Hm...I was thinking about how to make someone—everyone—smile." Kuu stretched as he answered.

"That would be simple...if you would just be open with your feelings. You're always so indirect; it's hard to tell if she's taking you seriously."

"Ooh...? What're you talking about?" Kuu asked, getting the sense they weren't talking about the same thing, which caused Leporina to tilt her head to the side.

"Huh? This wasn't about Taru?"

Kuu had been thinking about how to make the people of the republic smile, but Leporina hadn't been able to imagine he was thinking about something so serious, so she'd misunderstood and assumed he was thinking about the girl he loved.

Kuu realized that Leporina had misunderstood, noticed he had been thinking about something uncharacteristically serious for his ever-cheerful self, and since he was embarrassed to let Leporina know that, he decided to run with it.

"Hm? Oh, you're right there. Taru's been prickly lately. She used to be a little more willing to smile."

"You say that, but weren't you more honest with your feelings back then, too?" Leporina asked.

"Huh? I'm always telling her how I feel."

"I'm telling you that the way you do it is warped. When we were little, you gave her a crown of white flowers as a present, didn't you? That made Taru happy, didn't it? But lately you've been trying to get her jealous, making passes at furry girls like her, right? That's having the opposite effect."

"Ooh ah...but if I don't do that, she won't even look at me lately," Kuu said sulkily.

"I understand the feeling, but..." Leporina sighed.

She understood quite well why the two were on different pages. Kuu played at being a joker, but he had the potential to be the next head of the republic. Taru was working to master her trade as a blacksmith so as not to be left behind by him. The more Taru devoted herself to her work, the more she neglected Kuu, and the more obstinately Kuu tried to get Taru's attention, the more stubborn he made her.

They're the same type of people, you could say...ultimately.

The crux of the matter was that they were both stubborn. Neither would admit defeat to the other, and their stubborn attempts to make themselves look good to the other put them at cross purposes.

Well, that is what makes room for me, though.

Leporina had always had feelings for Kuu.

Kuu was the one with the greatest potential to carve a new future for this country, and Leporina always wanted to be close by his side, watching him. It might be fair to say she yearned for him. She wouldn't get in Kuu and Taru's way, and she meant to cheer them on, so she hoped she would be allowed to stay at his side.

But Master Kuu never tries to woo me...

In order to get Taru jealous, Kuu had been making passes at beastman girls with furry ears and tails like hers. In short, he was hitting on girls who were like Taru.

Still, if that was what he was trying to do, Leporina's rabbit ears should have fit the bill, too. However, Kuu had never hit on Leporina.

Am I so unattractive...Master Kuu?

While thinking about that, Leporina had unconsciously been patting Kuu on the head.

Ooh haaah?! Kuu was greatly surprised by this. That was because it was disrespectful for her, in her position as his servant, to be patting her master on the head.

When Kuu looked up at her, Leporina was staring off into the distance, her mind elsewhere.

What? Leporina... What're you thinking?

Realizing that she had acted unconsciously, Kuu opted not to say anything. He normally enjoyed seeing how his actions messed with people, but he didn't want to embarrass her by pointing out her mistake.

Man, that spooked me...

The reason Kuu didn't hit on Leporina was because, if he did make a pass at her, it wouldn't end as just a joke. If he did it to someone he was meeting for the first time, they would let it slide as mere banter. However, because of his close relationship with Leporina, if he made a joke of hitting on her, it would hurt her. The one he loved was Taru, but Leporina was important to him, too. That was why Kuu never tried to woo her.

So I wish she'd stop unconsciously trying to tempt me...

Leporina sighed to herself. *Do I need to show off my femininity more...?*

Kuu and Leporina, like Kuu and Taru, were also at cross purposes because of how much they cared for one another.

The numoth pressed on, carrying along two people who weren't on the same page.

HOW A REALIST HERO REBUILT THE KINGDOM

BONUS SHORT STORY 2

Liscia Writes a Letter

DEAR SOUMA, how are you? I hear you've headed for a cold place, so I'm worried you'll ruin your health. The weather here continues to be...

"Wait, this is way too formal!" Liscia crumpled everything she had written so far into a ball and tossed it on the floor.

This was Liscia's room in Parnam Castle, but the floor was scattered with similarly crumpled papers. She was wasting a large volume of paper that she could easily obtain, as a noble, though it was still a valuable commodity. But it was forgivable for today, at least.

She was writing a letter to convey something important to her fiancé, Souma. But, unable to put it into words properly, Liscia was clutching her head.

Souma was on a diplomatic voyage to the frigid Republic of Turgis in the south. Liscia had honestly wanted to accompany him, but because her health had worsened of late, she had ended up holding down the fort this time. Then she had been examined by Hilde, the best female doctor in the kingdom.

"Princess, about the reason for your feeling unwell. You're..." Hilde leaned in and whispered her diagnosis in Liscia's ear.

Upon hearing the word, Liscia's face had gone white with shock, then a feeling of euphoria had welled up from the bottom of her stomach. Finally, after calming down, she started to grow more and more uncertain.

Those around her were sent into a frenzy of activity by the diagnosis, but Liscia herself was now under orders to rest, and she had nothing to do.

For now, she was taking up her feather pen to inform Souma of the news, but she was finding herself unable to discover a way of wording it that she liked.

Then there was a knock at the door.

"Yes, come in!" Liscia called.

Naden, a fellow fiancée who was also staying behind, entered the room. "Liscia, are you all... Wait, it's kind of a mess in here, huh?"

She sounded exasperated, looking at the disastrous state of the room with all the failed letters scattered across its floor.

"Ha ha..." Liscia laughed awkwardly. "I was writing a letter to Souma to let him know about my diagnosis, but...it's not been going well."

"I understand how you feel, but if you overwork yourself, aren't you going to end up feeling sick again?"

"I'm feeling comparatively relaxed at the moment."

"Good grief..." Naden picked up one of the discarded papers and looked over it. "There's only one thing you need to tell him, right? Why not just write that?"

"But when I consider how Souma will feel when he reads it... I really can't write just that one thing."

"Well, fair enough. I'm sure he's going to be really surprised." Naden sat down on Liscia's bed. "So surprised he might come flying right back here. Not that Souma can fly."

"That's no good! Souma won't get many chances to take his time looking around another country, so I need to write to make sure he does his duty in this letter."

"Do you think warning him in a letter will be enough to make Souma listen?"

Liscia shook her head in response to Naden's question. Souma was family-oriented, and when a member of his family was involved, his field of vision narrowed. If he was informed of her diagnosis, she suspected he'd rush back to the country. Writing that he shouldn't do that in her letter was probably not going to stop him.

"I'll need to write to Aisha first," Liscia decided. She would write a letter to Aisha and have her restrain Souma.

As Liscia turned back to her desk, Naden shrugged. "I think we can rest easy with that."

"Can we really...?"

"Huh?"

The hand holding Liscia's feather pen stopped as she thought about it. "Aisha does pretty much anything Souma tells her to. She can hold him down with force, but if Souma seriously orders her to let go, I think she will. Hmm...in order to stop that overprotective Souma, I'll need to convince him I'm right with logic."

"Y-you will?"

Seeing Liscia come up with a multilayered plan to keep Souma from returning, Naden found it a little off-putting. In her heart of hearts, Liscia surely wanted Souma to come back home quickly, but she was firmly ordering him not to for his own good.

Who are you calling overprotective? You're being pretty overprotective yourself here, Liscia.

Ultimately, they were a like-minded husband and wife... No, a like-minded fiancé and fiancée.

Naden was exasperated, but Liscia went on mumbling without noticing.

"Maybe I shouldn't be in the castle, after all. If he knows he can't see me immediately by returning to the castle, I think that should keep Souma's desire to return home under control." Then something seemed to occur to Liscia, and she clapped her hands. "I've decided. I'm leaving the castle."

"Huh?! What're you saying?! You're supposed to be in a fragile state, aren't you?!" Naden exclaimed.

However, Liscia grinned. "I know why I'm feeling unwell now. It'll settle down in a little while. Besides, I said I'd be leaving the castle, but only to rest in the countryside where the air is fresher. My father's former domain, now part of the crown demesne, just so happens to be that sort of place."

"Oh! You're just going to rest, huh..."

Naden's relief made Liscia giggle. "It's a good opportunity, so I'll have Mother teach me all sorts of things while I'm there. From here on...I'm going to need that knowledge." With that said, Liscia turned back to the desk. "Now that that's settled, I need to let Souma know. If I write, 'You can't see me even if you come back now,' he won't force his way back here, I'm sure. Oh! I'll still have to tell Aisha not to let him come back, either."

Watching Liscia's feather pen dance happily across the page, Naden was filled with exasperation. "Oh, just do whatever you want." Unable to put up with any more of this, Naden left the room.

Now alone in the room again, Liscia quickly began writing.

I'm pregnant.

HOW A REALIST HERO REBUILT THE KINGDOM

BONUS SHORT STORY 3

Juno's Ridiculous Story

"COME TO THINK OF IT, there was that time rumors started spreading about Mr. Little Musashibo as the 'kigurumi adventurer,'" Juno said all of a sudden.

Juno and I were now meeting once a week for an hour or two to talk. We had been doing that ever since the first time.

I had brought a glass table and chairs out onto the terrace of the governmental affairs office in Parnam Castle, and I was talking to Juno over a light meal from Ishizuka's Place.

Also, the drinks were juice and tea—no alcohol. If we got drunk, there would be a security issue, not to mention the issue of whether Juno could get home properly. It was like a late-night tea party.

Juno sipped her tea as she recalled events for me. "There were other weird ghost stories, too."

"Oh? What would those be?" Aisha asked beside us. She was stuffing sandwiches into her face as she talked.

All my fiancées knew I was meeting with Juno, as was only proper, and I occasionally invited them to participate in our tea parties, too. I didn't want anyone wrongly suspecting these were romantic trysts and I was cheating on them.

Aisha and Juna (and Liscia, but she was away) were at least acquainted with Juno, and Roroa and Naden weren't exactly shy, either, so they'd gotten used to her in no time. If anything, I got the feeling that Juno was the one feeling tense.

"I-I'm Juno, and I often go on adventures with Souma...er, I mean His Majesty...er, not in person; I mean with his puppet..."

That had been her stammered self-introduction to Aisha, but, well, she seemed to get used to it after the third time.

But I digress. Let's get back to the ghost story Juno had to tell.

"Like, 'A giant snake was seen entering the castle at night,' or, 'The bones of the giant salamander in front of the museum move at night.'"

"The former must be Naden," I said. "No clue about the latter, though."

"You mean the skeletal specimen out in front of the Royal Museum? It moves?" Aisha asked.

"I don't recall installing that gimmick..." I muttered.

Aisha and I were both perplexed.

"It's just a rumor," Juno explained as she drank her tea. "They think the soul of the owner of the bones still resides in them and is making them move, apparently. Like a skull dragon, you know?"

A skull dragon was a monster made of the bones of a dragon that had died with lingering regrets. The bones would begin to move and would spread miasma around the area. In fact, whether they'd died with lingering regrets or not, if the bones were left sitting for many years, a dragon's bones might spontaneously transform into one.

"But that skeleton is a replica, you realize?" I said. "I sent the original out to be studied."

"Ohh, I suppose there's no way the original's soul could be inside it, then," Aisha said.

"I don't know," Juno shrugged. "I'm just saying that's the rumor."

Hmm...it sounded like it was just a ghost story. In my other world, there were stories like "the running statue of Ninomiya Kinjirou," or "the portrait of Beethoven in the music room that smiles in the middle of the night." Maybe people were just talking about something moving at night because they thought it would be creepy if it did.

I realized Juno was staring at me. "...What?" I asked.

"Oh, no. I just thought the bones thing might have something to do with you, too."

"Don't go blaming everything on me. Well, I'm sure I could move it with my Living Poltergeists, but I haven't."

"No, but a good percentage of the weird rumors up until now have had something to do with you or one of your people."

"I just can't see any point in making a skeletal sample move. No one would do something as pointless as... Ah!"

There *was* one person: the one standing on the thin line between genius and idiocy, who had created Mechadra with no way to move it.

◇ ◇ ◇

Later, when I had Ludwin bring her to the governmental affairs office for questioning, Genia answered without any sign of feeling guilty. "Ohh, I'm glad to see someone noticed."

I knew it had to be her.

"The setup itself is simple, you see. I put a rubbery material in the shoulders and other joints. The sample is in a spot that gets a lot of sunlight, so the material expands from the heat during the day, then it cools and contracts at night. That makes the angles of the arms and such change. If you check it hourly, you'll see it's moving, though just a little."

If people stood watching it the whole time, the change was too subtle to notice, but the gimmick was such that, if someone who saw the skeletal sample in the morning looked at it again in the evening, they would think: *"Huh? It's different from when I saw it in the morning, isn't it?"*

What did she do that for?

"The ghost's true identity was on the thin line between genius and idiocy..." I muttered.

"Genia...why do you do these things?" Ludwin clutched his head over his fiancée's bizarre antics.

Uh, yeah, hang in there, Ludwin.

◇ ◇ ◇

"I knew it had to be someone connected to you," Juno said exasperatedly when, later on, I told her how things had gone.

"I can't deny that, but I can't accept the way you say that like it's my fault."

"But you're the one employing that weirdo, right?"

"Well, yeah, but..."

While I was still unable to make excuses, Juno cackled. "You said you wanted to hear about the goings-on in the castle town, but from where I'm standing, it sounds like the more interesting stuff's going on around you. Doesn't sound like you ever get bored."

"Well, no, I'm never bored," I admitted. "I'm just swamped with work every day."

"That's good, isn't it? I became an adventurer because I'd hate to live a boring life, but it seems to me like maybe you can live a life without boredom no matter what job you choose. It's all a matter of how you go about it."

"Oh, are you up for quitting the adventuring life now?"

"Don't be silly. This life suits me," Juno said, sticking her tongue out.

I laughed. It really was fun talking to someone who normally lived a completely different lifestyle from me.

"Oh!" she said. "Now that we're on the subject, I think I remember another rumor that was going around!"

"What's it about this time?"

"There are these things running really fast across the roofs in town. There've been silhouettes like a monkey, a rabbit, and a deer or lizard thing, I hear."

"..."

Those were obviously people I knew. Honestly...there was never a shortage of things to talk about.

BONUS SHORT STORY 4
Juna's Nursing

"HUH?" Juna gulped.

In a hot spring in the town of Noblebeppu in the Republic of Turgis, when Juna and Souma were in the open-air bath together, Souma suddenly started to slump over.

"D-Darling?" Juna caught his head in her arms as it fell towards her ample bosom. He was red as a boiled octopus—the symptoms of someone who'd gotten dizzy from the heat. "O-oh, no! We need to get you out of the water, now!"

Juna pulled Souma out of the water and dragged him towards the changing room.

Having served as a commander in the marines, Juna could carry Souma by herself. When she did, his most private parts were clearly visible to her, but she didn't have time to worry about that right now.

Juna carried him to the changing room, put his clothes on, and went to call someone...and then realized she was buck naked, too. Though she had to hurry, as an unwed woman, she couldn't let any man other than her fiancé Souma see her bare flesh.

"I'm sorry, Sire, please wait just a moment." With that said, Juna hastily clothed herself and hurried to get someone.

Their companions had all either drunk themselves silly or were away, so Juna got help from the inn's staff to carry Souma to the room where they were staying. The staff concurred with her assumption, saying, "The heat probably just got to him," so she decided to let him lie down and cool off for now.

Thanking the staff as they left, Juna let Souma rest his head in her lap with a cool cloth on his forehead as she fanned his face.

While she looked at Souma's unconscious face, Juna lowered her eyes apologetically. "Is it because...I took too long to find my resolve, perhaps?"

The truth was, Juna had been ready to enter the bath as soon as Souma did. However, when the time came to do so, she'd suddenly gotten embarrassed.

"It... It was embarrassing for me, too..." she murmured.

Juna had boldly acted as if her feelings were "I don't mind being seen naked if it's by you," but she was a young maiden, and seeing him naked and being seen naked herself left her heart racing the whole time.

Because she'd hesitated, Souma's time in the bath had lasted longer than hers, making him get dizzy from the heat.

The truth is...I don't have that much extra composure from being the older one, Sire, Juna thought as she looked down at Souma with his eyes closed.

Souma and his other fiancées tended to look up to Juna like a big sister, but in some ways, she was trying to act more mature than she was. When she sensed that was the ideal vision of her that people held, she couldn't help but try to be that.

Lately, Souma had started to understand that aspect of her, so he had started to talk with her like they were the same age whenever they were alone, like they were just now, but...

The fact of the matter is, Aisha and Naden should both be older than me.

While those two members of the long-lived races were stubborn about not revealing their true ages, they most likely had lived far longer than Juna and the rest. She was a little dissatisfied that, despite that, they treated her like she was older than them. Yes, that had to do with Juna's high mental age, but...

Juna removed the cloth from Souma's forehead and patted him there.

"Oh, but being able to hear His Majesty's complaints may be one perk of that position."

Juna recalled what Souma said in the bath.

He had said he'd learned too much about Kuu and the others before learning about the republic. If a time ever came when he needed to become hostile to the republic, he was worried he wouldn't be able to give the order to fight. Even as everyone else was letting loose at the party, Souma was thinking about his duties as king, worrying without letting anyone else know.

Back then, too... You were worrying about things.

She recalled the night when war with the corrupt nobles and the Principality of Amidonia was drawing near. Juna had, at Liscia's request, sung a lullaby for a sleepless Souma.

You haven't changed since then. I like that.

There must have been many times since then that he had been forced to make a decision as king. The reason Souma was now at a loss for what to do was because, even after those decisions, he had not lost his natural kindness.

He was king, yet unable to fully become king. That was who Souma was.

That might be a weakness, and it was only in front of Juna that Souma could expose that weakness well. In front of his other fiancées, he always ended up trying to be tough.

"I think you would do a fine job of indulging a young boy who's trying to put up a strong front," Liscia had said back then.

When Souma was in front of Juna, he was willing to show a comparatively weaker side of himself. It made a sweet sense of superiority over the other fiancées spread through her chest. Feeling that, she thought, *Sorry, everyone.*

"It's okay, Sire," she murmured. "I will hide your weakness."

She spoke the same words she had spoken that time, with an awareness of her own feelings, which hadn't changed since that time… No, which had grown even stronger since then. And then…

"Juna-san…?" It looked like Souma had awoken.

"Oh! You were awake?"

Juna explained that he had passed out in the hot springs, and she had carried him here with the help of the inn's staff.

When he found out she had gotten a good look at various parts of him while he was out cold, Souma put on an embarrassed, forced smile. They were enjoying a quiet moment together after that, when...

"By the way, have Aisha and the others come back?" Souma suddenly asked.

Internally, Juna was a bit miffed. *Jeez...here we finally have some time alone together, and he's thinking about other people.*

She wanted to fill Souma's thoughts with nothing but her, so that...

"No. So we can do things like this." Juna pressed her lips to Souma's.

His surprised eyes only saw Juna. Satisfied, Juna let out a mischievous giggle. Her smile held enough power to entrance anyone who saw it.

"Shall we keep the fact we took a bath together our little secret for a while?" Juna asked charmingly, and Souma could no longer look away from her.

HOW A REALIST HERO REBUILT THE KINGDOM

BONUS SHORT STORY 5

Guardians of the God of Food

THE WAITING ROOM of the governor's mansion in the Kingdom of Friedonia's new city of Venetinova was filled today, like every day, with ambitious women confident in their beauty, aiming to become the wives of the Minister of Agriculture and Forestry, Poncho Ishizuka Panacotta.

"I'll take the position of head wife, with my beautiful face."

"Hmph! It will be I who wins Sir Poncho's heart."

The waiting women each believed that they were the one who would marry into wealth.

And yet, among them, one woman had a stern look on her face.

She was a woman of around twenty years of age, no less pretty than the boastful other women, but she had a desperate and almost tragic look on her face as she stared at the women around her.

This battle will not be nearly so easy to win.

Looking at the enthusiastic women around her who were here to discuss a potential marriage, the woman brought her hands together and intertwined her fingers.

She, too, had initially believed she could easily seduce a man like Poncho with her beautiful face. However, what separated her from the other women was that she did a thorough job of gathering information before this meeting, in order to ensure her quarry did not escape her. Thus, she quickly learned how difficult this meeting would be.

It's telling that despite the number of meetings he's had, no one has managed to secure an engagement to Poncho.

Though many women believed Poncho would be easily seduced, no one had yet succeeded in that task. She had tried to ask those who failed about their stories, but none of the women would speak a word about it, as if there were something scandalous about the truth.

However, there was just one thing she had learned in all of that. A maid who worked in the house of one such woman had heard her mistress mutter something:

"Poncho has a terrifying guardian."

A guardian. Remembering that word, this woman felt her body tensing up. There was no doubt about it. The one rejecting Sir Poncho's potential marriage candidates was this guardian, or whatever it was.

But if I know in advance there is such a person, I can take countermeasures.

She was betting on this meeting.

I'm going to marry well and change my destiny!

It wasn't that she had a pure affection for Poncho. She simply had greater ambition than the other women around her.

"Are you seeking to become Sir Poncho's wife?" a voice asked suddenly.

"Huh?!"

When she turned to look at the person who had suddenly spoken to her, there was a cute girl with her hair in braided pigtails. Her skin was slightly tanned, and her brightly colored dress looked good on her. Was this girl here to discuss a potential marriage, too?

"Yes... Is that wrong?" the ambitious woman said guardedly, but the girl with braids shook her head.

"Oh, no. I just had a feeling you were different from the other women. I thought you might love Sir Poncho."

"The world of the nobility isn't so easygoing that you can get married for mere love," the ambitious woman said, averting her eyes from the seemingly innocent girl with braids. "Both my parents and my elder brother are mediocre but good-natured petty nobles. There is no hope of them expanding their domain, and I can only see a future in which they eventually end up in debt to someone, and then I'll be wed off to a house that can shoulder their debt. I don't want that."

"..."

"That's why I want to marry Sir Poncho, who is so promising, and carve out a future for myself!" She didn't know why she was being honest about all this, but the girl's pure-looking eyes made her want to be straightforward.

The girl with braids looked at her with a gentle expression. "I see. I think that's a wonderful feeling."

A moment later, the ambitious woman was called in by one of the House of Panacotta's maids. Finally, it was her turn for a meeting!

As she walked down the corridor with the maid leading her, she passed by one of the women who had been boasting confidently in the waiting room. Where had that confidence gone now? Her face was twisted and she was rushing off in a hurry.

Aww, she must have gotten taken down by that guardian, the ambitious woman thought. *I need to steel myself for this...*

At last, when she was shown into Poncho's office, she encountered the rumored guardian. Standing behind Poncho, with a quiet smile, was a stunningly beautiful maid.

"Huh?!"

The intense wave of intimidation unleashed by that beautiful maid made her legs feel like they might freeze with fear.

B-but...I won't give up! She managed to endure that gaze somehow.

Then she heard a gentle voice from behind her. "Pardon me."

Had someone entered when they were supposed to be in the middle of her meeting? When she looked back in surprise, it was the girl who was in the waiting room before. The girl walked over to Poncho and stood behind him, opposite the beautiful maid.

In that moment, the ambitious woman sensed what had happened and her knees gave out.

"Oh! A-are you all right?" Poncho asked worriedly. "Yes?"

She couldn't even raise her face to respond to his inquiry.

I was being watched...all along...from the time I entered the waiting room...

There was no question that the girl with braids was connected to Poncho. The girl's mission must have been to probe the intentions of those in the waiting room. Because she had gathered information and learned of the guardian at Poncho's side, the ambitious woman had grown complacent.

No... Don't tell me there were two *protectors...*

As she knelt there, crushed, two lithe legs entered her field of vision.

When she looked up, the beautiful maid from earlier was there.

"I have heard the situation from Komain, and your grit and information gathering abilities are exceptional. How about it? Will you work as a maid in the castle?" With those words, Serina extended a hand to the woman who had been stunned into silence. "Many high-ranking nobles come and go from the castle. You may meet someone who is good for you, you know?"

The ambitious woman sensed an opportunity, and she didn't hesitate to take Serina's hand. "Ah! I'll do it!"

As a result of this strategy, where Serina recruited people who seemed like they might be useful, Poncho still had yet to find a fiancée, but the castle's maid force was gaining personnel and expanding.

Furthermore, though this is a digression, this ambitious woman would, in the future, meet the son of a great noble while working in the palace, and retire after getting married to him... but that is a story for another time.

HOW A REALIST HERO REBUILT THE KINGDOM